AUBREY STEPHENS & DALE KESTERSON
FOUR SCORE AND SEVEN
TIME GUARDS BOOK TWO

PRO SE ⚖ PRESS™

PRO SE PRESS

FOUR SCORE AND SEVEN: TIME GUARDS VOL. 2
A Pro Se Productions Publication

Four Score and Seven . Time Guards Vol. 2 by Aubrey Stephens & Dale Kesterson
Editing by Mike Hintze

Cover by Antonino Lo Iacono
Book Design by Antonino Lo Iacono
New Pulp Logo Design by Sean E. Ali
New Pulp Seal Design by Cari Reese

Pro Se Productions, LLC
133 1/2 Broad Street
Batesville, AR, 72501
870-834-4022

editorinchief@prose-press.com
www.prose-press.com

FOUR SCORE AND SEVEN: TIME GUARDS VOL. 2

This one is for Bob Asprin, who knew it was coming and is sorely missed. AS & DK

Many thanks to my fellow re-enactors that have shared heat, rain, snow, given sweat and on occasions blood to experience and show what our countrymen lived through in the fateful four years we now refer to as The Civil War. AS

My special thanks, as always to Jim for his love and encouragement. With love, DK

CONTENTS

PART ONE:
SUMMER OF RECOVERY
JULY AND AUGUST, 1863

CHAPTER ONE
THURSDAY, 9 JULY 1863

John Andrews fought his way out of a vivid dream. A professor of engineering at the University of Missouri, he had been dreaming he had been caught in a time eddy which placed him in Gettysburg, Pennsylvania in July of 1863, but he thought he heard a familiar voice addressing him. He moved his legs. Pain surging through his right thigh brought him to full consciousness.

"Hey, sleepyhead, I thought you wanted to go into town today. You're going to have to start moving if we want to get there before noon!" Cathy repeated as she prodded her companion. "Or are you planning to stay in bed all day?"

"What?" John sat up and looked around. He was lying on an old iron bedstead in a small room in a cabin. It all came back in a rush. He hadn't been dreaming.

He and Dr. Mary Catherine Howell, best friends from the age of four, had been transported through time from 2015 back to 1863 from a re-enactment they were attending. *No, transported was too mild. Drop-kicked was more like it.* Without warning, without knowing why or how, and just in time to witness one of the worst battles in the American War Between the States, it had been quite disconcerting. The two days before the battle were spent trying to find some logic to their predicament. None had come to mind. John never did believe in coincidences; he and Cathy had to be in 1863, in Gettysburg, for a reason. Passing as step-brother and sister, the pair had dealt with events as they unfolded.

Never in his thirty-five years of life had he imagined he would be participating in the real thing; nothing in his living history re-enactments had prepared him for leading a company of men – the 9th New York cavalry - into a real battle. His actions had saved the Union line on McPherson's Ridge until John Reynolds' relief troops had come up. The bonus was personal: he had insisted General John Buford leave the front line moments before a Confederate shot landed where Buford had stood. All it had cost him was a major wound to his right leg. A bullet had driven a silver dollar into his thigh. Cathy, who ran the Emergency Department at the University of Missouri Medical Center, had managed to put him put back together. The dented coin was now his lucky charm.

That had been eight days ago. A few days after the battle, an unexplained voice had come into their heads to explain, "*When the time is right, you will come full circle.*" He and Cathy had taken that to mean once they had done the task set - he had kept the battle line from collapsing and saved the general's life – and once he was healed fully – they would be restored to their own time.

John looked up at Cathy. Standing five feet tall, and petite, she was at his bedside, waiting for his reaction to her words.

"Well?" she prompted as her green eyes met his dark brown ones. She tossed her auburn hair over her shoulder. "Have you changed your mind about going into Gettysburg?"

John, still fuzzy from sleep, regarded her with curiosity; as what she said fully registered, he grinned. "You mean it? *We're* going to town? I can walk to town?"

"We're going to have to take it slow and easy, but yes. When I left yesterday, I told Mary and Miss Martha that I'd be late today because you would be coming with me." Cathy smiled at his enthusiasm as she rolled up her bed.

Cathy had been sleeping on the floor of the small partitioned room to make sure John wasn't bothered. She had worked hard – damned hard – to make sure he wasn't going to lose his leg, and she didn't want to risk injuring it by rushing the walk. "You'll get the hero's dinner of your life, too. So get dressed in your best civilian clothes. I'll be outside for a bit. Water for tea is on the stove."

"No problem." John swung his leg over the side with practiced ease, grabbed his crutches, and started getting ready. He realized that the exercises and walking Cathy had been encouraging had prepared him for the long journey into town. It was almost nine – he had slept past dawn for the first time since their arrival. As he dressed, he hummed what had become their private theme song: *Look for the silver lining when e'er a cloud appears in the blue….* They both regarded it as a piece of their childhood, as his mother used to sing it to them when they were sick or scared.

Cathy, for her part, checked the garden plot she had planted earlier that week. Knowing they had to stay until John's leg was fully healed, she had decided the best way to have fresh vegetables was to grow them. There were no spouts showing yet, but there were a few weeds. She watered and pulled the weeds before returning to the cabin to change her clothes; she realized that John's eagerness would not hear any delays. While John was outside at the sink, she gathered their faithful carry bag and John's empty knapsack, which he could wear across his body without it interfering with the crutch movement. The cabin, well out of the way in a clearing where two streams met, was ordinarily a forty-five minute walk from the home of their friends, John and Martha Scott. Martha's sister, Mary McAllister, lived with the Scotts; Cathy worked for Mary in her store. The walk would take twice as long today because of John's crutches.

John sat at the table and waited for his morning cup of tea and one of the leftover biscuits she had made. Cathy sat down with hers, and looked him over. It was the first time he had dressed fully since the battle, and he looked super.

"You look quite distinguished, Professor. Very much the wounded hero," she teased. "The sisters can't wait to see you."

He was always presentable; although not classically handsome, his dark, wavy hair and dark brown eyes had turned more than a few girls' heads on campus. The light tan he had when they had gotten to the re-enactment site – one hundred and fifty-two years from now? – had faded in the week he had been indoors since the battle, but even pale he looked good. At five feet seven inches, he was short for their own time, but almost above average for current circumstances.

"Should I bring the bench sketch?" he asked her.

"Absolutely, and also the sketch for the tables. I think Mr. John is looking forward to having another man to talk things over with – he hasn't been up and around himself long. His first real day up was yesterday, and only after I told him he could." Cathy sighed, recalling how she had risked breaking the timeline by giving their friend aspirin. "That virus took a lot out of him."

"Strange – he's not that much older than I am."

"Nutrition, medical care, and regular exercise make a big difference. Remember, John Buford was – rather, is – only two years older than we are." She sighed. "Such a waste. 'Back home' Buford would have meds to control the arthritis, and he'd be doing so much better." General Buford was the only person who knew they were from the future, and he had refused any medical help to ease the constant pain of rheumatoid arthritis.

"Scary. I know I can't walk on this leg yet – I think I moved it in my sleep last night and the pain woke me up briefly," he related. "I hope you know I'm trying to be patient."

"We'll see how you do today, and I'll make the decision whether or not to cast it." Cathy collected the table service items, washed them off, and dried her hands. She sighed as she looked down at them. "I'd love some hand lotion. Does baby oil exist yet?"

"Not sure about baby oil, but petroleum jelly and lanolin do, so we can contrive something," John replied. "I know you have your own stuff with you. Are you running out?"

"Not yet, but I don't want to wait until I do to find something to replace it. I'll put it on the list of questions for the sisters," Cathy said. "Oh, that reminds me – I want to bring your uniform pants. I mended the seam, so now they are just dirty and bloody with a hole from the bullet." She stuffed the rolled up pants into the carry bag between the molasses crock and the milk jug. "Ready?"

"I'm so ready I'm halfway there," he said with a big grin, moving to the door as she followed him, laughing.

***

The walk to town took a bit longer than the predicted hour and a half, and what John called the half-way log was welcome. As they approached the outskirts of town, both noticed the growing stench of rotting flesh.

"It was noticeable as a background smell on the first time I came in, and it's been getting steadily stronger," Cathy informed him.

"I've read accounts that describe it, but whew! This is nasty, and will probably get worse."

They made their way down Chambersburg Street and spotted Martha Scott on the front stoop.

"Cathy! And JOHN!" She ran to meet them, tears forming. "Oh, Captain, it is so good to see you!"

"Miss Martha, whatever is the matter?" Cathy gave the older woman a hug, lapsing into the more formal language she and John used in public.

"Nothing," she said, wiping her eyes. "It is wonderful to see the Captain up and around."

"What is happening? How are the soldiers?" Cathy asked, thinking of the men she had treated at the Scott home the past few days. She had been helping the sisters tend the wounded men sheltered in their home after the battle.

"The Confederate lieutenant died after you left yesterday. He passed quietly in his sleep."

"He is with his family now," Cathy said, swallowing hard, "which is what he wanted. I'm happy to know he died peacefully." One of the toughest calls in her professional career was to leave a major wound alone at the request of her patient, knowing his death might have been excruciating.

"The doctors came last night and took the rest of our wounded to hospitals. It almost seems strange having the house to ourselves after having the men underfoot for all that time," Martha confided. "Mary went to see if we need to provide food for the men still in the church, and I awaiting her to return."

"How's the young soldier Cathy helped?" John was curious. Cathy had used available tools and modern knowledge to try to save a man's arm.

"He's doing very well," Martha said. "He was taken to the hospital yesterday with the rest of the men, and they were talking about letting him go home for a spell."

"May he stay well," Cathy murmured, thinking of the young man whose arm she had treated despite the risk of changing the timeline.

"We wrote to his wife, and Michael hopes to be home next week," Martha continued. "He wanted me to thank you again. The hospital people said his arm looks fine." Martha spotted Mary coming down the street, and went to meet her.

"You did good, lady," John told her, giving Cathy a squeeze. "Real good."

Cathy sighed with relief. "Yep, I did. They both got what they wanted, and knowing the lieutenant died peacefully helps. Honoring his wishes was a tough call."

"Captain!" Mary called out as she came to the house. "We are so glad to see you. Go on into the house — you do not need to be standing out here!"

John made his way into the front parlor and sank onto the settee, putting his crutches to the side. "I cannot thank you enough for the loan of the crutches," he told the sisters. "It has made all the difference to me. I was really chafing to be up and around."

"He was becoming quite cantankerous," Cathy added with a smile. "I think the walls of the bedroom appeared to be getting smaller after almost a week."

"Have you had breakfast?"

"Miss Martha, I confess I was in such a hurry to make the trip to town I only had a cup of tea and one of Cathy's biscuits," John admitted. "I do thank you for giving her the instructions to make them and instilling the confidence she needed to utilize the recipe."

"I did relate that you were going to try one of my variations," Cathy told Martha, "however, I suspect he did not fully believe me."

Martha laughed. "We have certainly missed the banter between you," she teased. "John, if you will make your way to the kitchen, I shall get you a proper breakfast. Later, we'll have a nice early dinner."

Everyone was in the kitchen when there was a knock at the door. Mary went to answer it.

"Cathy, one of the men you tended yesterday would like to thank you. He's waiting in the front room."

Cathy went through and saw it was one of the amputees whose stump had suddenly begun to hemorrhage the day before. She smiled her greeting and gestured for him to sit.

"Miss Cathy, ma'am, I wanted to say again how grateful I am for your help with this," he began, lifting his left arm, which was in a sling. "They are letting me go home now."

"I am glad I was here to help. May I ask how you were injured? I didn't get a chance to inquire yesterday."

"I was hurt the first day, ma'am. I was on the front line with the cavalry, and the Rebels moved in kind of sudden-like. I got cut really bad, and the surgeon said he'd have to take off part of my arm. I reckon I'm lucky it was not worse, but I got some scared when the bleeding started yesterday."

"Cathy," John called to her as he came into the dining room, "Miss Martha wants to know...." He stopped, seeing the young man with her. "Bobby?"

"Captain!" Smiling, the young man rose and saluted. "Sir, I am so glad to see you! We feared the worst for you."

"Cathy, this is Corporal Bobby Healy. He was with me under Colonel Devin," John said smiling, coming forward on his crutches to shake the man's hand. "I see neither of us survived unscathed."

"No, sir, but we both made it," Healy said firmly, "and that is what counts. Captain, I seem to recall you arguing with the Colonel over who was going to tend to you. He made quite a fuss, ma'am," he told Cathy, "about how he didn't want the surgeon to touch his leg."

"So I was given to understand," Cathy said, smiling. "He can be most stubborn. I believe that once General Buford realized there was no arguing with him, he arranged to have my brother brought to where I was staying."

"I didn't realize that Miss Cathy is your sister, sir."

"She is indeed. Since she tended your arm, you perhaps can understand why I refused to let anyone other than my sister touch my leg," John stated. "She's the best nurse in Missouri."

"Yes, Captain, I'll give no argument." Bobby grinned, looking his age for the first time. "Sir, we held the line, and I'm proud to know you. I want to thank you both, as I reckon I wouldn't be standing here otherwise. I'm going home."

"It was an honor to serve with you," John told the boy sincerely. "May God keep you and yours safe."

Bobby Healy saluted once more and left. Cathy saw that John was touched at the man's honesty.

"That boy lost part of his arm because of me, Cathy," John said with a heavy sigh.

"Johnny, that man is *alive* because of you. That's how he sees it and I'd trust that, if I were you," Cathy told him gently. "Now, we'd best get back to the kitchen or Miss Martha will come after us with her rolling pin!"

While Martha cooked, Mary popped her head in to say she would be at her store if needed.

"Well now, Captain," said John Scott, coming into the kitchen from outside, "I was told you were up and around." He offered John his hand, and the men shook. Their host got himself a cup of coffee and joined them as they ate.

"It is good to see you up and around too, sir," John echoed, smiling. "I heard from Cathy that you did not precisely follow her advice."

"And rued it most sincerely," the other man stated. "Captain, it is my understanding that you have designed a few pieces of furniture for what Martha calls the uncivilized cabin."

"Cathy has insisted that we have a few comforts above bare survival," John said, winking at her. "To be candid, I can agree with the notion. However, Miss Martha's generosity has already given us a few touches of home. Even before the battle, Cathy had put up curtains."

"It's surprising how a few simple things can make a big difference. Lest Johnny leave you with a false impression," Cathy put in, "we have found the cabin, as rustic as it is, to be a quiet haven in these tumultuous times. We did not have to bear direct bombardment or dodge stray shots the way you in town did, and I, for one, am heartily grateful."

"With our primary needs fulfilled," John told the older man, "I feel we can now turn our efforts to some of the comforts, hence the design for the small tables and bench for outdoors. I should be grateful for your opinions, if you would care to venture any." He handed the sketch sheets to Scott.

Cathy, figuring she could leave them to it, told John she was going to see if Mary needed help at the store, located across Chambersburg Street from the house.

Scott studied the designs for a few moments. "Can you walk a few blocks? I'd like to show these to a friend of mine."

"Mr. John," replied John as he picked up his crutches, "I walked here from the cabin, so I suppose I can walk a few blocks." The men set off together.

In the midst of helping straighten out the mess in the store left by both sides, Cathy glanced out the front window just in time to see them leave. She pointed this out to Mary.

"I would guess that John wants to show the Captain's designs to Edward Fahnestock. He has another store not far from here – it's more in the way of a dry goods store with some hardware. It is also being used as the headquarters for the new Sanitation Commission, but knowing John you will have your bench by tomorrow," Mary said, chuckling. "I think they both need to do something useful. John has been busy with the telegraph, but he's been looking for an excuse to get out of the house."

***

Amidst the confusion of setting up the Commission, Scott introduced John Andrews to some of the town's men who were getting supplies to repair or rebuild what had been destroyed as a result of the conflict. Asked to relate his battle experience, John gave the short form: he had been with the NY 9th New York under Colonel Devin and General Buford, and had been wounded on the front lines the first day of the battle.

"His sister told us that General Buford wrote a letter commending Captain Andrews' service with him," Scott added, as it wouldn't hurt to have these men realize the newcomer should be considered a hero.

"My sister is proud of my service, sir. However, I am just as proud of what she did. After I was wounded," he told the proprietor, "the General had me taken to her because she's a nurse. I want to try to make the cabin more of a home for her, as she not only saved my leg but my life."

"Miss Cathy also helped Martha and Mary with the wounded at our house, and nursed me when I was sick."

"What may I do for you, Captain?"

"I wanted the Captain to show you some designs he drew," Scott said to Edward Fahnestock.

"What would it take to build them?" John asked.

"All it would require is the wood and a few nails," he replied, studying the bench. "I like the look of this, Captain – it's different, not flat boards or simple slats. I see you have listed what you need, lengths included. This will not be at all hard to construct."

"That's my hope." John leaned on his crutches. "I'm an engineer, not a carpenter. How much will you charge for the wood and nails?"

"Let me keep the design for use and you can have the materials. I'd be honored to put it together, seeing as how you are on crutches."

"Begging your pardon, sir," John interrupted, "as much as I appreciate your kind offer, I am staying in a cabin outside of town, and once built, the bench would be impossible for me to move. I was hoping to take wood, nails, and a hammer back with me and build it there."

"Where's the cabin?"

"It's not easy to describe," he replied hesitantly. "It sits in a clearing near a spot where two streams meet."

"John, if the bench is built, I'll make sure it gets to you." Scott turned to Fahnestock. "Please look at the sketch for the tables."

"If I can get the wood and nails, I can easily build these if Mr. John will loan me a hammer," John said, pointing to the second sheet. "I kept the table simple and traditional. My sister has asked for two side tables, and I would hate to disappoint her."

"It looks sturdy. This should be easier to build than the bench," Scott commented.

"That was my intention."

"Did I understand you to say you are an engineer?" Fahnestock inquired, thinking out loud.

"Yes, sir. I teach civil engineering at the University of Missouri, or did until the war shut down the school." John regarded the man behind the counter. "If there are any local projects, or rebuilding to be done due to damage from the battle, I hope you will inform me as I would be pleased and honored to help."

"We have a railroad bridge out. The Confederates blew up the bridge over Rock Creek the week before the battle, and our rail is now useless," Fahnestock explained. "Work has begun on the repairs, but we would be obliged if you would lend your expertise."

"Mr. John, can you take me out to see it?"

"Let's get the materials for the tables. While you wait for the order, I shall return to the house for a cart and take you out to the bridge. We can drop the wood off at the cabin, as it is more or less on the way. For now, Edward," Scott said to Fahnestock, "put the wood and nails on my account, and the Captain and I will settle up later." As John started to protest, Scott put his hand. "You were wounded defending this town, and we owe you. More personally, I owe Miss Cathy for taking care of me when I was poorly." He left.

John turned to the proprietor, who was handing the list of materials for the tables to his assistant, a teenaged boy who introduced himself as Dan Skelly. Fahnestock told Dan to put the order together and have it ready for pick up. "Cut the wood to the lengths on the sheet. That will make it easier for the Captain."

"Sir, my sister and I have been overwhelmed by the generosity of the town. I hope to repay you in kind," John said sincerely.

"You help us get that bridge back in order, and we'll show you real gratitude," the proprietor responded. "Ah, here comes Joseph Broadhead. He works for the railroad."

"Morning," said the man coming up to the counter.

"Joseph, this is Captain John Andrews. The Captain was wounded the first day of the battle, and he and his sister are good friends of John and Martha Scott. She helped tend the wounded they sheltered."

"My sister will also be working for Mary McAllister at her store," John put in as he shook Broadhead's hand.

"I heard telling of a nurse helping out at the Scott place. My wife Sallie has been going to the hospital at the Seminary, and your sister would be most welcome there."

"I will relay that to her. I must confess to being shamefully selfish in keeping her to myself. After the first day of the fight, she was busy taking care of me," John said. "She insisted she could save my leg."

"Understandable," Broadhead commented. "What do you do, when you are not in the middle of a war?"

"Captain Andrews is a civil engineer," Fahnestock replied. "I thought he might be of some help getting the railroad bridge back up."

"We would be mighty grateful if you could, Captain. From where do you hail?" Broadhead asked.

"My sister and I both teach at the University of Missouri," John said. "Or at least we did until most of the school was shut down due to the war. I was with the Third Missouri Cavalry until I fell sick in Arkansas, and Cathy came out to nurse me. We made our way across the war so I could join General Buford's troops. I had hoped to serve with them for more than a morning," he added ruefully.

The men were talking about the rail damage when Dan Skelly came to the counter to report he had the order completed; at the same time Scott entered to announce he had the cart. John was told to go to the cart and the other three moved the wood to it. The cart was hitched to an old pony that looked so bedraggled John guessed both sides left it alone.

"She is stronger than she looks," Scott said with a smile, seeing John's skepticism. "If we had cleaned her up, the Rebs would have taken her, too."

"Mr. John, I hope you told the ladies where we are going and why."

"Captain, I've been married for many years. The reason it has been happy is because I remember to do things like that," his host chuckled.

The drive out to the railroad bridge was not long – John realized that the long walk to and from the cabin was only long because they were walking – and over uneven terrain. He saw the turnoff they used for the shortcut, but didn't comment.

There was a work party of men at the destroyed railroad bridge. John was introduced by his host, and took a quick tour of the damage, partly by cart and partly on his crutches. He was able to give the foreman of the railroad's team a few tips on what needed shoring up in addition to the work which was already in progress.

"I am concerned there may be a good chance that there is some hidden damage in the rails beyond what is visible," he cautioned. "To be safe, I would recommend you pull the rails from another forty yards on either side. Check the beds to make sure they have not shifted, and if you have the available rail, replace that which is closest to the bridge." *Metal fatigue would be increased with the impact of the explosion, although that concept was decades, if not almost a century, away.*

The foreman quickly realized he had an expert to consult; he brought over the original construction drawings of the bridge. John looked them over and made a few suggestions for future use. He kept them simple – nothing drastic, for fear of really impacting the timeline – just simple ideas that logically followed the designs. His history classes were clearer than ever, and he wondered if the textbooks would change any.

John was sitting on a makeshift bench, looking over the spec drawings when one of the workers approached him with a cup of water. Taking it and drinking, John was about to hand the cup back when the man asked if he had been wounded during the battle.

"I caught a bullet the first day," John replied.

"You are fortunate you have your leg," the man stated flatly without being unfriendly. "Most do not."

"I am aware of that and grateful," John said simply, and extended his hand. "John Andrews, Captain, formerly with the 3rd Missouri and 9th New York cavalry."

"Bartholomew Scovel," the man replied. "You are being mighty helpful to us, sir. Some lengths of rail we are pulling up is not as good as we thought it was, and the bed needed leveling. You probably kept a few accidents from happening." Scovel was about John's height, maybe a bit taller, with a serious manner.

"I'm happy to help. This town has been good to me, and I wanted to find a way to thank the people here."

"I think this will come close to clearing whatever debt you feel you owe," Scovel said with the barest of smiles. "We have workers, but the Army took our engineers."

"The same way I was – I'm an engineer yet they placed me in a cavalry unit," John replied, with a wry smile. "At times I fear there is little reasoning behind some of the military policies."

"Yes, sir." Scovel hesitated. "I regret you were hurt in the fight."

"My sister would agree with that," John explained, nodding, "yet as you say, I'm one of the lucky ones."

"I will tell you frankly, Captain, I'm getting real tired of seeing good Union men being killed, maimed, and crippled fighting this war. I love my country, yet I wonder if it would have hurt to let the Confederacy stand on its own. The way I reckon it, the states wouldn't make it for long and would be forced to come back peaceable."

"I can understand your frustration," John admitted, wondering where this was going. "I saw a lot of good men fall the day I was hit, and I know there were many, many more killed and wounded over the next two days. I guess I never thought of letting the Confederates leave. This war is supposed to pre-serve the Union, or at least that is what I heard."

"There are a lot of men who feel it would be for the best to let the South go."

"After experiencing the horrors of battle, I can see how that might appeal to folks," John murmured, recalling that some northerners embraced that philosophy. "Mr. Scovel, do you work for the railroad?"

"I've been on the rails since I was sixteen. I'm from over towards Hanover way, and I ride these tracks a lot." Scovel regarded John and the crutches. "Will you be able to work again after the war?"

"I am told I will make a full recovery," John replied, "and I am thankful."

"Are you staying in one of the hospitals?"

"My sister and I are living in a cabin not far from here," John said. "She is a nurse and took care of me after I was wounded."

"Probably why you still have your leg," Scovel observed with a smile. "Smart of you not to let the surgeons work on it."

"To be fair, they have to work fast, and she took her time. She used to help her father, who is a doctor." John realized how naturally their cover story – Cathy's father was actually a lawyer – came out.

"If I see you in town, I'd be proud to buy you a drink, sir."

"I would enjoy that," John said. They shook hands again and Scovel rejoined the work party, leaving John to think about what had been said.

After over three hours on the site, John Scott suggested they get going. The foreman, Daniel Adamson, thanked them for coming out, and John made sure the man knew how to reach him – through Scott – if he could be of further help.

"I cannot believe how good it feels to be useful after this past week," John commented with a sigh as they left the site. "I'm tired, but it's a different sort of tired."

"Captain, I wasn't wounded but I have been laid up, so I do understand how you feel," his host replied.

"I was glad to hear of your recovery, sir. I know Cathy was concerned."

"My good lady was as well. I had hoped to be of more use – the Lord knows help was needed – but that sickness really laid me out." He shuddered as they followed the pathway John and Cathy used the first day. "Here's the cabin. Martha was afraid it was a shack, but this looks fine. Once we get this unloaded, we'll head back to the house. There's a big dinner for you and Cathy."

***

Cathy was helping set the table when the men got back to the house. Once glance at John's face told her the story. "I'm glad you were able to help," she greeted him with a smile.

"He did," replied Scott, entering, "and we are grateful."

Once they were seated at the table, their host said grace, including thanks for the deliverance of his family, friends, and town from the ravages of war. The 'amens' echoing around the table were heartfelt.

John brought up his conversation with the worker. "I was wondering if there is much agreement with this thinking."

"There is some, especially with the way the war is going," Scott replied. "There are people who see it as wrong to force the secessionist states to stay."

"I spoke with some of the wounded soldiers," Cathy started, "and some of the Union men are just plain tired of fighting what they see as a losing war."

"You'd probably find more of it in Maryland, as it is on the Confederacy border," added Scott.

"I never thought the fighting would get this far north," Mary stated. "I do not mind saying that I was scared. Even Saturday, there were sharpshooters around. The man across the street was shot even as he called a warning to me as I crossed to my store."

"I would like to propose we speak of other things," Martha said, passing around a bowl of potatoes. "This is a time for celebration, and I, for one, believe it might help our digestion if we cease discussing the war!"

"Hear, hear!" Mary agreed. "Cathy, how is your garden coming along?"

The subject of the war was dropped. John related some anecdotes from his childhood with Cathy, who noted that he carefully hedged places and time. He was a good storyteller, and she joined in the laughter.

After the dishes were cleared and washed, Scott offered to take the pair back to the cabin in the pony cart.

"As much as I would appreciate the ride," John began, "I think we had better walk. I must to get used to this."

Cathy looked at the clock on the mantle, and realized that as much as she'd like the ride, John meant it. "If we leave now, we ought to make it back by dark," she agreed, somewhat reluctantly. "I guess I knew that once he started walking, he would insist on continuing to do so." She made a face.

"We shall walk slowly and I promise I'll let you rest," John said, and as the comment elicited chuckles, he asked, "Do we have the bags?"

"Here they are," Mary said, handing him the knapsack and Cathy the other one. Both were full.

"Miss Mary, ma'am, your generosity is overwhelming," John assured her sincerely. "We shall endeavor to find a way to repay you."

"Nonsense," Scott stated firmly. "With your help, the railroad bridge will be operational by Saturday, and Miss Cathy has done her share of nursing besides helping at the store."

Cathy regarded their hosts and turned to her companion. "Johnny, one certain sign of intelligence is to realize when you have lost a debate. I do believe we can call this one over," she stated amid laughter. "Mary, I shall see you tomorrow at the store."

The pair took their leave, Cathy walking to John's pace as he thumped along with his crutches. They had gone a few blocks when a man hailed John from across the way, at the Globe Tavern.

"Captain Andrews!"

John looked across the street and murmured to Cathy, "That's the worker I mentioned."

Scovel crossed the street to where they stopped. Cathy saw he was slightly taller and stockier than John, clean-shaven, with wavy brown hair and solemn blue eyes.

"Mr. Scovel, this is my step-sister, Miss Catherine Howell. Cathy, this is Bartholomew Scovel, one of the men I met at the railroad bridge project."

Cathy bobbed a small curtsey, fully aware the man was studying her with marked interest.

"Miss Howell," Scovel said, "your brother is a right smart engineer. He spotted a problem with the tracks we had not considered."

"I am delighted he could be of service, Mr. Scovel. After being laid up for a week or more, I am certain it also did him a world of good."

"Cathy and I are returning to our cabin," John told the larger man. "It's been a very long day for me." The fatigue was showing on his face.

"I was going to offer you that drink – the Globe serves a good ale – yet I won't keep you now, sir. You do look a bit peaky."

"Perhaps another time," Cathy said. "We really should try to get back before it gets dark. The pathway is not even, and I should hate to see my brother trip and fall on his wounded leg."

"I would be happy to accept your offer, Mr. Scovel, I assure you. It has been a while since I've been able to relax over a pint," John said with a grin, "however we should get a move on now. Will you be in town tomorrow or Saturday?"

"I'll be at the bridge site tomorrow. We hope to get it finished by sundown," Scovel explained.

"I shall be working in Miss McAllister's store tomorrow, if you wish to get a message to John," Cathy stated quickly, heading off any response of John's. "I suspect today has taken more out of him than he realizes at the moment. I shall encourage him to do as little as possible tomorrow."

"Ma'am, I will make a point of stopping by to see how he fares," Scovel replied. "Until then."

Goodbyes were said. Cathy and John continued on their way. John started to speak once they were out of earshot, but Cathy told him to save his energy and concentrate on not tripping over anything.

***

It was past dusk, almost dark, when they reached the cabin, which looked like a haven to John. He collapsed into a chair, not resisting when Cathy asked him to take off his pants. Checking the dressing, she sat back on her heels with a sigh.

14

"I know you're exhausted and in pain, but the dressing looks clean. Any burning sensations?"

"Nope. Just aching pain."

"Let's get you to bed, and I'll go ahead and make a cast splint," she told him. "I think it will help support your leg, which should cut down on the amount you have to do to keep it in the slightly bent position you need for walking."

"Won't that make it harder for me to sleep?"

"No – it'll be removable."

An hour and a half later, John looked at the splint now drying on the floor. The engineer in him appreciated the flexibility of the design, simple yet supportive.

"That's amazing. I can use it when I'm up or walking, and take it off when I want to sit or lie down." He looked at Cathy. "I'm really impressed."

"It's a hard plastic. Once it dries, it will be lightweight and we can hold it in place with elastic wraps, all of which are hidden by clothing. It's not what you would call period-specific, but it will help." Cathy smiled, delighted she had succeeded in surprising him. "I learned this from an orthopod in charge of some residents last year. It's not quite a half-clamshell, which is sometimes used after surgery, but it's close. I don't want to cast your leg because we do want some muscle mobility and I have to be able to get to the dressing, yet I wanted support for it. Best of both worlds."

"It should also help protect me in case I do fall," he observed.

She nodded.

"I can't wait to try it out," John said, yawning widely. "Tomorrow?"

"Tomorrow." Cathy stretched. "As for now, I think a snack and then bed. I'm almost as tired as you are."

John noticed that Cathy was singing "Look for the Silver Lining" to herself as she settled onto her bedroll. He smiled, recalling the number of times his mother had sung it to them both when they were little.

"*So always look for the silver lining, and try to find the sunny side of life,*" Cathy finished. "Good night, Johnny."

CHAPTER TWO:
THE SECOND WEEKEND AFTER THE BATTLE

10 July through 12 July 1863

Friday, 10 July

The bell on the door to Mary's store called Cathy from the storeroom where she had been since ten, stocking shelves with a new shipment. Mary had gone across the street to ask Martha a question, confident that Cathy could handle any situation that presented itself.

"May I be of assistance?" Cathy asked, wiping her hands on a damp rag as she came into the main shop. Recognizing her customer, she added, "Oh - good morning, Mr. Scovel."

"Miss Howell, I was wondering if your brother will be coming into town today," Scovel questioned.

"Mr. Scovel, I am afraid John wore himself out by overdoing yesterday," Cathy replied, "and I insisted he stay at the cabin rather than making the long walk into town. He asked me to relay his regrets to you when I saw you. I believe once he does return he would be pleased to take you up on your offer of a glass of ale at the tavern."

"I understand, ma'am, although I am sorry he will not be in today." Scovel's solemn face was a picture of sincerity. "Please relay my regrets."

"I shall. I would be remiss if I did not inquire how the work on the railroad bridge is progressing. I trust it is going well?"

"We have it almost completed now. They are planning to test it tomorrow by running a locomotive across it. Mr. Broadhead will be bringing the engine over in the morning."

"That is wonderful! John will be pleased," Cathy said. "I know he was happy to help with the project."

"Please let him know we are very grateful to him," Scovel said. "Will you and he be coming into town tomorrow?"

"I know he hopes to, and I have already promised Mrs. Scott that we will take supper with them. As most homes did, they took in wounded after the battle and are now trying to settle back into normal life again." Cathy looked up at the man who seemed to loom over her. "Perhaps you and he could get together after that?"

"I don't see why not," he replied. "The Scotts live across the street. I can call for Captain Andrews there."

"My only concern would be the trip back to the cabin. I would prefer John not walk on crutches after dark." Cathy gave it some thought. "I believe I could ask Mr. Scott for the use of the pony cart you probably saw yesterday."

"There is no need for that. I have a cart and horse I was planning on bringing to town myself. I have to pick up some supplies." Scovel smiled and added, "If you would care to stay with the Scotts while your brother and I have our ale, I can easily take you both back home."

"That is most considerate of you. I shall tell John it is all arranged, which will no doubt please him. He's had little company besides me for over a week," she said with a chuckle. "As I remarked yesterday, I believe it would be good for him. You mentioned supplies. Will you need anything from here?"

"I have a list," the man answered and reached into his pocket. "I'll be needing bacon, salt pork, beans, molasses, and flour." He showed her his list.

"I can pull all this together for you so it will be ready to pick up." Cathy copied the items Mary carried onto a slip of paper. "Did you want it today or tomorrow?"

"Tomorrow will be fine, ma'am, and thank you. I'll see you then."

As Scovel approached the door, Mary McAllister opened it on her way in. They greeted each other briefly as they crossed paths.

"Bartholomew Scovel," Mary commented after he had left, "is a good man, hardworking. He takes care of his mother. They live in the country between here and Hanover. Did he leave a list?"

"Yes, I told him I would have the order ready tomorrow. He and Johnny are going to go out for a glass of ale tomorrow after supper. They met at the railroad bridge yesterday, and Mr. Scovel has offered to buy him a drink. Since he's going to come into town with a horse and cart, he has also offered to take us back to the cabin afterwards."

"It will do them both good. I don't think Mr. Scovel gets out much."

***

Cathy related the day's events to John back at the cabin while they were sitting at the table.

"Mr. Scovel seems eager to buy you that drink," she teased gently. "Mary and I agreed it's probably going to be good for both of you – apparently he doesn't get out much other than work."

"I'm looking forward to it, actually," John stated with a grin, "considering it's been one hundred and fifty-two years since I had a beer. But, a boys' night out is good. Not that I am in any way complaining about present company, you understand. I just wish I could see that test. "

Cathy waved her hand, dismissing that. "So, what did *you* do all day?"

"I read and took a walk. The cast works really well," he said. "Oh, and if you go into the bedroom, you'll see something new."

Cathy wasted no time; John smiled as he heard her yell.

"*Tables!*" She came back to the main room and gave him a hug. "Johnny, they're great!"

"I didn't know where you wanted them or what you wanted on them, so I just put them together. The kid at the store did a great job cutting the wood to size – it was like using a kit."

"I'll take care of all that once we have supper. What did you do for lunch?"

"Uh, I grabbed a food bar. I was busy with the tables, so I didn't fuss."

"Handy, aren't they," she commented. "Well, I'll do better than that. Let me get some things from the cooler," she said, referring to the pail with a flat rock cover she had buried by the creek and was now using to keep some items cool. "I'll be right back."

John maneuvered on his crutches enough to dip water into the tea kettle, and put it on the stove. He added some wood to the stove before he realized Cathy was taking longer than expected. Going to the door, he looked out.

John Scott was outside sitting in his pony cart, talking to Cathy.

"Johnny!" she called. "Stay inside – I have invited Mr. John inside for tea."

"Captain," Scott said as he climbed out of the cart and approached the cabin, "Daniel Adamson came by the house late this afternoon. He would like you to inspect the project before the test and act as observer for it."

The men sat at the table while Cathy began to prepare supper.

"I would be honored," John said.

"Mr. John, don't let him fool you. Only a short while ago he was saying that he wished he could see the test," Cathy related, placing a plate of biscuits on the table. "I'll have your tea in a moment, gentleman."

"What time are they planning to run the locomotive over the tracks?" John asked as he helped himself to a biscuit.

"According to Daniel, the final inspection will be done at eight o'clock, with Joseph running the engine over the bridge at nine." Scott chose a biscuit and took a bite. "These are right tasty, Cathy. Martha would be proud."

"I know the site is not far from here," John began, "so if I leave here at seven, I should get there on time."

"Johnny, I do not believe you should walk it," Cathy stated. As he started to protest, she quickly added, "I know you are capable, it is not that. I feel you should arrive fresh and alert, which will not be the case if you walk." She set two cups of tea on the table for them.

"Captain, I was planning on coming out with the cart to take you over there. Once we are finished, we can pick up Cathy before going into town." Scott smiled at the pair. "Martha told me that dinner will be waiting for us when we get back to town, and you are both expected."

"Mary made it sound more an order than an invitation this morning," Cathy acknowledged with a chuckle, "however, we would be happy to accept your plan if you don't mind company for the afternoon. Johnny also has an engagement following supper."

"Mary told me that Bartholomew has offered to bring you both back here afterwards, which is fine." Scott rose. "I'll be heading back now. I shall let Daniel and Joseph know you will be present at the bridge site in the morning, Captain. I'll see you about half past seven."

Cathy walked their guest to his cart and saw him off while John waved from the doorway.

"Johnny," she began as she resumed dinner preparations, "are we screwing up the time stream?"

"I don't think so. The bridge was put back into operation about a week after the battle. Since there were no more incidents with the tracks, I assume it was done right. If they did find problems with the rails after I suggested their replacement, it all fits."

"Score another one for our side," Cathy murmured thoughtfully.

"This is a very complex time period," John observed. "So many overlaps of things happening, and all of it chaotic. All we can do is follow our instincts and hope we maintain the proper sequences of events."

"No pressure...."

"Yeah, tell me about it," John replied. "Anything you can tell me about Scovel?"

"He seemed genuinely disappointed you didn't make it to town today, but I think he understood. Mary said he lives with his mother and takes care of things for her, so he is probably looking forward to tomorrow as much as you are. Other than that, he's polite. Sorry – I only had about five minutes with him. Nothing jumped out."

"My conversation with him yesterday was odd – he's really concerned about the war continuing."

"Well, you can sound him out tomorrow," Cathy said as she put their supper on the table.

"Hey, you're getting good at this. It looks wonderful." He dug into the meat and potatoes dish she had made, with fresh beans on the side.

"I'm glad you're impressed. Just don't ask for Chinese food – we don't have carry-out!"

"Can you do a pizza?"

"Watch it, buddy – I'll hide your crutches!" she threatened with a grin.

"That's cold - I surrender," he said laughing and holding his hands up. "How about a hamburger?"

"You don't know when you have it good," she retorted. "Tell you what, though. Figure out how to bring home some beer and I'll make a real treat!"

"Like what?"

"Nope, no hints. Just do it and you'll find out, so there."

"Okay, be that way. How about a game of cribbage after we eat?"

"Great. Oh, damn. I forgot to ask if the Scotts play cribbage. I thought it might be fun to play when you are whiling away your time at the tavern."

"We can bring the board with us tomorrow. I think the cards will pass."

Saturday, 11 July

Cathy saw John off with John Scott, and immediately changed her clothes into the young boy outfit she had worn the day she and John walked into town. John had gotten it for her for the re-enactment so she would be comfortable while running the First Aid tent; now she preferred it for gardening. All her seeds were sprouting! Even the spinach, radishes, and lettuce – long shots because they preferred cool weather to grow and it was the middle of summer – were coming up. Pleased, she weeded and pulled some more soil up around the sprouts to support them, smiling as she recalled trying to pass as a young teenaged boy, a ploy which didn't last long the first time she and John had visited the Scotts' parlor. A bird started chattering in a nearby tree.

"Good thing I know what I planted where," she remarked to the sparrow, "or we'd be playing mystery plants out here." Laundry was next on her list of domestic chores. "Want to watch me do some laundry?" The bird flew off. "Be that way, then."

***

John and his host arrived at the bridge well before eight, and were met by Daniel Adamson, who introduced the newcomer to the railroad men he hadn't met yet.

"Captain Andrews, thank you for coming. I would appreciate it if you would join us while we do a final inspection. If you see anything we need to address, please speak freely," the foreman said.

"I assure you, I shall," John replied.

Once the walk-through had been completed, they grouped around the small table holding the plans of the bridge.

John realized all the men were looking at him, waiting for him to speak. "I saw nothing untoward. The bed is level, the rails appear solid, and the bridge structure is sound."

The men nodded. Adamson turned to a young boy mounting a horse.

"Let Mr. Broadhead know we are ready for the engine."

The boy took off.

"Joseph is waiting at the last junction, in case we had something to correct. He should be here shortly," explained Adamson.

"A wise precaution," John agreed.

"Here she comes!" yelled the boy as he raced back to the bridge site.

The engine's whistle sounded as the locomotive came towards the bridge. Broadhead slowed as he made the final approach and moved carefully over the tracks, stopping once he had cleared all the repaired rails. Then he blew the whistle three times as the men cheered.

***

Cathy heard the locomotive's whistle as she was changing back into her civilian clothes. Cocking an ear, she realized that the cabin was indeed close to the tracks. As the whistle sounded again, she guessed the test had worked – no crash sounds.

***

"Catie! We did it – the bridge is back in operation!" John yelled as he and Scott drove up to the cabin.

She ran out the door to the cart, and gave him a big hug.

"I heard the whistles and guessed as much," she said. "I listened for cheers; however I suspect we are just too far away to be able to hear those."

"We did cheer, I assure you," said Scott with a grin. "I am surprised you didn't hear it – we hollered really loudly!"

"We would have been back sooner but Daniel and I decided we should do a second inspection after Joseph backed the engine over the bridge. It all appears fine," John told her. "Are you ready to leave?"

"I shall be right back," she replied, turning to go back into the cabin. She stopped as a horse and cart, driven by Bartholomew Scovel, pulled into the clearing.

"Mr. Scovel," John called out in greeting. "Welcome."

"Miss Howell. Captain, I saw you at the testing and I wanted to make sure you had a ride to town if you needed one," Scovel looked slightly embarrassed as he alighted from his cart. "I did not mean to intrude."

"It is no intrusion, Mr. Scovel, I assure you," Cathy said as she came forward again. "I believe you know Mr. Scott?"

Both men said yes, and nodded to each other.

"I was just going to get my things so I could spend the day in town," Cathy explained, "and Mr. John and my brother were waiting for me." *Johnny, it's not fair to have Bartholomew Scovel hang out like a flat fifth tire – he's uncomfortable. Think of something!*

"Mr. John, would you mind taking Catie into town? I believe I would like to ride in with Mr. Scovel and discuss the railroad situation," John said.

"That would be fine," Scott said. "I don't mind waiting for her, and I'll take her to the store."

As he hobbled over to the horse-drawn cart, John managed to wink at Cathy. She held the crutches while he maneuvered up and onto the seat, and handed them up to him.

"Do be careful, now, when you get down – this is higher than the pony cart," she admonished. "I should not take it kindly if you were to further injure yourself by falling."

"I shall take every care," John replied. *Yeah, she'd make good on her threat to suture me up without using a local for doing something stupid.*

"I shall ensure he does not fall, Miss Howell," Scovel said with a smile. "I think between us we can manage." He slapped the reins gently on the horse and left.

"Cathy, do you and your brother have the ability to communicate between your minds?" Scott asked.

"Now, Mr. John, you know that is not possible. I believe it is more a matter of simply thinking alike," she replied, thinking fast. "We have known each other all our lives, you know." She gave him what she hoped was a warm and innocent smile. "I won't be long. I gathered everything up before you got here."

***

"Captain? Shall I take you to the Scott house?" Scovel asked when they approached town. "I have to pick up some supplies at Miss McAllister's store. I left a list with your sister yesterday and she told me she would have it ready for me today."

"Cathy shouldn't be too far behind us, but maybe we had better give her some time in case she didn't pull your order before she left yesterday," John replied with a smile. "She's a wonderful nurse but I am not altogether certain how she fares as a shop assistant."

"Perhaps you're right."

"Do you have other errands in town?"

"Not immediately - I was going to meet a few people later this afternoon, after I picked up the rest of what I need to buy." Scovel hesitated. "If you wouldn't mind, I could stop at Fahnestock's first, pick up what I need there, and then we can go on to McAllister's."

"Mr. Scovel, I was cooped up in that cabin for a week. There are two rooms in it – the main one, and a small bedroom. I can tell you every board and nail in the bedroom after spending six days in there." John grinned. "I do not believe I would mind anything as long as I don't have to stay in bed in that tiny little room inside the cabin."

"Captain, I've never been that poorly so as to have to stay in bed for that long a spell," Scovel said with a grin of his own, "and I guess I hope I never have to do so. Errands?"

"Errands."

John insisted on getting off the cart at the larger store. The proprietor thanked him for his help with the bridge repairs as young Skelly got Scovel's order for him.

"Captain, we are working on the bench design you drew. I should be able to get it out to the cabin later today."

"My sister and I shall be spending the day in town," John informed him. "Mr. Scovel has offered to take us back after dark." He turned to his new friend. "Would it be possible for us to pick up the bench here before supper? I would rather not put anyone to the inconvenience of delivering it all the way out to the cabin as we are going back that way ourselves."

"That won't be any trouble at all," Scovel assured him. "I didn't know you designed furniture."

"I'm an engineer, and Cathy wants a bench so she can sit outside." John chuckled. "I count myself lucky that she hasn't decided she wants a larger porch!"

"Sir?" Dan Skelly was beside him with Scovel's order, which consisted of, among other things, some patterned material. "I hope the wood for your tables was correct."

"Dan, the wood was cut perfectly, and my sister loves the tables. I was able to put them together sitting in a chair." John gave the boy a big smile and the teen beamed.

"Captain, make sure you come here if you need anything else for you or your sister," Fahnestock said as the men were leaving. "Joseph Broadhead was in here earlier telling about your help with the bridge. A fair portion of my stock comes by rail, and I am grateful."

The next stop was the McAllister store where they were greeted by both Cathy and Mary.

"I have everything ready for you, Mr. Scovel." Cathy put a bundle on the counter, "It's on your account."

"I appreciate it, ma'am," he replied, taking the bundle. "The Captain told me that you will be here for the day."

"Miss McAllister was kind enough to offer me this position as a means of living, for which I am grateful," Cathy explained. She nodded towards John. "My brother may be at loose ends for the rest of the day, unless Mr. Scott would like to play cribbage."

"Cribbage?" Scovel's face lit up for the first time since Cathy had known him. "Captain, do you play?"

"Truthfully, we both do, although he's a much better player than I," she admitted as John nodded. "Once we are finished with the noon meal, perhaps you and he can spend some time playing this afternoon."

"Mr. Scovel has plans for this afternoon. Later he and I will be picking up your bench from Fahnestock before supper." John turned to Scovel. "Would it be permissible to play over a glass of ale at the Globe?"

"I was about to suggest it. I shall come for you shortly before five o'clock so we can get Miss Howell's bench." He bowed slightly to Cathy, shook hands with John, and left.

"Johnny, you seem to have made a friend."

"Yes, I believe I have. He seemed dour, almost surly at first, yet as I have talked with him, I have come to realize that most of it is simply shyness," John said thoughtfully. "Miss Mary, I hope you do not mind if Mr. Scovel calls for me at your home. He has offered to assist getting the bench to the cabin."

"You are quite correct that Mr. Scovel has always been shy, but he can be quite determined. His father and his wife both died of a fever a few years back, and he has taken care of the farm and his mother single-handed."

Scott appeared in the doorway. "Martha sent me to remind you folks that dinner is ready and you have just enough time to clean up before eating."

"Well, I shall race you all across the street. I only ask that you not eat everything before I get there," John said with a laugh.

***

At the Globe after supper, John found the camaraderie very similar to that which he enjoyed at re-enactments. Men greeted each other freely, asked about family members, exchanged jokes and anecdotes. After a game of cribbage and over their second glass of ale – which was great, John discovered – Bartholomew, as he suggested he be called, asked if his guest was at ease.

"I don't feel a stranger in any way," John confided, "and I must confess that it is most welcome."

"Word of how you assisted with the bridge has spread, along with the story of your service in the battle. These are hard times, and although Gettysburg is a fair-sized city, in many ways it is still very much a small town." Scovel smiled as he took a sip of ale.

"We are grateful, I can assure you. The Scotts and Miss Mary took us in immediately," John said, and proceeded to relate how the pair had been welcomed and given the means to live even before the battle commenced. "Even the knowledge of the cabin came through them. We have been truly blessed in our friends, you among them."

"You have both given freely of yourselves, something highly regarded in these parts. I also heard that General Buford himself has commended your actions in the fight."

"The general was generous."

"Captain, I understand if you are reluctant to speak of those events."

"To be honest, there are some aspects of that day I still cannot recall clearly. Cathy has suggested that when I am ready, the memories may return."

"She seems a remarkable woman."

"That she is," John returned with a broad smile. "The General and I shared an observation of Shakespeare's about her: 'though she be but little, she be fierce.' It sums Cathy up completely and quite possibly explains why she remains unmarried. She and Miss Mary found they have several attitudes in common, and became strong friends."

Scovel laughed aloud, which drew some surprised looks from a few of the other men around them.

"I can tell you that my sister would recommend you laugh more often — she says it is good for the soul," John commented, noting the reactions. "However, if you are considering any interest in Cathy, she would probably tell you to not bother."

"Bartholomew!" A man approached their table, ale in hand. "May I join you?"

"James, please do." Scovel introduced John to James Weston, another railroad worker. The newcomer shook hands and pulled a chair to the table. Weston was a bit taller than Bartholomew and as broad in the shoulders. He had a boyish face, framed by curly, sandy blond hair, and his eyes were blue.

"Bartholomew, I am pleased to see you here, and enjoying yourself. Your mother is well?" Weston smiled, showing a dimple in his cheek.

"Yes, very well, thank you."

Noting the confusion on John's face, the newcomer hastened to explain, "Bartholomew rarely comes out in the evening, and I cannot remember the last time I heard him laugh. You seem to have accomplished both."

"Alas, I cannot claim full credit for either occurrence. Bartholomew invited me for a glass, and the laughter came from a description of my sister,"

John returned. "However, I am enjoying my first evening out in longer than I care to relate, so I guess he and I are even in that respect."

"Your sister is the woman now working for Miss McAllister?" At John's nod, Weston continued, "I met her at the store yesterday, and I'm curious. Miss McAllister informed me she's a nurse."

"Cathy was teaching nursing before the war, as well as working at the medical clinic at the university where we both taught. According to her students, she's more than efficient – she can be downright formidable."

"Captain, I'm sure you do her a disservice," Weston protested. "She's lovely."

"James, apparently even General Buford agreed with him," Scovel said with a chuckle.

"Miss McAllister told me she is not married. Is she courting?"

"Not to my knowledge, Mr. Weston," John replied with a smile. Remembering what he had told Randy Thomas at the re-enactment – one hundred and fifty-two years from now – he repeated the gist of it. "Cathy may look small and helpless, but I assure you she is more than capable of anything she puts her mind to accomplish."

"I wonder. Would you object to my interest?"

"Mr. Weston, I have been told off – more than once, I'm afraid - for trying to interfere with her life, and dare not do so again," John replied, again smiling. "I would ask you to remember that she is a strong lady in more ways than one. Cathy operated on my leg after I was wounded, doing more than a military surgeon would have taken time to do, and I owe her my life. If you have any notions of courting her, I won't tell you not to do so, but bear in mind she is very independent."

"I may see if she would be interested."

"There is one more thing I would like to add. We are not from this area, and I know she does plan to return to her position at the University once she can, as she has hopes to attain the directorship of the nursing school." John leaned back in his seat, hoping that would do it. Inside, he was grinning. Weston was handsome and intelligent, but he knew Cathy would not consider giving up a smidgen of her independence even if the man came back to the twenty-first century with them. "If you will be guided by me, keep to the idea of friendship, rather than courting her."

Weston's face, which had darkened a bit, broke into a smile. "I must seem very forward to you, speaking of courting your sister on our first meeting."

"Mr. Weston, I am well aware that Cathy is an attractive and intelligent woman – I am her brother, but I am not blind. I take no offense, either on my part or on behalf of hers, I assure you." John saw that the other man was supremely confident in his opinion of himself.

"Leaving that subject," Scovel said diplomatically with a smile, "James, I wanted to ask you if all is well at your place. We missed you this afternoon."

James Weston shot a quick glance at John Andrews before replying.

"I had to tend to a sick calf," he replied in an offhanded manner. "She'll be fine, but I had to make sure. After all the Army took, I need every animal I have left." He looked at Scovel meaningfully.

John knew that if he hadn't seen the sharp look exchanged between his two companions, he would have taken Weston's answer at face value. Yet there was an undercurrent he could not identify. He decided to let it slide for now and question Scovel later.

"I know both armies took most of what they could carry," he said in what he hoped would be taken as candidly casual. "I helped Miss McAllister move stock from her store to her basement storeroom before the battle broke out, and I know Cathy has been helping restore order to the stock that was left."

"General Early demanded money, and when that was refused, the Confederates sent a written list to the borough's council before the battle. They were told to take what they could from all the merchants. When the Union soldiers came, they took a large part of what was left," Weston explained bluntly. "It's enough that we had to do that, but when the wounded were sheltered here, we tried to take care of them. When people charged for things like bread, we were told that wasn't right. Even if they paid, we were left with next to nothing." He grimaced.

John nodded in understanding. "The Scotts made sure Cathy had enough to keep us fed during the days after I was hit," he said, "and I know Cathy was worried that they had given us what they needed for themselves. I find myself hoping that all of it was worth it – that the Union will hold together."

"I see you have crutches," said Weston. "Did you lose your leg?"

"Thankfully, no. My sister was able to remove the bullet in my leg and stitch me back together. She told me it took her longer than she expected, but I spent the first six days after that in bed."

"They're living in the grandfather's cabin in the woods, out near Rock Creek just northeast of town," Scovel informed his friend.

"Oh, you're the engineer who helped with the bridge repair! It was General Early's troops that blew it up."

"I was happy to assist, I assure you," John nodded. "I offered my services because this town had been very generous to us in these hard times, and as I said, we are very grateful."

"We are much obliged," Weston said with a smile. "Joseph Broadhead was impressed with the way you spotted the problems with the track and bed."

"Call it experience," John said with a small shrug.

"You're too modest," Scovel observed. "I was out there when the Captain was looking at the drawings. He's every bit as impressive in his own field as his sister is in hers."

John was becoming embarrassed and said so, making his two companions chuckle. Weston offered to buy another round of ale.

"What unit were you with during the fight?" Weston wanted to know as he set down the new glasses.

"I was a replacement officer with the 9th New York Cavalry, under Colonel Devin's brigade of General John Buford's cavalry division. They are good men, and I was honored to lead them. General Buford is one of the finest officers and men I have ever had the pleasure to meet."

"Would you have stayed with the Army if you hadn't been shot?" Weston persisted.

"I would have been proud to have stayed with the unit." John paused for a moment, taking a sip of ale before continuing. "I have heard telling of officers who did not take their men's lives into consideration in pursuit of their own glory, but I can assure you from my own observations that John Buford is not one of them." He smiled and continued, "in fact, I had to force the general to withdraw from the very front of the lines so he wouldn't be shot. I called it a discussion, but he later referred to it as an order bordering on insubordination on my part!" He chuckled with the others.

"Many men have died or been maimed for life in this conflict," Weston said, growing serious. "I still cannot see that the war should have been started over slaves. Not that I agree with slavery, mind you, but if those states wanted to form their own country, maybe we should have let them."

"Bartholomew has expressed similar ideas," John said. "I confess I never considered it from that viewpoint, but after being shot myself, I have been giving it more thought." *Damn, what the hell is going on here? This seems to be landing in my lap. Another coincidence?* He forced his mind back to the conversation.

"You may well want to do so. Hopefully, you will make a full recovery, but there is the thought that if you do, you might well end up back in the fight if the war continues."

"Yes, I can see that," John commented, trying to make it sound a bit hesitant. "In a way, it already happened to me. I fell ill when I was with the 3rd Missouri Volunteer Cavalry – we were in Arkansas. The doctors there said they couldn't help me, and I sent for Cathy, who came out and nursed me back to health. Then I joined Buford's cavalry and now here I am, on crutches. Without Cathy, I would either have lost my leg or my life." He shuddered, something totally real.

"There are many men who feel this way," Scovel stated earnestly.

"Probably more, too, but some are afraid to say so openly," Weston commented sourly.

"It's hard to know what's best and what to do about it all," Scovel observed sadly.

"There is a group of us who meet to talk about it," Weston told John. "We'd be honored if you would like to join us."

"I shall give that some thought," John assured him. Glancing out the window, he noted it was dark and pulled out his watch to check the time. "Good heavens, it is past eight!" He turned to Scovel. "As much as I have enjoyed this evening, I believe we really should be going. We still have to pick up Cathy at the Scotts' home before going out to the cabin."

"I'll apologize for keeping you out so late," his host said with a smile, "and maybe she won't blame you!"

All three men laughed. Weston handed John the crutches and watched as the wounded man carefully started for the door, with Scovel following with the cribbage board. John was helped up onto the seat of the cart, and they shook hands and exchanged compliments.

Arriving at the Scott home, Scovel went to the door so John didn't have to descend from the cart. Cathy had been right – it was higher than the pony cart. Cathy came out with the Scotts, the faithful carry bag in hand.

"I'm glad you enjoyed your evening. Did you remember my request?" she asked with a smile.

John's stricken face was all the answer she needed, and she was glad he didn't pop a modern colloquialism in trying to voice a reply.

"No matter," she said, waving it off with a laugh as Scovel handed her up into his cart.

"Let me take care of it for the Captain, seeing as how he hasn't had an evening out in quite a while," Scott said with a chuckle. "After all, we wouldn't want to see him in trouble, would we, Martha?"

"No, John, absolutely not." Martha didn't laugh out loud, but the humor was in her voice.

"What did you forget, Captain?" Scovel asked as he climbed to the driver's position. "Might it still be had tonight?"

"It really is of little consequence, Mr. Scovel," Cathy explained, still chuckling. "I had asked Johnny to bring me some ale or beer. I wish to use it in baking."

"I was looking forward to that experiment of yours," Martha put in. "Let John get it tonight and it will be here tomorrow."

"Mrs. Scott, allow me settle this by stopping at the Globe on our way to the cabin. I'll buy a small keg to take with us tonight," Scovel suggested with a teasing grin. "I would not want my friend in trouble with his sister."

"If you would all stop treating me as if I weren't here, I would have suggested that myself," John broke in, attempting to pretend his feelings were hurt. It didn't work – everyone laughed, including him.

"Let's go," suggested Cathy. "We shall be happy to return tomorrow, if you have not yet tired of us," she called to the Scotts.

"Let us judge if and when you wear out your welcome," Scott called back. "We shall let you know, I promise!"

Moments later, stopped in front of the Globe, Cathy noticed the bench for the first time as Scovel disappeared into the tavern.

"Oh – you have the bench, too! I can't wait to see it in place!"

"The men at Fahnestock's did a great job with it," John told her, and lowering his voice, added, "and I have lots to tell you once we get back to the cabin."

"Meanwhile I give you full points for not saying 'cripes' or 'shit' when you realized you had forgotten the beer," Cathy teased in a low voice. "You did enjoy the night out, though, right?"

"Oh yeah, I had to bite off 'cripes.' Big time. But here he comes." John raised his voice to say, "I am glad you aren't cross with me, Catie. Truthfully, I did enjoy my evening out. I met more of the folks here, too."

"Thank you, Mr. Scovel," she said, taking the small – and cute – keg from him. "Who won the cribbage game?" Cathy asked once they were on their way again.

"I did, Miss Howell," Scovel replied proudly, "although it wasn't by much."

"You are to be congratulated, sir – I fear my brother is quite the fiendish player. Most of the time he wins our games, or holds me to a narrow victory."

Scovel chuckled. "I am certain he will win our next match. Perhaps some time you and I can play, thereby practicing between us so we can beat him?"

"Please, Bartholomew, do not give her any ideas," John said with a mock groan. "She has enough of her own."

"John, please – you will give Mr. Scovel quite the wrong opinion of me," she shot back.

"I doubt that very much, Cathy. However, I shall say to Bartholomew that everything I relayed about you to his friend Mr. Weston also applies to him as well." John then folded his arms and refused to explain any of it to her.

Scovel threw back his head and laughed. "You two remind me of the way my wife and her brother used to bicker all the time, but we all realized they didn't mean a word of it."

"Mary told me you lost your father and your wife during an outbreak of fever. Please accept my sympathy on your loss," Cathy said sincerely.

"Thank you, ma'am," he acknowledged, "that is most kind of you."

At the cabin, Cathy had to insist on helping Scovel unload the bench, arguing that she was stronger than she looked. They lifted it down together, placing it along the side of the cabin just to the right of the door. John promptly sat in it and pronounced it comfortable.

Cathy laughed at his antics and asked Scovel if he would like a cup of tea before he left.

"No, ma'am, I think I'd best be getting home. My mother might be getting a tad concerned about now, although I did tell her I was going to be late." Scovel offered his hand to John. "I suspect Miss McAllister told you I don't get out much. I want you to know I enjoyed it, too."

Back inside the cabin, after a detour to the outdoor sink, John headed straight for bed, asking Cathy for assistance in taking off the splint.

"I was wondering how you were holding up," she said as she unwrapped the elastic bandage. "Any chafing or burning sensations?"

"Only a little chafing at the top of the back of my leg where it hits. No burning. Not to worry, though – I suspect I did better with it than I would have without it. It really does hold my leg in position, and I can still tighten my muscles." John raised himself up a bit to look at what she was doing. "Do you need to change the dressing?"

"After all you have done in the past few days, that's not a bad idea," she agreed. "Let me change, wash up a bit, and get stuff together. Then you can tell me what you have been biting back since you got back to the Scotts'."

While she bustled around getting her materials ready, John wondered – again – if she knew him better than he did himself. On the flip side, though, he reflected that he probably knew her better than she did, so it evened out.

"Are you going to look this time?" she asked as she removed the dressing. "I think you should – it's clean and healing. Honestly, it looks fine. No signs of anything nasty, no cellulitis, no infections. Just an incision with stitches."

John propped himself up and cautiously inspected his thigh. He immediately looked up at her in surprise. "What happened to that big, gaping hole?" he demanded. All he saw was a neat healing suture line with stitches, just as she had described.

"I closed it, silly." Cathy chuckled at the astonishment on his face. "You saw it the first time I did the dressing, and haven't looked since. It's been getting better while you still had that first image in your mind. All I'm going to do now is check the sutures, and pad it with a dressing."

"No bread mold?"

"Nope. We won," she said with a grin. "Or we will," she cautioned, "if you will give the muscle time to heal."

"Wow," he mumbled as he leaned back, "Catie, you're the best."

"While you are so impressed, let's do your exercises. I want to make sure everything still works, and after being in the cast splint all day, you should rotate your ankle if nothing else. You don't want leg cramps."

"Oh, no – not like the ones I had a week ago," he winced, remembering the excruciating muscle cramps two nights after the battle. John dutifully went through the series of muscle stretches and contractions she had devised for him, and she helped him with the knee movements. They still hurt, but nowhere near as much as they had.

"Wait a minute! You didn't give me any pain meds before that."

"Nope. Did you miss them? "

"Uh, no." He frowned slightly. "What's going on?"

"Johnny," she laughed as she gathered up what she had used, "you were shot on the first of July. Today is the 11th. Pain is strongest the first week, and you're past that. You've been up and around, so your circulation has been maintained. You've also been distracted. You'll probably need a half a pain tab tonight – that's what I've been giving you lately – but that's it. Back in a moment, and I'll wrap you up."

Cathy left the room, and he heard water splashing as she began to soak the bandages.

"I'm really better?" he asked skeptically when she returned and began working on the elastic wrapping.

"Johnny, you're over the worst. It's still going to take time, but the real mess is behind you." She grinned at the puzzlement on his face. "Kinda snuck by you, didn't it."

"Yeah, I guess. So everything worked?"

"You mean the penicillin bread mold, the oral antibiotics, and such?" She continued at his nod. "Yep. And now that you're past the crisis point, I have a confession to make." She sat in the chair she had brought in earlier.

"Oh?"

"Johnny, being here, without the backup I'm used to – labs, equipment, nurses, x-rays, and such – I feel you should know that I've been making a lot of this up as I went along. There were times I was scared that I wasn't going to be able to do right by you." She sighed, and studied her hands in her lap. "I hope knowing this doesn't undermine your confidence in me."

"Uh, Catie?" John waited until she looked up at him before continuing, "Nothing could make me trust you less. The circumstances were horrendous, and you've been amazing."

"I just wish we knew for certain if saving Buford and the Union line was why we ended up here." She regarded him closely. "Okay, let's have it. What happened this evening?"

John related his conversation with Scovel and Weston.

"You think there's something going on with this group of theirs."

"Exactly. There are copperheads all over the North, people who believe that the South should have been able to secede peacefully. I don't know if that's exactly what these men believe, but since I have been invited to attend, I think I should."

"I agree you should check it out. I've overheard some murmurs at the store in the past few days that fit with this, although I put it up to grumblings about what happened to the town before, during, and after the battle." She paused. "I can't blame them for feeling abused – this town was ransacked, twice, in addition to being bombarded and occupied."

32

"Most battles took place outside of places like this and few lasted for three days of active fighting. Here the battle shifted from one side of town to the other with a running battle in between. Other places were decimated as Sherman tore through, burning things to the ground, and Vicksburg was under siege and devastated for a long time – that was broken last weekend – but although there was no outright fighting in the streets here, there were snipers doing target practice." John shook his head slowly. "Gettysburg was one of the big ones, and the civilian population took it right on the chin. They were occupied by each side at least once, caught in the crossfire, and both sides grabbed supplies."

"And here we are, smack in the middle." Cathy rose. "Do you need anything?"

"Water would be nice." John tried – unsuccessfully – to stifle a yawn. "I'm bushed."

"The ales helped relax you – and I'm really glad you enjoyed your evening," she said as she came back with a cup of water. "Scovel seems nice, if a bit of a loner. Looks like he's opening up a bit with your help. What's the other man like. Weston? If he's the one I think he is, I waited on him in the store yesterday."

"You did. Tall guy, curly sandy hair, blue eyes."

"Yep – dimple in his cheek when he smiles."

"That's him. And he'd take the fact that you noticed the dimple as encouragement to court you. He asked some pretty pointed questions about you this evening, including my permission to court you."

"*What?* Oh, damn! This we don't need."

"I did my best to strongly discourage him." John laughed at the sour face she made. "I don't think it had occurred to either of us that this could happen once things calmed down."

"I'm too old for this nonsense," she mumbled crossly.

"So am I, but be prepared. I suspect we are both going to have to rebuff advances, as the saying goes." John made a face of his own. "It doesn't help that neither of us looks thirty-five."

"Yep, our thirty-five looks more like contemporary twenty." Cathy grimaced. "Mary finally asked me how old I am. I knew she wouldn't believe that she's only six years older than I am, and I was right."

"Were you honest?"

"Hell no! I scalped it down to thirty, and she still didn't believe me. I told her all the women in my family have always looked younger than their years." She sighed. "At least she understands that I don't want to be courted."

Suddenly, John yawned. "Damn, I'm tired."

Cathy laughed, and announced she too was ready for bed.

Sunday, 12 July

Cathy awoke first. A light rain was falling, although an occasional bird could be heard. If the ground was wet, they couldn't walk to town, though. Crutches got stuck in mud. She sat up and peered at the clock. Eight o'clock. For her, that was sleeping in. She regarded John, still sound asleep. He was lying on his side, facing her. Man, if she was attracting attention from the local men, wait until the local single ladies got a look at him! She had always envied him his long, dark eye lashes – his looked better than hers, even after she applied mascara.

His eyes opened, bleary as they usually were first thing, and he smiled.

"Good morning," she said with a smile. "It's about eight, and it's raining."

"Good for the garden, bad for walking."

"Yep. We can't walk in, I'm afraid. Let's get dressed anyway."

"What do you know that I don't?" John got up and grabbed the jar on his bedside table.

"Nothing – but I'd be willing to bet that Mr. John comes out for us. It's Sunday, and although the church still has wounded in it, Miss Martha was wondering if there would be some sort of service somewhere in town." Cathy rose, rolled up her bed, stretched, and began to dress.

"So, what's this great experiment you are planning for the ale we brought back?"

"Ah – something that Gran taught me how to do the day she wanted to make some bread but didn't have any yeast. Grandad always had beer, so I learned the world's simplest recipe."

"Your beer bread! I should have guessed! Mom loves the loaves you make at Christmas." John handed her the jar, got his crutches and stood up. "I'll wash using the pitcher and bowl in the main room. That will save you bringing it in here."

"Thank you. I'll grab a pail of water from the stream and see how muddy the ground is."

The rain was no more than a drizzle, but has been going on most of the night judging by the softness of the ground. Cathy got a pail of water, took a look at her garden – growing nicely – and went back inside. She wiped her shoes on a spread of cut tall grass she had placed on the edge of the porch Friday. Some sort of doormat would be nice, she thought. If necessary, she could weave tall grass or wheat stalks.

John was dressed and at the table. He had the tea kettle on the stove and mugs set out. After a light breakfast, she put together two loaves of beer bread, making one plain and the other with molasses, ginger, and cinnamon. They were playing a game of cribbage, enjoying the smell of the fresh bread that was now cooling, when they heard the sounds of a carriage pulling up outside.

Cathy automatically glanced around to make sure nothing modern was showing – she pocketed her watch and stashed one of her books in a dresser drawer. John had gotten up and was opening the door when Cathy came to stand beside him.

The Scotts and Mary McAllister were getting out of their carriage, and all three were carrying chairs. The two women came inside and Scott went back to the cart to get a large picnic hamper.

"Please excuse the intrusion," Martha began. "It is my doing – I insisted on coming out here to see the cabin about which I have heard so much. I had to see for myself that you are not tenting in the woods. John told me that you only had two chairs, and we thought it would only be polite to bring extras since we figure to stay to dinner."

Scott handed Cathy the hamper. "My lady would not presume to arrive empty-handed, so we also brought the dinner," he said, smiling. "I have some canvas and rope. With your permission, I'd like to see if I can fashion a small shelter for the pony, although the drizzle is letting up." He sat down at the table. "Where would be the best place?"

"Why not extend the lean-to of the woodshed, using some trees as anchors?" John grabbed his pad of paper and a pencil, quickly sketching what he had in mind. "This may work."

Scott took the sketch and studied it for a moment. "I believe you're right, Captain. I shall give this a try." Refusing offers of assistance, the older man went back outside.

Martha, having already taken a tour of the small cabin, started unpacking the hamper. She set dishes on the table while Mary placed serving dishes on the stove.

"Cathy, it smells wonderful in here," Martha observed. "Is this the bread you made with ale?"

"My Gran ran out of yeast one day, and decided to try to use the beer that Grandad always had on hand," Cathy explained with a grin. "He initially fussed like a wet cat, but once he tasted it, he quit and behaved himself."

"May I have the recipe?" Martha asked.

"It's so simple it's embarrassing," Cathy confessed. "I use three cups of flour, four and a half teaspoonful of baking powder, a half a teaspoonful of salt, a tablespoonful of sugar, and a cup and a half of beer or ale. Mix the dry ingredients first, add the beer, and pour it into a greased loaf pan. Gran discovered that beer – or ale – has enough yeast in it to make it rise."

"You do not knead it?"

"No, and it does not have to rise. That is the beauty of it." Cathy looked at John's watch on the sideboard. "It takes about an hour to bake. These are cooling. I was going to bring you a loaf when we came into town today, but the weather had other notions."

"Captain, your design for the shelter worked just fine," Scott reported as he came back in. "Cathy, that smells as good as anything Martha makes."

"That is beer bread, John, or rather ale bread," Martha informed him. "Cathy gave me the recipe, and I can't wait to try it."

"Personally, I can't wait to sample it," Scott commented as he sat down.

"The real fun to this bread is playing with it," Cathy confided to Martha. "You can add almost anything to it. One loaf is plain, but I added molasses and some spices to the other. Gran adds honey, fruit, raisins, nuts, and such to hers."

The warm ale bread – immediately pronounced a success – made a terrific addition to the meal brought out by the visitors. Chatting long after they finished eating, the cleanup was quickly accomplished.

"The sun's coming out," John announced as he opened the door.

"Cathy, may I see your garden?" Martha asked.

Cathy showed her small plot to the sisters, leaving the men to relax on the bench after they dried it off.

"I must confess the cabin is much better appointed than I had feared," Martha commented, "and you have done wonders with this garden. That does remind me – we brought something you might find useful."

Mary went to their carriage and returned holding a garden hoe.

"I have no idea how you managed all this without one," she said as she handed it over.

"Oh, this is delightful! It will be well-used, I assure you. I know we have thanked you before, but we shall forever be grateful for all your kindness and generosity," Cathy said sincerely. "Without your gifts, this would be a much more primitive place. We are really quite content here. My only envy of you in town is your gas lighting!"

"What about water?" Martha asked. "The tea was remarkable."

"It's spring water."

"Spring water?" Mary asked.

"The evening before the battle I made a wonderful discovery which has been a true blessing," Cathy explained, taking them behind the cabin. "It was very quiet and I heard a low, gurgling sound. When I investigated, I found this."

"Well, I'll be – your own spring!" Mary stooped to taste it. "It is wonderful!"

"It almost makes up for not having gas lighting," Cathy said with a laugh, "but not quite!"

The visitors left soon after. Cathy had been unable to convince the sisters that the dishes and chairs should go back to town. Mary declared that the chairs weren't needed, and Martha stated that the dishes should be used the next time the siblings had company, which Scott pointed out, might be they. John smiled to see Cathy overruled, which she did accept with grace.

"Once again, I can't believe how lucky we are to have found such friends," she commented as she put the new dishes up.

"Mr. John asked if Bartholomew Scovel was interested in you," John informed her.

"Yikes. What did you tell him?"

"I told him we were actively trying to discourage anything like that on the grounds we won't be staying here."

"Cripes, I hope we can get that to stick," Cathy replied, getting the cribbage board out again. "Maybe…"

There was a knock on the door.

"We appear to be Grand Central Station," John commented, getting his crutches.

"Does it exist yet?" Cathy queried.

"For the record, no. Grand Central Depot won't open on that site for another eight years." John opened the door. Both Scovel and Weston were there, having arrived on horseback.

"May we come in?" Scovel asked. "I hope we aren't intruding."

"This seems to be our day for callers. Please, come in," John said with a smile. "Mr. Weston, I believe you know my sister, Miss Howell. Cathy, this is James Weston, a friend of Bartholomew's."

"We weren't introduced at the store," Weston said, bowing slightly. "Miss Howell, I'm pleased to make your acquaintance."

"Johnny, now that the rain has stopped, I thought I'd see how the garden is doing. I didn't get the chance to weed this morning."

"Fine, Catie," he said, as she went outside. "May I offer you gentlemen a cup of tea or a glass of water, and perhaps a slice of Cathy's bread?"

Both men shook their heads, and Weston, who had followed Cathy with his eyes as she went by him, added a verbal "no thank you". They sat at the table while John stood his crutches against the wall.

"Captain, James wanted to know where your cabin was, and the easiest way was to show him," Scovel began. "I hope you and Miss Howell don't mind. We seem to have chased her out."

"Pay that no mind," John said, chuckling, "as I suspect that is exactly what she would have done even if you hadn't come by. Cathy planted a vegetable garden last week, and she didn't get to it yesterday. I believe she has declared war on the weeds, and knowing her, she will prevail."

***

Cathy hoped that John realized she was trying to put some distance between her and the two men, and she turned her attention to the garden. She weeded and pulled some soil up around the sprouts on the hills, finding the task much easier with the hoe. For one thing, she was able to do it without kneeling – always a plus. Once she finished, she washed her hands in the stream, wiped them on one of the privy cloths, and wandered in the woods for a while picking wildflowers. Checking the watch that was still in her pocket, she saw she had given the men a good half-hour, yet when she got back to the cabin, the horses were still tethered. *And here we go. I'm not ready for this.*

Scovel and Weston stood as she entered. John asked if her chores were done, and she nodded as she placed the flowers in the container she regularly used for them. She noted that the conversation had ceased abruptly.

"I hope I'm not interrupting anything, gentlemen," she said as she put the tea kettle on the stove. Scovel sat down, but Weston remained standing.

"Miss Howell, you have made this rustic cabin a true home for your brother," Weston commented, "and you are to be commended."

"Mr. Weston, while I do appreciate the compliment I feel I must add, at the risk of impertinence, that I too live here, so my motives in making it a home are not quite as pure as you would make them sound." Cathy happened to catch John's eye, and he winked.

"My admiration still stands," Weston said with a smile.

"I thank you, sir. You, on the other hand, may be seated." Cathy knew she was bordering on a breach of centuries, but she had the feeling that this man was not going to be deterred easily. *He's charming, but not nearly as charming as he thinks he is. Oh well. Maybe Mary was right about leaving the chairs here.* She made herself a cup of tea and joined them at the table. "Mr. Scovel, I would like to thank you once again for offering my brother an evening out," she said truthfully. "He truly did need it."

"At times I fear that my sister knows me better than I know myself," John commented with a smile.

"I am hoping we can prevail upon the Captain to join us again in the near future," Weston said, "with your permission."

"I trust I have not given the impression that he needs my permission," she replied. "Since I will be working at Miss McAllister's store, time is bound to lie heavily on his hands, especially since he is still recovering from his wounds."

"How serious were his injuries?" Weston asked.

Cathy looked at John with a raised eyebrow. "I would have supposed that he had already informed you of this, unless you want the medical assessment and are seeking confirmation that I am what I claim to be."

Weston looked uncomfortable. "I do not wish to test you, yet most wounds severe enough to excuse a man from returning to duty also end in amputation."

"John took a bullet in his leg, which was partially deflected by a silver dollar he was carrying in his pocket. I cleaned the wound, removed the bullet and the coin, stitched what I could, and set a dressing." Cathy noted that Scovel was taking deep breaths, so she smiled. "Gentlemen, I am a trained nurse, and I am not squeamish – for the sake of those who come under my care, I cannot afford to be." She looked at Weston, who nodded.

"Please, ma'am, forgive me. My only excuse is an error of judgment, entirely my own. Your appearance belies your qualifications."

"Cathy, I believe you should translate his words to mean you look too pretty and ladylike to get your hands bloody in my leg wound. Or words to that effect," John put in, smothering the urge to smile. "You need not be so severe on him, as I suspect he meant it as a compliment. I suggest you consider it as such and accept it."

"Mr. Weston, I am well aware that most people who see me take me as I appear." Cathy gave a small shrug with the ghost of a smile to soften her reaction, "yet my brother is undoubtedly correct to imply I am over-reacting."

"Again, I would ask your forgiveness," Weston said, shifting uneasily in his chair.

"Gladly given, sir." Cathy felt sorry for the man, in a way. *He's more likeable when he wasn't trying to shower me with compliments and charm, but he didn't let it happen enough. Oh well.*

"Perhaps you should also understand that most men would be heartily uncomfortable with the notion of having a severe injury treated by a woman," John suggested gently.

"Perhaps," she said. "Fortunately for you, you are not among them."

"I learned to accept you as an equal long ago, beginning with the first time you beat me in a race around the apple orchard," John commented. "We were on horseback, and she was six years of age."

Cathy laughed. "If memory serves, you were crushed for a week or more."

"At the lofty age of almost, um, eight, it was hard to admit I had been soundly trounced by my little sister," he admitted, chuckling, hoping the men didn't notice his stutter over his age. "The knowledge that it was I who had put her on the horse did not increase my complacency."

"How odd – it did mine," Cathy said in all innocence as the visitors laughed. "Johnny, did you not offer your guests some refreshment? Perhaps tea and some of the bread with honey?"

"Ma'am," said Scovel, "we appreciate the hospitality, but we only came by so I could show James the cabin."

"Most of the folks in town know of the grandfather cabin, but few can agree on its actual location," Weston explained. "I myself believed it to be closer to the rail bridge." He rose, offering his hand to John. "Captain, I would be pleased if you would meet us at the Globe this Wednesday evening."

"I would be honored. Would it be possible to let you know that day to confirm it? As my sister continually reminds me, I am still healing, and I do find myself getting tired. I find I also have to take the weather into consideration as I have discovered that crutches and mud are not compatible. I shall send a message into town with her for you, if that would be acceptable."

"Of course," replied Scovel. "We shall hope to hear from you then."

After the usual parting salutations, the men left.

"Okay, what the hell is going on?" Cathy asked as she stoked the stove. "I got out of your way, partly for my own reasons, but your faces when I came back in were screaming volumes."

"I told you that there seems to be a group of men who are, let's say, dissatisfied with the war and how it is going. They gather every now and then – nothing super regular, usually once every other week or so - but vary the day and place. I've been invited to the next gathering."

"Wouldn't a tavern be a bit too public?"

"Yeah, but just because we meet there doesn't mean we stay there – or at least that's the impression I'm getting." John gave a heavy sigh. "I don't know where this is going, but every instinct in me is telling me I have to check it out."

"I agree. Just be careful."

"No problem." He got up from the table, grabbed his crutches, and went outside.

Cathy set up the board and shuffled the cards.

"Where'd the hoe come from?" John asked as he came back in.

"Johnny, where does anything that shows up here come from? Mary thought it might be useful, and I admit it was lots easier doing the garden stuff with it."

As they began the game, John told Cathy that she had handled the situation with Weston well. In return, she asked for his take on it.

"It's obvious that they are both interested," he replied. "Can you be prickly without getting hostile?"

"That's asking a lot – there's a fine line between the two. Maybe I can intimidate with brilliance. For some reason, Weston makes me feel a bit uneasy, probably because he pushes. I wonder why he has not married."

"Who knows – maybe his standards are too high."

"Mr. Scovel is more low-key. He seems patient, and much more genuine."

"Good luck. Weston is a bachelor and Scovel is a widower." John grinned suddenly. "Oh, as you suggested yesterday, my turn at the romance thing may come after all. Apparently, Weston has a sister who is single. She's out of town at the moment."

"Great. Back home, I know exactly how to deal with this, but here I'm totally hampered by etiquette, especially if you are getting involved in something with them." She put down her last card for thirty-one. "Count 'em up."

"If this group thing goes deep, I may have to play along in order to deal with it," John said as Cathy pegged twice his score.

"Just keep me up to date so we can decide how I should handle it." Cathy shuffled and dealt. "Have you considered that this group, and whatever they want to do, is another part of why we're here?"

"That was one of my first thoughts last night at the tavern. If it is, I definitely need to get involved."

"Cripes, nothing is simple for us, is it?"

CHAPTER THREE:
THE REST OF JULY, 1863

As the days passed, John and Cathy realized that their lives had settled into a pattern, which Cathy decreed a good thing. She pointed out that life is easier once this happens because humans can stress out if they have to plan each day as it comes, rather than letting it fall into set parameters.

"And you called me a show-off," John grumbled the evening this came up.

"I am, after all, a doctor. It's...."

"In your job description," he finished for her, laughing. "Yeah, I know."

Cathy's job at the store gave her the opportunity to be busy enough to begin to avoid her would-be suitors, as she was able to remind them that she was, after all, working. Mary McAllister, who recognized that Cathy was genuinely not interested, lent her considerable experience in this vein to back Cathy's decision about it. John noted that Cathy started to let her own personality creep slowly out from underneath the social etiquette of the era, gradually enough so she didn't set off any major alarm bells.

Wednesday, 15 July

John's stitches came out at two weeks, a bit longer than normal but Cathy decided to be cautious, especially since they hadn't all gone in at the same time.

"Okay, they are out," she informed him as she cleaned up. "It's a milestone, but that doesn't mean everything is fully healed."

"Do I still need the splint?" he asked as she reapplied a dressing and the elastic bandage.

"Probably."

One day without it convinced him she was right. When he admitted it she told him he was learning.

Monday, 20 July

After another week of staying home while Cathy worked, John found a job of his own, volunteering at the Sanitary Commission headquarters in town, now located at the Fahnestock Store.

He was known for his work on the rail bridge, but it was his natural sense of order and organization, coupled with the fact that he was an officer who was wounded in battle, that kept him there. It didn't hurt that once in a while his engineering skills were utilized, and he came to be well-regarded. Still on crutches and using the cast splint, the people around him assisted him as much as he would let them.

Thursday, 23 July

At noon, Cathy looked out the front window of the store, stopped in the middle of a step, and dropped the bundle she was placing on a shelf. It hit the floor with a dull thud, drawing Mary's attention.

"Cathy, is something wrong?" Mary came out from behind the back counter, where she had been weighing and packaging bacon. Wiping her hands on her apron, she approached her friend, who was staring out the window.

"I don't believe that 'wrong' is the correct word. I prefer to say I was startled," she explained. She pointed out the window before picking up the fallen package.

John had just pulled up driving a small, partially covered wagon which was drawn an animal. Cathy couldn't decide if it was a small horse or a large pony. As the women watched, he drew his crutches from behind his seat, and began to make his way to the door. Upon seeing the two women in the window, he gave a big grin and bowed.

"Goodness, where did he get that?" Mary asked, staring at it.

"I have no idea – this is the first I have seen it. I assure you I shall find out once he comes in here."

Mary chuckled. "May I assist?"

"Oh, please do. Better still, why don't you perform the honors? He contends I tease him enough as it is."

As John opened the door to the shop, Mary greeted him with her hands on her hips, while Cathy moved to stand beside her.

"Captain? Is that your cart?"

"Yes, Miss Mary, it is."

"You do not own a cart."

"I do now." John reached into his jacket and pulled out a letter. "Before I explain, however, Cathy needs to see this." He handed it to Cathy. "It arrived today."

"It's from – Myles Keogh!" Cathy looked from the envelope in her hand to glance at John. "It is addressed to you in care of the Scotts. How in heaven's name he get the address?"

"I gave General Buford the Scotts' address when I first signed on with him. I had asked Miss Martha if this was acceptable, and Mr. John spoke to Mr. Buehler," he replied referring to the town's postmaster. John's grin got wider. "Read it. You're mentioned, too."

As Cathy read the letter, John explained to Mary that Major Keogh was General Buford's aide. Cathy groaned, almost on cue, as John added that the former Captain had begun to show interest in Cathy.

Mary snickered and murmured, "Completely understandable. I wonder if he is aware he's standing in line."

"He wouldn't be surprised," John murmured back. "He might even be at the head of it."

"Johnny, he says you have received a brevet promotion to major, you've been honorably discharged, and" she looked up with wonderment, "you got back pay!"

John reached into his pocket and pulled out a larger envelope. Cathy took it and shook out shoulder boards for major. Eyes shining, she gave him such a big hug she almost knocked him over.

"Take care! If I fall, you'll have to do more surgery!" John teased, laughing.

"How is all this possible?" Mary asked.

"According to Major Keogh's letter, General Buford felt obliged to honor John for his actions in the battle," Cathy explained, carefully choosing her words. "The promotion and discharge were a matter of paperwork, apparently."

"The general is about to go on personal leave, and they managed to push it through channels before he left. Captain, excuse me, Major Keogh, was ordered to arrange the pay voucher, which I cashed at the bank," John added.

"So you used the money to buy a cart?" Mary inquired.

"No, ma'am. Last week some children found what was left of a wagon in a ditch. The base of the box was fine, the wheels were off but still useable, and the rest was broken and splintered. With carts being scarce, I told Mr. Fahnestock I thought I could build a working cart out of it, and he said if I could, I could keep it in order get to town more easily. Young Dan helped me with the actual work after I sketched it. When I reported to the Commission this morning, it was waiting for me."

"Well, that explains the cart but not the horse," Mary stated, repressing a smile.

Cathy noted that John's grin was, if anything, getting broader. *He's enjoying this interrogation as much as Mary.*

"That is a nice, but odd-looking animal," Mary continued. "Is it a large pony?"

"Dizzy is a small horse. She is too small to use for plowing or hauling much, and much too small for most to ride. She belonged to James Weston's aunt." John turned to look at his rig and the animal hitched to it. "She's very nice, well-behaved, and seems to like me."

"Did you buy her?"

"I paid a little less than half of what a normal-sized horse would have cost. We needed something to pull the cart," he explained. "Mr. Weston offered her to me last week, but I told him I couldn't manage to ride yet. When I knew the wagon was going to work, I asked him if she was still for sale. Come outside and meet her. She's very gentle."

The two women followed him out to the rig. Cathy went to Dizzy, and petted her. John was right – she was gentle, and seemed to enjoy the attention. For her part, Mary examined the wagon itself.

"Captain. Oh, I do beg your pardon. Major, you seem to have crafted something that is not quite a wagon and not quite a carriage."

"That, Miss Mary, was precisely my intention. Going back and forth to the cabin, we needed something smaller than a wagon because most of it is just a pathway, yet I wanted it to have the capacity of a small cart. I also designed it to be sheltered enough for use in case of rain."

Cathy turned from the horse and studied the cart. At first all she could think of was a station wagon, akin to an old El Camino. No, it reminded her of something else…a pickup truck! Peering into the bed, she saw a piece of canvas rolled up and secured to the side, ready to cover the open bed. A pickup with a cap! She gave him another hug, and murmured, "Toyota, eat your heart out." Out loud, she said to Mary, "I'm going to call it a carriage cart!"

John laughed. "I'll be back to pick you up at closing time." He got back into his creation and guided Dizzy onto the street. More than one person turned to look at the odd vehicle, but if he was aware of it, he ignored it.

"I must admit he's never dull," Mary commented as she and Cathy returned to the store. "Oh, here come Martha and John."

Martha craned her neck to watch John go down the street as she opened the door; her husband was still on the street, staring at the receding vehicle.

"What on earth is that?" Martha asked when they were both inside.

"That, dear sister, is Major Andrews' new carriage cart, complete with his new horse."

"Major?" Martha echoed.

"That's a horse?" asked Scott.

Mary and Cathy looked at each other and laughed before offering explanations. Scott wondered aloud if that sort of wagon would ever catch on. Cathy just smiled to herself. Yep, the nineteenth century version of a small pickup truck was exactly what they needed.

Over lunch, Scott asked Cathy when John was going to be able to start walking without the crutches.

"I honestly cannot say. It's been less than a month since the battle and the muscles in his leg were badly torn. They need time to mend. I am hoping he'll be able to start using only one crutch next week, but I do not imagine he will be walking on his own until the middle of August." She smiled. "At least that is what I told him last night when he asked that very question. He's getting impatient, yet he is at a stage of healing where he could do some serious damage if he's not careful."

"As I did by getting out of bed too soon," Scott said quietly.

"That is a good analogy, Mr. John. If John starts to bear weight on his leg too soon, the muscles which are not fully healed could tear even more." She shuddered. "I would not care to speculate on that. We discussed this at length, and I believe he understands the risks. Meanwhile, he has gotten quite agile with the crutches."

***

Late in the afternoon, Cathy was sweeping the floor in preparation for closing when the door opened, admitting James Weston.

"Mr. Weston, good afternoon. How may we help you?" Cathy asked.

"I was wondering if your brother would be free this evening."

"I wouldn't presume to speak for him, sir, however, he will be coming to pick me up at closing time, which is not far off," she replied. "Have you seen his new wagon? I understand he got his horse from your aunt with your help."

"Little Dizzy – yes, she was belonged to my aunt. We named her Dizzy because when she was a colt she kept going around in circles," he explained with a smile. "I have not yet seen the wagon myself, but I've spoken to at least three people who have. It must be quite a sight."

"It is that, certainly," Cathy laughed. "I have named it a carriage cart, and it's unique. I suspect it will be exactly what we need for our journeys between the cabin and town. Did you try to find John at the Sanitation Commission? He is usually there on Thursday afternoons, although they may be asking him to make a few deliveries now that he can get around town."

"Ma'am, they recommended that I see if he was here, not that I needed an excuse to come in and say hello to you."

"Mr. Weston, I thought it was understood that I am not interested in being courted, by you or anyone else," Cathy kept her tone light, but the words were serious.

"Miss Howell, you cannot blame a man for trying," he replied, and as she started to speak again, added, "please, I mean no disrespect."

"Mr. Weston, you are a friend to my brother, and I hope to me, but I

46

must insist that we keep it at that. I sincerely hope you will honor my choice, as that is all I can or intend to offer." She hoped that was firm and clear.

"What about Bartholomew?"

"This is not a competition with me as the prize, I assure you." Cathy knew her tone was getting sharp, and tried to soften it. "I had this very conversation with him over the weekend." *And he took it far more gracefully than you seem to be doing.*

The shop door opened.

"James! I heard you were looking for me," John greeted his friend, needing only one look at Cathy to realize what he had interrupted.

"I was wondering if you were free this evening," Weston said. He looked out the window. "So *that* is what all the talk is about!"

"Come outside and see for yourself." John showed his friend the features of his odd vehicle, which was admired for being different yet functional.

"The bench you designed is the same way – you can see it is a bench, but it is different." Weston nodded his head towards the store behind them. "I may have angered her again."

"James, you must give up thoughts of courting her, please for all our sakes." John shook his head. "You may take some consolation from knowing it is nothing against you. Cathy simply does not wish to marry. She prefers friends to suitors and making her own living to being dependent on anyone. Who is to say – in years to come, her way of thinking might become normal for women." *How about women's liberation, a century early. Sheesh.*

"So it's not against me, or Bartholomew, or...."

"—or any other man she's ever met. I have seen many men try, and she's never found one for whom she was willing to trade her independence." John realized that his words were basically the same now as when he had tried to explain this to one of Cathy's admirers, a friend of his at the university 'back home'. He knew Cathy had a similar speech about him.

"Please tell her I'm beginning to see what you both mean," Weston said slowly. "I meant no harm."

"I believe you will find she knows you do not," John said. *Geez, I hope like hell the lecture will take this time.* "Now, you wanted to know if I am free this evening." He was wondering if this was to be another meeting of the disgruntled.

"Yes. My sister is back in town, and I am planning to visit. I thought you might like to accompany me. She's staying with my aunt – the woman who sold you Dizzy."

John, realizing that the other man meant well, got out of it as gracefully as he could, knowing if he went it would be taken as the first step of courtship. *Things were much easier, when it came to this aspect of life, in their own society, where independence was better understood.* The invitation was declined with no lumps to the friendship. Thankfully Weston took his refusal better than he had Cathy's and went on his way.

Returning to the store, John perched on a stool. "Miss Mary, why does everyone assume that a single person is unhappy in his or her unmarried state?"

"I have no idea, although I have been striving to answer that question for years. Did anything specific prompt it this time," she asked, smiling, "or are you merely offering it as a topic for conversation?"

"After I made another attempt at the lecture with James regarding Cathy's aversion to being courted, he invited me to go with him to visit his aunt and sister." John's sigh was a first cousin to a moan. "Miss Mary, you have successfully maintained your independence. My diplomatic skills are withering as we speak. Are there any tricks I should know?"

"Shall we go across the street and discuss this over a cup of tea?"

***

On the way back to the cabin in John's new conveyance, Cathy asked what John had expected Weston's invitation to be.

"I thought it was going to be another group meeting, and I would have accepted that. Frankly, I'm beginning to get worried. There are two real hotheads, and I seem to spend half my time keeping things calm."

"You've mentioned them before, although not by name."

"You don't need to know any names, at least not yet. It's strange, because most of the men are there simply to blow off steam, voice their fears about the war continuing, and grumble about how conditions in town are bad. These two seem to really want to incite some sort of action."

"You mean a protest or demonstration?"

"I'm not sure. If they want to send a few guys to Washington to meet with the president – that can be relatively easily done now, it's not like the background checks and body searches we have back home – fine. I'd even offer to go with them, and Lincoln would probably listen. But they seem to be waiting for something to happen that they can turn into a rallying cry for drastic action, and that's what has me worried."

They reached the cabin in silence. John climbed down from his seat, and the two of them unhitched and unharnessed Dizzy. He took a halter and leading rope out of a leather bag in the back of the wagon and tethered her under the tarp John Scott had put up. Cathy put an armful of grass and a bucket of water in her reach. They both talked to her and fussed over her while they were working.

"She really seems sweet," Cathy observed, "and gentle. I hope she likes it here."

"I'll see what I can do about putting together a corral of some sort tomorrow. I mentioned it to Mr. John today and he may come out to help me.

Once that's done, I'll go into town and pick up the other things we'll need to take care of her."

Inside, John removed his splint while Cathy got supper together. They were enjoying radishes from the garden, and the spinach and lettuce were almost ready. Cathy had discovered that cooking the radishes in a stew or soup added extra zip, but John preferred them raw.

"Catie – I'm really proud of you," John told her as they started supper. "I know this hasn't been easy."

"I could say the same about you, MAJOR. That's impressive, Johnny, really." Cathy spread some butter on a piece of her ale bread. "But I've got to ask: what is a brevet major?"

"I guessed you didn't quite catch that. It's pretty simple, really. A brevet promotion is usually given in the field as an acknowledgment of outstanding service or meritorious conduct. You get the rank and you are called by the rank, without the authority or pay of the higher rank. Buford could do this pretty much on his own, and Myles probably did the paperwork." John smiled thoughtfully. "In a way, I am not surprised they did it. The real shock was the back pay. They got me more than just battle pay, Catie. I don't know how they did it, but I have six months of back pay."

"General Buford was concerned about us having some income," she said, recalling that officer's question the evening he had paid his surprise visit to the cabin the day John was shot. "I told him I would be working in the store, but I don't think that satisfied him. Okay, how much does a Union Captain make?"

"At this time of the war, captains make about $115 a month. To give you a comparison, Union privates make $13 a month. We have enough to live on for at least six months," he said, grinning. "Is there anything you need?"

"I'll think about it, but it's nice to know we can start buying our own groceries, and with the chairs and dishes here, we can invite the Scotts over for dinner once in a while. I know they'd never accept outright repayment, so we'll have to get sneaky about it." She grinned back at him.

"We even have the means to bring things home now, too. I'm sure Dizzy won't mind as long as we don't try for a load of bricks."

"Weston told me how she got her name – I love it."

After she cleaned up their dishes, with John helping put them away, Cathy said seriously, "Tell me more about your hot-heads."

"The men, in general, would like to see the war end. Period. The two hot-heads seem willing to do something, anything, to precipitate it - and that really concerns me. I think they see any means as justifying the ends."

"Fanatics of any kind are scary. Any idea of what they want to try?"

"No. So far I've eased in as someone from outside who has been through the horrors, and I have agreed that the war is bad. They don't trust me enough yet to let me into the deep stuff, but I'm making progress. That's why I haven't told you everything – most of what I have are suspicions, and you see most of these men at the store."

"I was getting a bit anxious about that, to be honest – but I can understand your reasoning."

"If and when more substance shows itself, I'll let you know, I promise. Meanwhile, each time I'm with them, I become more certain that it's tied up with why we're here."

"You know, I'd really kill for a script of this," Cathy said, frowning. "I hate having to feel our way through it. I keep thinking I can completely obliterate the world we know by cleaning a cut on someone's finger."

"Time. I've always enjoyed movies and shows that focus on time travel, but I guess I never fully appreciated how easy they make it look. It's really complex."

"If that entity – the one whose voice I heard in my head? – if it turns out his name is Al, I'll quit."

"Wibbley, wobbly, timey-wimey…" John began with a grin.

"Johnny, your stitches may be out, but don't press your luck."

Thursday, 30 July

Under Cathy's watchful eye, and using all the tips she offered, John carefully maneuvered around the main room of the cabin on one crutch. She had agreed only after he was able to demonstrate using his leg muscles to move his injured leg, and suggested he keep using the splint until he got used to it. He had wanted to place the crutch under his arm on his right side – to use it in place of the injured leg – and she let him try it. Then she told him to shift the crutch to his left side and move his bad leg with the crutch, and decide for himself.

"You're right. It's better this way," he said, moving the crutch back to his left side.

"You need to start bearing a bit of weight on that leg, but not much. Use your toes to balance – that'll be enough for a start."

"Gotcha." He went around the room again, and sank onto a chair. "Is it okay for me to go to town today?"

"As long as we both go, yes, since you know how to reach me in case you have problems." Cathy got breakfast on the table. "You've been awfully quiet about last night."

"Not much to report. One of the hot-heads wasn't there, and we stayed at the tavern. It was mostly social." He smiled as he ate. "Frankly, it was a relief. Just a guys' night out. I figured I needed to listen and be friendly. You know, build up my acceptance."

"You still feel this is part of the whole thing?"

"More than ever. It could be the key." He rose as she collected their dishes. "I'll go out and get Dizzy hitched up. Having only one crutch should make it easier."

"I'll be out shortly," she said.

***

Cathy looked up as Mary called to her that John had just pulled up outside.

"Has the day gone by so quickly?" she called back. "Truly, it does seem as if I just arrived."

"He's early – it is only three o'clock," Mary informed her. "However, if he is ready to go back to the cabin, you can leave now. We have accomplished what needed to be done today."

Cathy came to the front window. John was sitting in their cart, making no move to come in. "Mary, let me see if there is something he wants."

At Mary's nod, Cathy went out to the cart.

"Johnny, what's wrong?"

"Can you leave? We need to talk."

"Easily – I'll be right back." Cathy wasted no time in the store, and with Mary's blessings, was back outside in less than five minutes.

"I hope you know that you're scaring me," she said as she got on the seat beside him.

"Brace yourself, because I'm going to make it worse," he replied, "but let's get back to the cabin first."

Cathy waited, not patiently, while they made their way along the well-marked shortcut trail to the cabin. Once there, they unhitched Dizzy, putting her into the corral John had built with the help of John Scott and Bartholomew Scovel, which included a small lean-to that provided shelter for the small horse during rain.

John sat on the bench, motioning for Cathy to sit beside him.

"We are going to take a trip to Washington, D.C.," John began. "I have to meet the president."

"Whoa! Can you back up a bit? I assume you have uncovered a plan or plot being developed by your hot-heads, but it's quite a leap from 'oh, it was social' to 'we need to meet the president'. Can you be more definite?"

"Sorry, you're right, of course." John looked up at the sky, then down at the ground, which Cathy recognized as something he did when he was searching for words. She kept quiet, knowing the tale would flow once he was ready.

"Bartholomew came to the Commission today and confided that another man in the group had just told him that one of the hot-heads, the one who didn't show up last night, was planning to plant some sort of explosive in the White House."

"When....what..., er, why...." Cathy stopped to let the logjam of thoughts in her mind steady out a bit. "Let me try that again.... Why did Bartholomew come to you?"

"He trusts me, he trusts you, and I think he believes I can do something about it." John shrugged. "He feels, and I agree, that most of the guys in the group don't want this kind of action. Grousing is one thing, but terror is something else."

"When is this supposed to happen?"

"Sometime in mid-August." John sighed. "With Washington basically surrounded on three sides by Confederate states, this was almost inevitable, and Maryland is not exactly clear of copperheads. We apparently have some time, but not much."

"It looks like it would be easier to block this mess before it's implemented, but if you can't, is there anyone in Washington you can approach to get you an appointment with the president?"

"You lost me. Like?"

"Oh, say a general, or someone fairly high up in the military, who would listen and take you, as a wounded and honorably discharged soldier, to meet someone in the president's office?" Cathy paused a moment to let her idea take hold. "If you are escorted in, you can always claim that it was not your doing and only happened at the behest of said officer. You could also claim to be scouting for the group, nosing around a bit."

"That's worth considering. If I can reach General Stoneman, or General Pleasanton, it may just work. Both men were, I mean are, friends of General Buford, and I can use Myles Keogh's name to get to them," John said thoughtfully. "Thanks, Catie – you really do have a devious mind, even if it is in your job description."

"If you do end up going, I'm going with you," she stated.

"No arguments." John gave her a hug. "Oh, I did ask Bartholomew to come by. He's so uncomfortable with this whole idea, it's really scaring him."

"It's scaring me, too. Does he know you confide in me?"

"I think he takes that as a given."

"Good. Does he have any specifics as to where this thing will be planted? D.C. is a big place, and so is the White House."

"We may have to wait for that. It's going to be hard to act as though everything was normal while we do wait."

"I don't want to know the hot-head's name," Cathy said firmly with a shudder. "Damn, we were right, though – this has got to be part of why we got stuck here. Oh, I just remembered something that I wanted to tell you."

"Good or bad?"

"Probably good. I heard two people in the store talking about the national cemetery that David Wills is organizing. Apparently, the plans are actively in the works."

"I've heard about it too, and --- oh, my God!" John suddenly sat up straight. "THAT'S IT!"

52

Cathy was about to demand an explanation when they saw Scovel riding up. He dismounted and tethered his horse to the rail of the corral.

"Miss Cathy, John," he said by way of a greeting, "I hope I'm not intruding.

"Not in the least. We were sitting here, enjoying the afternoon sun," Cathy replied. "Why don't we go inside? I made some lemonade."

Sitting around the table with glasses of lemonade, Cathy exchanged glances with John. The larger man looked totally dejected and was studying his glass. John nodded to Cathy.

"Bartholomew," she said quietly, "John has related what you told him. We are as disturbed as you are at the thought of such violence. I do not know the particulars, as I have asked him to withhold the names of the men involved, yet I feel I must ask: would this act, if perpetrated, be intended as an assassination or simply to create horror?"

"Miss Cathy, I feel it would be done to inflict as much damage as possible," he replied slowly. He sighed deeply. "Please believe me when I say that I never, ever expected this when I invited John to join our discussions. Now, though, I think he is the only one who can help stop it."

"Your faith in me may be misplaced," John said. "I am a newcomer."

"That's part of the reason why you might be able to stop him. He may listen to an outsider before one of us," Scovel insisted. "He respects you. There are three of them involved, but he's the leader, and the others will follow his dictates. It is he who must be stopped."

"Do you have any more information as to when this would be attempted?"

"I believe it would be in two weeks or so. He has called a meeting for Sunday afternoon, after the church social."

"Sunday? Isn't that a little unusual?" Cathy asked.

"I think he hopes that some won't make it and he will therefore have a better chance of riling up those who do come."

"Not bad strategy," John murmured. "I have an idea, which may take some time to implement, but for now be assured that I shall attend the meeting. Does he know you're inviting me?"

"I told him I would let you know if I saw you. I did not say that I was planning on coming out here."

"Bartholomew, I shall do what I can – you have my word."

Scovel drained his lemonade and stood. "John, thank you – I feel better for your knowing. Good afternoon, Miss Cathy." He left.

"Oh, my God," mumbled Cathy, "this is nuts."

"I'm going to write to General Stoneman directly – it'll take less time this way. I'll use Buford and Keogh as references and ask for a letter of introduction we can take to the White House, and at least meet with John Nicolay."

"Johnny, before Bartholomew arrived, you had just exclaimed, 'that's IT!'

What is IT?"

"Let's see how this plays out," he replied. At the look on her face, he quickly added, "I don't want to jump the gun. I may be wrong."

"You think we have to make sure President Lincoln gets to deliver the Gettysburg Address."

"Catie, if we head off a conspiracy to detonate a bomb in the White House, we may be doing just that. There's the devil to pay, as General Buford would say, and I want to make sure he gets his due."

CHAPTER FOUR:
AUGUST, 1863

Tuesday, 11 August: Washington, District of Columbia

At about one o'clock in the afternoon, John's letter of introduction from General Stoneman was in the hands of President Lincoln's secretary, John Nicolay. John was sitting outside the man's second-floor office in the White House with a very nervous Cathy beside him. John had explained to Cathy on the train trip down to Washington that the only access to the president was through Nicolay, who guarded his idol from anyone who might be an annoyance, up to and including the First Lady. Nicolay had taken the letter and John's information to the president, and they were now waiting to see if Mr. Lincoln would see them.

"Johnny," she whispered as she fidgeted with the ribbon on her bonnet, "I can't believe we are really here."

On the trip, John noticed that Cathy's appearance was more than equal to his own. He was back in uniform with his major's insignia on a new jacket and sporting a new pair of uniform pants – with one crutch and no splint. Cathy was wearing her pretty summer day dress – the one she had worn to meet General Buford – and a shawl, along with a bonnet the sisters had helped her choose. In addition to her usual crinoline petticoats, she had rather begrudgingly agreed to wear hoops. When Scovel had come to take them to the train station, he had been speechless with admiration. Thankfully, Cathy had been so anxious she hadn't noticed.

John had his packet of correspondence with him, and the reason they had given for the trip was to sort out a mistake in the discharge and payment papers. He knew that the timing was going to be close, and he wasn't sure if he had convinced the three men responsible to drop the attempt to plant a bomb in the White House, although he had tried. What really worried him was talk that one of them had not been seen in Gettysburg for a day or two.

"Mr. Nicolay seemed to believe me," he told Cathy quietly as they waited. "At the moment, it is out of our hands. I gave him the information I have, and told him that one of the men has now left Gettysburg."

"Here he comes," Cathy said, nodding down the hallway.

"Major, I would like you to speak to Robert Eldon, one of the men assigned by Pinkerton's to see to the president's safety. His office is in the basement, directly below mine. Will you excuse us, Miss Howell?" Nicolay, a man of slight build, bowed slightly to Cathy, who rose and helped John with his crutch.

The two men went down the hall and turned to the stairs.

In an office less crowded than Nicolay's, John was questioned by the Pinkerton man in the presence of the president's secretary.

"Major, how did you come by this information?" Eldon, a slim man no taller than John, seemed to be grey all over – grey suit, mostly grey hair, grey eyes, and skin so pale as to reflect grey. Yet for all that, John sensed determination. The man was a force to be respected.

"Sir, I was invited to join a group of men who, for the most part, got together intermittently to talk about the unfairness of the conflict which ransacked Gettysburg. I believe I was asked because I was wounded during the first day's fighting there, and it was assumed that I would be sympathetic to their sentiments. I let them continue in that belief, hoping I could avert trouble if any appeared."

"Were all these men belligerent?" Nicolay asked.

"No, sir, to the contrary. Most were grumbling about the treatment the townspeople received, yet there were two men who seemed determined to stir up feelings with a third willing to act with them. When I discovered that there was a plot forming, I sought the interview with you after securing a letter of introduction from General Stoneman."

"Why General Stoneman?" inquired Eldon.

"The General knows General Buford and his aide, Myles Keogh, and they know my service," John replied simply. "I felt I should have credibility from at least one person known to you."

Nicolay and Eldon nodded, Nicolay adding, "a wise move on your part."

"Assuming you are not merely crying wolf," began Eldon, "why bring it to the White House?"

"Gentlemen, I am a loyal Unionist and I undertook this journey to apprise you of the situation in the hope of avoiding, at best, needless damage to the White House and at worst, an attempt on the life of President Lincoln." John felt himself getting defensive. *Stay calm, stay calm. Don't get frustrated....They have to be sure you're on the level.* "Would there be another, perhaps better, place to present this?"

"Major," Nicolay said soothingly, "I do not believe Mr. Eldon is suggesting that you should have done anything other than bringing it to us. I would not have wanted you to stay in Gettysburg and wait for news of an incident." He shot a glance at the Pinkerton's agent.

"No, indeed, Major," Eldon confirmed. "I do not mean, in any way, to cast aspersions. You must, however, be aware that we receive intelligence of this kind almost daily. Acting on vague information can be as detrimental as not acting at all."

"I understand," John began, spotting a 'good cop/bad cop' routine, "and I...." He was interrupted by a knock on the office door.

"Johnny?" Cathy's voice came, low and slightly breathless, through the door. "Are you in there? Please – this is important."

"My sister is outside," John said, "apparently with some information."

Nicolay, closer to it, opened the door. "Miss Howell?"

"Forgive me, gentlemen, but I thought you should know that I have seen someone I recognize carrying a bag or satchel. He is upstairs in the main hallway near Mr. Nicolay's office and acting most furtively," Cathy reported quickly. "Johnny, I have seen the man in the store with James."

Eldon came around his desk, and taking Cathy's arm, started out the door. "Show me," he commanded.

Cathy was used to dashing down a hospital corridor without giving the appearance of running, and she almost out-walked the agent. As they reached the second floor and turned a corner, she stopped and forced him to do the same. Further down the hallway, they could see a man in the act of coming out of a room. He wasn't carrying anything.

"Office?" Cathy asked in a whisper as they observed the man slowly closing the door.

"No, that's the reception room," he replied just as softly.

The man turned and, spotting the pair watching him, broke into a run towards them, as if to force his way past them. Eldon tried to thrust Cathy behind him just as the stranger grabbed her. Biting her lip to keep from swearing as she was tugged from two sides, Cathy forcibly jerked her arm out of Eldon's hand.

"Let me," she snapped at him. Turning inside her assailant's reach so her back was to him, she jammed her heel into his instep as she squatted and pushed backwards, knocking him over. Turning again to face him, she fell against him, and planted a knee in his groin just as John and Nicolay appeared in the hallway. She wasn't sure – and didn't care – how it had happened, just that he now lay still.

Eldon, who for his part was not sure he wanted to know – much less discuss – how the man had been incapacitated, reached down to help Cathy regain her feet in the midst of a flurry of petticoats and hoops.

"My apologies, Mr. Eldon, for snapping," she said for his ears only. "He already had hands on me and I had no wish to be pulled apart between you." She looked down at the semi-conscious man. "I hope he will recover enough for questioning," she commented as she straightened her bonnet.

"Miss Howell? Are you injured?" Nicolay approached her with John behind him as Eldon stepped over the assailant and went into the room. "What happened?"

"Catie?" John reached for her hand, and whispered, "Did you do that?" He nodded to the prostrate man.

"You're damned --, er," Cathy swallowed, edited her response, and said aloud, "Yes, Johnny, I believe I did. It all happened so fast! I felt faint and I guess I fell against his legs." She looked at John, rolled her eyes, and added in a whisper, "I think my knee landed where it did some good."

Stifling a laugh, John watched Eldon exit the room carrying a satchel.

"I found this in the small storage area inside."

"Mr. Eldon, I am a civil engineer – if that is an explosive device, I may be able to help disarm it safely."

"We have military explosive experts," Eldon began, as he tried to gain some control over the situation, "and I shall send for one."

"Sir, with all due respect, if there is a chemically delayed detonation device in that bag, we may not have the time for that luxury," John pointed out. "Whatever you decide, however, it should be removed from the building. Perhaps outside?"

"Of course, Major," the Pinkerton man agreed. "First let me get this man under guard." He pulled out his pistol and handed it to John. "If you will ensure he doesn't escape while I call for assistance, I'd be obliged."

"My pleasure, sir." John held the pistol at the ready, and Eldon nodded approval.

"I believe I hurt him when I fell against him," Cathy murmured.

"Miss Howell? How did you come to be involved in all this?" Eldon asked.

"May I present Miss Mary Catherine Howell, my step-sister," John performed the introduction with a slight bow. "Miss Howell tended my wounds after the battle."

"As I reported, sir, I recognized this man as someone from Gettysburg, and he was acting in a strange and secretive manner." She shuddered. "I was not prepared to be assaulted."

Eldon left at a trot, returning shortly with two armed guards. Cathy's assailant – or victim – was still unconscious.

Cathy managed to convey to John that they shouldn't be seen enough to be identified by the man. "You may need to go back to the group, you know," she pointed out in a low voice.

"Gotcha," he whispered, "but can you manage to at least act as if you are fussed about this?"

"Johnny," she said as close to pleading as she could, "will you take me back to Mr. Nicolay's office? I don't wish to look upon that awful man again." *Cripes, talk about over-the-top damsel in distress. Yet these guys take it in stride.*

"Mr. Eldon, I would suggest that Mr. Nicolay and I escort my sister back to his office," John stated as he offered her his free arm.

They followed Nicolay while Eldon's guards picked up the barely conscious man. Eldon ordered him taken to his basement office, and caught up with John at Nicolay's door. Cathy, who had been totally turned around, finally figured out the reception room was two doors down from the office in which she now sat.

"Major Andrews, I would appreciate your assistance with this as my expert is not immediately available. Would you follow me outside?"

Seated on a chair, Cathy assured John she would be fine. "I simply need to sit and collect myself for a few moments," she said. "Please, lend your assistance to Mr. Eldon, but I do beg you to be careful."

Nicolay offered her a cup of tea, which she accepted, and while she sipped it, he asked her questions about the discussion group. Cathy truthfully replied that she did not know the names of the men John had talked about, nor was she able to put a name to the man who had attacked her.

"I have seen that man in the store where I have secured employment for the time we remain in Gettysburg. I took him to be a railroad worker from another location, as we get those coming through the city."

"I see. I thank you for your quick-thinking in bringing his presence to our attention." Nicolay's European origins were evident in his accent.

"Mr. Nicolay, I am aware that my brother came to you with little proof of the plot, and I understand if you and Mr. Eldon were inclined to put him off. I can but hope that these recent events have lent him considerable credibility," she said.

"To be sure, yes," he replied. "As a matter of curiosity, were you in Gettysburg during the battle?"

"We are staying in a small cabin just outside the town itself. General Buford had my brother brought to me after he was wounded. I tended his wounds and stayed by his side to care for him, therefore I did not get back into town until after that weekend. In truth, it was General Buford who strongly recommended that I stay, as he put it, indoors with my head down until the shooting stopped," she said, smiling at the recollection.

"You met the general?" Nicolay sounded mildly surprised.

"Yes, sir, we met the afternoon before the battle. The general acceded to John's request that I be allowed to accompany him when they met at his headquarters so John could officially offer his services. I understand his agreement was most unusual of the general." Cathy looked at Mr. Nicolay, taking in for the first time the fatigue on the thin man's face. "If I may be so bold as to make a suggestion?"

"Of course."

"General Buford and his troopers performed heroically the first day of battle, and from what I have gleaned listening to my brother's recollections, it was the general's actions in choosing the ground that led to the eventual Union victory. I am not a soldier and I do not pretend to understand all the military nuances, but if it would be at all possible, I would urge you – or anyone in authority – to promote General Buford to Major General." Cathy's earnestness was real. "This may be untoward on my part, but John Buford is a loyal Union man, and an honorable one."

"Pardon me, Mr. Nicolay," said a slightly high-pitched, male voice behind Cathy, "I was just passing your door and overheard your visitor. May I come in?"

"Of course, sir." Nicolay rose behind his desk.

Cathy, with a feeling of growing excitement, rose and turned to see Abraham Lincoln standing in the doorway. She immediately dropped to a curtsey, rising slowly.

"Mr. President, may I present Miss Howell?"

"Sir, it is a great honor to meet you," she said, realizing how much of an understatement it was.

Nicolay pulled another chair forward for the president and as the tall, awkward-looking man sat, he indicated that Cathy should also. She did so gladly, having found that her knees had suddenly turned to jelly.

"Am I to understand that you think John Buford deserves a promotion?" Lincoln held up a hand. "Before that, however, I should ask if you were party to the fracas that happened here a short while ago."

"Miss Howell was accosted by the man Mr. Eldon is holding in custody," Nicolay explained. "It was Miss Howell who, in a manner of speaking, apprehended the man."

"Really." Lincoln regarded the petite woman. "Would you care to elaborate, starting with why you are here?"

"Mr. President, my brother is Major John Andrews, lately an officer attached to the 9th New York Cavalry under General Buford at Gettysburg. He was wounded during the action on the morning of the first day, and we are staying in Gettysburg for a time until I am certain of his full recovery. He became aware of a plot to create havoc here in the White House, and I accompanied him on this trip as his wounds are not yet healed. Mr. Nicolay took John to see Mr. Eldon, and while they were in Mr. Eldon's office, I saw a man – whom I recognized as someone I have seen in Gettysburg – carrying a satchel of some size in this hallway. It appeared to me that he was moving in an odd, furtive manner, so I ran downstairs to Mr. Eldon's office to let John know. Mr. Eldon and I saw this man, whose name I do not know, coming out of a room down the hall now empty-handed. The man saw us, and came at me. Mr. Eldon tried to protect me, but the other man grabbed me. In my struggle, I knocked the man over, although I am uncertain how I did it."

Cathy took a deep breath and let it out slowly. She reached for her teacup and noted her hands were shaking. *Not even acting.* She drained the last sip. Nicolay offered to refill the cup, and she declined.

"There's no need, sir, truly, since I would undoubtedly only end up spilling it," she said with a smile. "I fear the encounter has left me somewhat unsettled. I do beg your forgiveness."

"Most ladies would have swooned." Lincoln chuckled. "I understand it's considered very fashionable."

"I cannot recall ever having done so, and I appear to have missed the current opportunity," Cathy replied. "I suppose I should credit, or perhaps blame, the lack feminine wiles on my nurse's training."

"I say it is to your credit," Lincoln said firmly, with a smile of approval. "Let us return to the subject of John Buford. You have met?"

Cathy recounted what she had related to Nicolay. "It was a privilege to make his acquaintance, sir. He is a most honorable man. Indeed, he saw to it that my brother, sorely wounded, was brought to me as he had promised."

"You tended your brother on your own?"

"Assistance was not readily at hand, sir. I did what had to be done," Cathy replied simply.

"I believe the general to be a Kentucky man originally, but raised in Illinois," Lincoln said, thinking aloud.

"So similar to your own background," Cathy murmured, not aware she said it aloud.

"You are quite correct, Miss Howell," Lincoln nodded. "Thank you for bringing this to my attention. Look into it for me, John."

"I shall, sir. In the meantime, I would like to bring up another matter related to this disturbance today, with Miss Howell's assistance."

Cathy heard the familiar thump of John's crutch and the murmur of voices in the hallway.

"Mr. President, I believe my brother is coming down the hallway," she said, rising. "If Mr. Nicolay is going to broach the subject of the plot, I would suggest you include John in the discussion as he knows more than I. With your permission, I shall see he joins you."

At the tall man's nod, she left the room. John was walking with Mr. Eldon, and she saw that both men looked relieved. They stopped as she approached them.

"Gentlemen, your presence is required at a conference with the president in Mr. Nicolay's office," she said, watching John, whose eyes widened. "I was given leave to inform you. Mr. Eldon, I would suggest you proceed ahead of us and allow me to walk with my brother."

Eldon hurried off.

"Catie? Lincoln? Himself? Catie? You met? For real?" John spluttered and gulped. "What's he like?"

"Johnny, he's…, well, he's exactly what you would expect him to be. Down to earth, intelligent, and TALL." Cathy was beaming. "He towers over me."

"You're so calm…."

"Only on the outside, I promise." At the door, she let John precede her and slipped in behind him. "Mr. President, may I present my brother, Major John Andrews?"

John came to attention and snapped a salute to the commander-in-chief of his dreams. "Sir! At your service."

"At ease. I thank you for your service, Major Andrews," Lincoln greeted him, hand extended. They shook hands. "I am told you are recovering from your wounds, for which I am grateful. Please, be seated."

The men started to sit. Cathy realized there would be little, if any, room for her and stayed standing. The men who had started to be seated jumped back up. *Awkward, very awkward.*

"Gentlemen, I believe I shall withdraw. This office does not appear to be large enough for the four of you and my skirts." Cathy curtseyed and drew the door closed behind her. She thought she heard Lincoln's chuckle along with John's as she sank gratefully onto the bench outside the office.

The conference lasted for another twenty minutes, not overlong in her estimation, which was reassuring because she noted it was getting late and they had a long train trip back to Gettysburg. *Strange, 'back home' it would be little more than two hours of driving, even taking traffic into consideration. With the changes of trains, it had taken close to four hours to get to the capitol.*

She rose as the door next to Nicolay's office opened. The President thanked her for her assistance with the fracas, and shook her hand before he headed off past the reception room.

"Miss Howell," Eldon said as he came forward, "I, too, want to thank you for your courageous actions. You have assisted us in preventing what would have been a terrible act of violence. Major Andrews assures me you are re-covered from your ordeal."

"Oh, yes, I am quite recovered, and I thank you for your concern. If you are finished, my brother and I should see about our return to Gettysburg."

Eldon nodded, shook hands with John, and headed to his office.

"I shall have you escorted to the train station," Nicolay said.

"A plain carriage would be better," John replied. "If any other discontents were to see us being escorted, I fear our safety would be compromised."

"I understand. I shall see you out myself."

***

On the train, Cathy turned to John. "Well, was it a bomb?"

John nodded. "Sort of a canister with black powder and shrapnel mixed up in it, with a chemical fuser. I was able to dismantle it. Eldon is good at his job, and all is well on that score. He was confused and impressed with you, by the way. What the hell did you do to the man you downed?"

"Remember those self-defense classes you insisted I take? Shoe heel to his instep, a deep crouch to the floor, and pushed back against his knees to knock him over. I meant to stand up right away, but my foot got caught in my skirts and I ended up twisting around and kneeing him in the groin, not exactly deliberately." Cathy gave a wan smile.

"Cripes! The good news is that he didn't recognize you and he didn't see me."

"So, what happened at the conference?"

"War council might be a better description. Apparently small groups of dissidents are cropping up all over the northern states, and Eldon's belief, based on his experience, is that this failure won't stop these guys. We all feel that this could be the first move by the hotheads, and now that it's been thwarted, I am to keep an ear open for more trouble. If I have anything to report, I'm to write to Nicolay, and he or Eldon will use general delivery in Gettysburg to reach us." John smiled at her.

"I'm glad you've earned their confidence."

"By the way. The room where the bomb was planted is the reception room. The room in between it and Nicolay's office is the president's office."

"Crap – my lousy sense of direction strikes again." She sighed. "Oh well. I did manage to find Eldon's office."

"I won't ask how."

"I appreciate that. I used the windows at the end of the hall as a clue, I think." Cathy sat for a moment. "Wait a minute – you came out of Lincoln's office!"

"Yeah, I know. I'm savoring that thought. I also have an idea I would like to discuss with you once we're home." John took a sharp breath. "Catie, that's the first time I have really thought of the cabin as home."

"I know what you mean." She leaned against his shoulder. "It is home for now, though."

"It really does beat the crap out of a tent, doesn't it," he agreed.

"Frankly, I can't wait to get back there. I'm whacked."

"It's been a long day," he said, moving his arm around her shoulders. "I'm proud of you, though. You did good, lady. Again. Even the president was complimentary to you."

"Mmmmmm."

"You're not excited? I mean, I got all goofy. You're almost too calm."

"Johnny, we met Abraham Lincoln," she said quietly. "He joked with me, he shook my hand. I can't quite grasp it – it's too much, too big for me to wrap my mind around."

"I understand. He asked my opinion, and listened to me," he replied. "Amazing, totally amazing. He's so real – no, that's not right. He's so human."

"We were raised to think of him as an icon," she agreed, "and we met a genuine man. I'm sure he's a true politician – he'd have to be – but you're right. He's become a real person to us." She sat reflecting on the memories for a moment. "Oh, I may have screwed the timeline."

"How?"

"I brought up the idea of a promotion for John Buford. I was telling Mr. Nicolay about it, and that's when Mr. Lincoln came in. He has asked Mr. Nicolay to look into it."

"It'll probably be okay – the whole thing will get hung up on Stanton's desk. He was totally skeptical that anyone with any kind of Southern background would be worth promotion."

"Including the president?"

"Especially the president." John thought about it. "If the promotion does go through a bit early, it shouldn't make a huge difference. Buford really deserves it, but if memory serves, Stanton wanted to make sure he was dying before awarding it."

"That's cold."

"That's Stanton."

***

The train station was not quite deserted when they got off the train as dusk fell. Cathy alighted and was reaching up to help John when she realized that Bartholomew Scovel was standing next to her.

"Miss Cathy, please allow me. You must be right tired after such a long day."

"Thank you, I am." She stepped to one side as the larger man assisted John down.

On their way to the cabin, John broke the silence.

"We didn't expect you to be waiting for us – the hour is late."

"I wanted to see you got home safely," Scovel replied. "I also wanted to find out if all went well with your business."

"All is as it should be. We were in time to take prevent what we had feared would happen. We shall talk more about it another time, but without you, it might have been another story entirely. For now, please excuse us from giving more details. It has been a long, exhausting day." John noticed Cathy had leaned against him again and shifted a bit to make her more comfortable. She was doing her best, but the fracas – he liked Lincoln's term for it – had cost her.

"Thank the Lord you were in time."

"Yes, thanks be to God, we were." John heaved a sigh of relief as the cabin came into sight.

Scovel helped the pair down. "I won't come in, unless you need something."

"I feel we owe you a cup of tea at least," Cathy said with a tired smile.

"I appreciate the offer, but as John said, we'll have time for it another day," he replied with a return smile.

On their own, Cathy helped John change into what he called his invalid clothes. She was shocked when she looked at their clock in the bedroom. John saw her staring at it, and checked his watch.

"Umm, it's correct. It's just eight thirty."

"Feels like it should be at least eleven. Uh, Johnny? You've been asking when I was going to move back to the bed. If that offer is still open, I think I'm sore enough to need it."

"No problem. Remember, I'm an officer and a gentleman," he said with a salute. "Seriously, did you get hurt in the scuffle?"

"I think it was the push-back – I may have stretched a muscle. I know I put everything I had into it. Meanwhile, are you hungry?" Her question was muffled as she pulled a tee shirt over her head.

"At this point, I'll settle for a protein food bar and a glass of water."

"Glad you asked for that, because I think that's about all I can manage." She dragged the faithful duffle bag out from under the bed and dug into it for the energy bars they had used to survive their first week in 1863. "Here." She tossed a bar to him, picked one for herself and looked at the wrapper. "Hey – they don't expire until January 2016!"

"Now *that's* a silver lining...."

Wednesday, 26 August

John woke with feelings of mixed emotions. Eight weeks ago, he had fallen in the thick of battle. Today was the day Cathy had designated for the beginning of his serious physical therapy. Today was the day he would try to bear his full weight on his bad leg. Today was the day he was going to try to walk. He admitted to himself that he was scared. *Just a bit. Maybe more than just a bit. Maybe a lot.*

"Good morning," Cathy greeted him as she rolled over to face him. "Ready?"

"For breakfast first, if that's okay."

"Aw, I figured you could try walking to the table." Cathy got up. "You've been raising your knee on your own, the suture line is healed, you've quit using the splint, and you've started to bear some weight on that leg while you used the single crutch. If it will make you feel better, I'll get something Mr.

John sent for you."

She disappeared for a moment. When she came back to the bed, she handed him a very handsome walking stick.

"This is lovely," he said, examining it. "The ornamental handle looks like silver."

"It belonged to Mr. John's father. When I told him you were about ready to start walking, he offered to loan it to you." Cathy stood back. "Go ahead."

John stood up, and leaning on the walking stick, slowly put all his weight on his right leg. Standing normally, he looked at Cathy and grinned. "Damn, I can't believe how good this feels!"

"Take a step."

He started to and stopped. "I can't remember how...."

"Johnny, you're thinking about it too hard. Just do it," she told him with an understanding smile. "You're okay. Use the stick the same way you did the single crutch, on your left side, and move it with your right leg."

He made it to the door and back to the bed. Sitting on the chair, he looked at her. "It's stiff."

"That will get better. Any pain?"

"A bit of discomfort, not much more. Are you going to leave it strapped?" He felt the elastic bandage. "I hope?"

"For now. You need to work up your muscle strength, and until you do, the bandage will support the quads and hopefully prevent you from twisting your knee." Cathy grinned. "It's only been eight weeks. You're actually ahead of schedule. The exercises you've been doing have paid off."

"Can I have breakfast now?"

"Get dressed. I'll see to it."

A few minutes later, Cathy watched as he carefully, but steadily, walked to the table and nodded her approval. She put the tea kettle on the stove.

"I'll be back," he said, heading out the door.

"Dear God," she said to herself, praying as she sat down, suddenly shaking, "thank you. I didn't screw it up." She hadn't realized how much tension she had been holding since doing his surgery. She took a deep breath, let it out slowly, and got up to get their breakfast, singing, *"a heart full of joy and gladness will always banish sadness and strife...."*

***

John pulled up in front of Mary's store, climbed down, and handed Cathy down. They were almost to the door when Mary came striding out of it, clapping.

"Major! You're walking!"

"Yes, ma'am," he acknowledged, grinning even as he blushed beet red, "and it feels wonderful!"

"You must go across to the house – I know Martha and John will want to see this," she told him.

John offered Cathy his arm, and they made their way to the Scott house, knocking on the door.

"Major! Oh, it's good to see you walking," Martha greeted him with a wide smile.

"Martha, you're embarrassing the man," her husband commented. "After all, he's only doing what a year-old child can do." He winked at Cathy as he reached to shake John's hand.

"John Scott, if I didn't know you were joking, I'd burn your dinner," Martha retorted.

John laughed. "Believe me, Miss Martha, he can tease me all he wants. I do want to thank you, sir, for the use of this handsome walking stick. I find I still need a bit of assistance."

"Mr. John, the crutches are in the wagon. I'll bring them over later," Cathy said. "Johnny, I'd best be getting to work." She gave him a hug. "Take is easy – and don't try any foot races!"

Mary, who had watched the pair cross the street, greeted Cathy with a hug. "You should be proud of what you did for him," she said.

"Mary, truthfully, when I saw him walking in the cabin this morning, I suddenly felt shaky. I am so thankful he's all right. I would never have forgiven myself if I had done something amiss." Cathy sighed with relief.

"I would say you have no more worries about that," Mary replied.

***

John walked into the Sanitary Commission office, hoping there would be little fanfare, but several people came up to shake his hand. It took a while for things to settle down to the work for the day.

"Major," Scovel greeted him later in the day, smiling broadly, "I believe it's time for another quiet glass of ale to celebrate. I am so pleased to see you without crutches."

"I assure you I am more than pleased to be without them, and I would gladly raise a glass to that! Shall we say Friday after supper?"

"Agreed." Scovel hesitated for a moment. "Before that, however, I should like to come by the cabin to pay my respects to your sister."

John didn't need a neon sign to realize Scovel had something to tell him. "Perhaps you would like to come by later today? I'll be picking my sister up at closing. Why don't you meet us at home?"

"I'd like that very much. Until later."

The day got away from him, and John didn't have time to let Cathy know they were having company until he pulled up at Mary's store.

"Sorry, I couldn't get word to you," he said getting ready to hand her up into the carriage cart. "We were swamped."

"If Bartholomew needs to speak to you, no problem," she replied quietly. "I think Miss Martha wanted to have us to supper, but I think we can make do with Friday."

John nodded. "That was my thought."

"I'll run in to let her know – be right back." Cathy dashed into the Scott home, returning a few minutes later. "No problem," she reported. "We're set for Friday supper."

Their guest was sitting on the bench outside the cabin when they arrived. He greeted the pair, and offered to tend to Dizzy.

"I would be grateful," John accepted, "as I'm a bit tired." He sat on the bench.

Cathy bit back her reply, as she couldn't figure out how to phrase it in contemporary terms. Somehow, she knew "Brainiac" wasn't part of nineteenth century colloquialisms.

"Will you stay for supper?" she asked their friend.

"No, thank you. Best not."

"How about joining us for a cup of tea with a slice of bread and honey?"

"Now that I will accept," he said, his face lighting up with a warm smile. "I gave my mother your bread recipe. She didn't believe it could be that easy until she tried it. Now she tells me to stay out of *her* ale!"

Cathy went into the cabin laughing. She put the kettle on, grabbed a pail, and headed for the garden to pick radishes, lettuce, and spinach. "Part of supper," she said, brandishing the pail as she went back inside.

The two men watched her as they conversed in low tones.

"We have to do something," Scovel said. "We cannot let this happen."

"Let's go inside. I want Cathy to hear this," John told him. "She might be able to assist us, if you would permit that."

"You know I have the utmost respect for Miss Cathy, yet I would hesitate to involve her. It may prove dangerous."

"No more so than when she assisted with the apprehension of Jake Reissen." John rose, and when Scovel didn't stand, he glanced at his friend. "Oh, I beg your pardon; I forgot that you were not aware of that. Cathy asked me to withhold the fullness of her involvement in the incident from you."

"She apprehended him?" Scovel was torn between shock and admiration.

"John," Cathy said sternly from the doorway, "you weren't to mention it."

"You have my profuse apologies, sister dear. It slipped out," he replied with a shrug. "It's been a long day."

"Please, would you both come inside? I have our afternoon tea set out," she said, "and if there is anything to discuss I would prefer to do it at table."

As she poured out, Cathy regarded their guest. "I do not know how much John has told you, Bartholomew. I hope you do not think I am overmuch the hoyden for having played a part in the fracas at the White House. Most of it was simply a matter of being in the way."

"We have told you she's stronger than she looks," John added, eyes full of mischief.

"Miss Cathy, John asked if I would permit him to tell you that which I have just informed him," Scovel began, "and I must admit that my instinct was to shield you from involvement."

"If I may contribute in any positive way, I should be pleased to do so," Cathy replied. "My brother often confides in me. There are times when the very act of voicing ideas helps to solidify them."

"John, will you inform Miss Cathy of the latest plot? You tell things better than I ever shall."

"Our two agitators have decided to attempt assassination."

"This would be a direct threat on the president's life!" Cathy wondered how much John had told their friend – and until she knew, she couldn't advise contact with Nicolay or Eldon.

"It will be, if they take this forward. The two men have apparently decided that Mr. Lincoln is all that stands in the way of an honorable peace. They believe that Vice-President Hamlin would be willing to compromise and negotiate terms. Whether this is true or not does not matter; the only thing that is important is their belief that it is true – and they are willing to act on it."

"Dear heavens," Cathy murmured, forcing herself to stay 'in character'. "Do we have any idea how this would be attempted? Would it be another explosive device?"

"After what happened at the White House, they have abandoned that method. They want to shoot the president," Scovel sighed deeply. "They have asked me to do it."

"Oh, no," Cathy moaned.

"Bartholomew, you did not tell me that," John said slowly. "May I ask why they came to you?"

"I'm the best shot in the group," he admitted. "They are looking for a good marksman. I'm a sharpshooter."

"Johnny," Cathy said after a period of silence, "we may be able to use this."

"Talk to me," John commanded, leaning forward.

"Imagine there is a conspiracy to assassinate President Lincoln and the man chosen to pull the trigger, who agrees to do the deed," she said slowly as she carefully picked her phrases, "is planning on deliberately missing his target so that the real conspirators can be apprehended."

The two men stared at her.

"Catie, your mind truly works in strange ways," John muttered. "That has real potential."

"You are saying I should go along with this?" Scovel asked Cathy, astounded.

"Not precisely," John replied for her. "She is suggesting you *appear* to agree."

"What better way to stop this – or at least make certain it does not succeed – than to pretend to join them?" Cathy regarded the larger man. "This will not be easy for you."

"I do not believe I can pretend well enough to fool anyone," Scovel said. "My wife always told me I was not born to lie." He smiled shyly. "I never could fool her about anything."

"Hold on," John interrupted. "I have a thought. Bartholomew, I'm a fair shot. Would you be willing to coach me with the goal of being able to say that I would be a better choice as the assassin?"

"And you say my mind works in strange ways," Cathy mumbled.

"I apologize for being slow," Scovel began, "but I am confused. You wish to be the assassin?"

"No, absolutely not. However I believe it would be easier for me to dissemble." John regarded his friend. "Bartholomew, will you take me for shooting practice? If I can reach the point of being as good as you are, you could recommend me. The group knows we are good friends, so it should not strike anyone as odd."

"I could recommend you anyway," Scovel said. "Why not keep it simple?"

"That would not fit the case," Cathy put in. "If I were in charge of the conspiracy, I would want proof the shooter was capable of completing the task set. They know you, whereas John is an unknown quantity. You two should have a contest. If you suggest it yourself, it would be more believable."

"I couldn't have said that better myself," John mumbled to himself. *Don't scare him, Catie.*

"You are correct, of course," Scovel agreed. "All right, we get you accepted as the shooter. What would happen after that?"

"I shall have to consider that for a while," John stated.

"What shall I do now?" Scovel asked. "I told him I would think about it."

"How much does 'he' – and please remember I do not want to know who he is – know about what happened in Washington?" Cathy inquired. "Does he know we helped thwart the explosive attempt?"

"No, he does not. He believes that you went to see General Stoneman," Scovel replied, "and that the general took you to the White House so you could see it."

"If I may suggest something?" Cathy asked. At their nods, she turned to Scovel. "First, I believe you should take full advantage of the time you have to think it over. Wait until the last possible moment to give him a firm answer. This will give you and John time to train, and for John to gain their trust. Bartholomew, you need to let it be known you are concerned because the task is so important the best way to ensure its success, the plan – whatever is decided – should have the best shooter available. And you then openly wonder if Johnny would be the better man."

"That might just work," Scovel said thoughtfully as John nodded again.

"Yes, but let us make sure I am at least as good before that comes up," John cut in, nodding.

"If I know you, brother dear, you will hone your skills quite quickly," Cathy assured him. "You could always volunteer to act as a second to Bartholomew, or the other way round." *Okay, I've done enough for now – time to go back to being the hostess.* "Now, if you both will excuse me," she said, rising and collecting the tea things, "I had better start getting supper together. Are you sure you will not join us?"

"No, I'd best be getting home." Scovel rose. "Thank you both – I do feel better about all of this. You're right, Miss Cathy. Sometimes it helps to be able to talk about a problem."

John got up and walked him outside.

"John, can you take some time off tomorrow afternoon? We need to get you used to my Sharps."

"When you're ready, come get me. I know there will be no argument."

John stayed to watch his friend ride off across the stream, before he went back into the cabin.

Cathy, busy with their supper, spoke over her shoulder. "Okay, give. Do I get to hear the plan you couldn't tell Bartholomew about?"

"Oh yeah – because I'm going to need your help. I haven't fine-tuned it yet, either." John sat down at the table. "Meantime I'm going to be introduced to a genuine Sharps rifle tomorrow. Bartholomew is going to pick me up at the Commission sometime during the day and we're going out for my first lesson."

"You sound nervous."

"I am, although it's the least of my problems." He scowled. "Damn it! I am about to volunteer to assassinate Abraham Lincoln and audition for the privilege."

The meal was eaten in silence. After cleaning the dishes, Cathy got out the cribbage board and skunked John two games in a row, something that had never happened before.

"Johnny, if you were playing against yourself, you'd both lose," she observed candidly. "Look, if nothing else, we'll be able to alert Mr. Nicolay – and the entire Pinkerton Agency if we need it. You won't be alone, and if everything else fails, you can always miss. Besides, nothing is in concrete yet."

"I'm sorry, Catie. It's really hitting me," he muttered with a shudder. "This is getting ugly, really ugly."

"I see that." She saw John was still deep in thought and frowning.

"This is getting ugly, really ugly," he repeated glumly.

"HEY!" she called out sharply.

John jumped. "What?"

"Damn it! Remember right after you were shot we shook on being honest about getting down and such?"

"Yeah," he admitted as he wondered what was coming.

"You're an engineer, right?"

He nodded, absolutely certain something was coming – like the proverbial 'other shoe' at his head.

"I bloody well did my share – your leg is okay and you can walk again, right?

John nodded again, convinced that the proverbial other shoe was about to turn into a very large and heavy boot. She got up and slapped her hand on the table.

"I want a hot shower!"

She disappeared into the bedroom. It took a minute, but finally penetrated. John threw back his head and laughed. As he laughed, he felt some of his anxiety fade away.

"I'll see what I can do," he promised, wiping away tears of laughter when she came back into the room. "I owe you at least that much!"

PART TWO:
CONSPIRACIES

CHAPTER FIVE:
SEPTEMBER, 1863

In the first few days of the new month, John designed what was probably the first hot shower stall in history and showed it to Scovel, explaining that he wanted to see if he could make some alternative for bathing which would save them from toting pails of water to heat on the stove. Scovel, impressed with the design and curious to see if it would work, immediately volunteered to help build it. Gathering up the materials from all sources, they constructed an odd-looking water tank in a tree behind the cabin; John told Cathy to keep her nose out of it. Realizing he was trying to make good on his promise, she complied. Her demand had done precisely what she had hoped: it gave him something else to think about.

Scovel, now a regular visitor, had privately told her that John was every bit as good as he was with the rifle after three sessions. John confided that he felt comfortable with the weapon, and the two men had agreed on how to broach the idea of transferring the job from Scovel to John when the time came.

Additionally, a letter to Robert Eldon had been written, outlining the assassination plot. John was waiting for a response. He knew communication was not instantaneous, but was impatient to hear back from the Pinkerton agent.

Friday, 4 September

Hearing Mr. Fahnestock call his name, John looked up from his desk at the Sanitary Commission to see his friend escorting Robert Eldon, wearing a major's uniform, to his cubbyhole.

"Major Andrews?" Eldon extended his hand. "I am Major Robert Eldon, attaché to General Stoneman. I was sorry to have missed you on your recent trip to Washington. General Stoneman asked me to bring you up to date on your discharge and pay status. He also wanted me to see if you are recovering from your wounds."

Edward Fahnestock was openly regarding John with new respect, which John suspected was part of Eldon's purpose. *The CIA couldn't have done it any slicker.* Inwardly, he grinned.

"Major Eldon, please sit down," he said, indicating the chair by his desk as Fahnestock withdrew, "I am honored that General Stoneman would send a representative all the way to Gettysburg to see to this."

After a few moments of small talk, John suggested they proceed to the tavern for refreshment and easily secured his superior's permission. Outside, John offered the choice of walking or riding in the carriage cart. Eldon took one look at the oddity and chuckled.

"I take it this is your own design?"

John nodded. "My sister calls it a carriage cart. It was, I admit, a major source of curiosity when I first used it; however as with all things, the novelty has faded with time. Shall we?"

"Speaking of your sister – is she anywhere about?"

"She is at the McAllister store. We can go by there first, if you wish to include her in our discussion."

"I do. We should also find a place where we can speak in private."

"I believe I can prevail upon the Scotts to loan us their parlor. We trust them implicitly, and John Scott is the telegrapher, so they are used to confidentiality."

"You seem well-placed for strangers in town," Eldon said thoughtfully. "May I ask how this was attained?"

As they drove to the store, John explained how the Scotts had taken to them and his role in putting the railroad bridge back into use. "We feel we earned our way into the community." Eldon nodded as John got out of the driver's seat.

"Major, you no longer need a crutch?"

"My sister did a remarkable job," John grinned. "My leg is almost as good as new, and as you can see, I'm now only using a cane. She insists that I have it handy to avoid any missteps."

"Why, then, did General Buford put through your discharge?" Eldon stepped to the store entrance. "Does he know something I don't?"

"Yes, he does." John acknowledged as he opened the shop's door. "Cathy! There's someone I wish you to meet. General Stoneman sent him from Washington."

Cathy came out of the storeroom, wiping her hands on her shop apron, and stopped as she saw Eldon. Taking only a moment to sort out the situation, she bobbed a small curtscy as John performed the introduction.

"Mary stepped across to see if Miss Martha needed anything," she explained when John told her of Eldon's request. "Oh – here she comes."

John introduced Eldon to Mary, explained his cover purpose, and asked if Cathy could be given leave to join him. Mary, surprising the visitor with her intelligence, suggested they cross the street. "I'm sure my sister will readily agree to the use of the front parlor and you can draw the doors closed."

Within fifteen minutes, the trio was ensconced in the parlor with a tray of tea, bread, and slices of sausage, all gratefully accepted. As Martha drew the doors shut, Eldon regarded the siblings.

"The time has come for some frank speaking. Your letter was concise, yet I felt impelled to make this trip." He accepted the cup of tea Cathy poured out. "Forgive me for being blunt, but with the president's safety at stake, I need more information. Who are you and why do I have the impression there is much more to this than I am yet aware?"

"If we are wrong about you, there will be the devil to pay and Heaven alone will be responsible for Mr. Lincoln's life," John began. "Forgive my hesitation, but I agree there is much more at stake than would appear at first glance."

"We are dancing around being able to trust each other," Eldon admitted. "Too many things are at odds. I see a soldier with a discharge who is fit enough to return to duty. I have a one-star field general who vouches for him unconditionally, and higher-ranking general who blindly backs the judgement of the first. I saw a small woman take down a large, aggressive man with moves I could not follow or duplicate. Finally, I have word of a conspiracy which threatens not only the life of our president but the continued existence of our country as a whole. If I am to prevent a catastrophe, I repeat, I must have more information."

The twenty-first century friends exchanged glances, akin to sharing thoughts.

"I don't see any alternatives, John," Cathy said slowly, breaking the tense silence. "If we don't trust him, it puts everything at risk."

"You questioned me about how we took our place in the community," John began, "however, it goes deeper than the simple acceptance of strangers. We are not from Gettysburg, as you know. We are indeed from Missouri, as we have said. Yet, although we are from Missouri," John took a deep breath before plunging ahead, "we are not from this time." He sighed. "I was forced to explain this to General Buford, who was able to understand it."

"He believes you truly did save his life."

"Yes, sir. I know as a fact of history from my own time that the general had to survive that battle."

"You are from… the future?" Eldon was frowning.

"Yes, sir, we are," Cathy confirmed. "We cannot tell you how or why we were chosen, or how we were thrust back over a century of time into this era. All this remains hidden even from us, and we may never know. Please believe it has been as disconcerting to us as this concept must be for you."

"You have knowledge as to what should happen," Eldon stated, struggling to understand. "Why not come forward with it openly?"

"Time is a fluid concept. We appear to be here to keep history, as we know it, flowing in the way it should." John shrugged. "One misspoken word, one wrong action, could change the course of history so drastically as to disrupt the world Cathy and I know as our present; indeed, it might be destroyed completely. We might even cease to exist ourselves."

"You told this to John Buford?"

"In much simpler terms, yes. I had to make him understand why I had placed myself in direct jeopardy in order to protect him, and why I was insisting I be taken to Cathy instead of allowing one of the army surgeons to operate on my leg."

"Uh-oh," Cathy muttered, "here we go again."

"I beg your pardon?" Eldon turned to Cathy. "Why would it make a difference?"

"Mr. Eldon, in my own time, I am not a nurse. I am a fully qualified doctor in charge of a facility at the university hospital and clinic. I have a staff of resident doctors and nurses under me, and I supervise what we call the emergency department. John knew I could operate on his leg and save it. You have probably noticed he is close to being fully healed well before time and with no complications of infection."

"Yes, I have. Of course, I do not know the severity of the wound."

"A bullet tore the muscles in his thigh, chipping the bone. His recovery will shortly be complete." Cathy paused. "Johnny, perhaps we need to show off my handiwork. I believe it may help to convince Mr. Eldon more than words."

After John lowered his pants, Cathy assisted by undoing the wrap she still had around his thigh, offering the rolled up bandage to him for examination. "I had this and other medical supplies from our era with me when we arrived here."

Eldon examined the bandage and scrutinized the almost completely healed injury it had been supporting, before he straightened up. "I can find no alternative explanation for all this, but that doesn't mean one doesn't exist."

"He's a hard sell, this one," John murmured as he re-wrapped his thigh and dressed. "Catie, show Mr. Eldon what you have in your pocket."

"Oh!" Cathy smiled a bit mischievously as she put her hand in her pocket. Carefully checking to make sure the safety catch was on, she pulled out the

Beretta John had given her the day before the battle. She popped the magazine, took the cartridge out of the top chamber, and drew the slide as a final check to be sure it was empty. She handed the gun and a bullet to Eldon, who was obviously stunned.

"You are holding a Beretta Bobcat semi-automatic pistol, which was manufactured about one hundred and forty years from now," John explained. "It can fire eight twenty-two caliber long rounds as fast as you can pull the trigger. The bullet in your hand is a special type called a hollow point stinger round. The magazine in Cathy's hand holds seven rounds. Nothing like it exists in this day and age, as I am sure you will agree. I had it with me when we were transported in time, and gave it to Cathy for her personal defense. I assure you, she is quite capable of firing it accurately."

Eldon handed the weapon back to Cathy, who inserted the clip and the extra round before putting it back in her skirts. John was correct – the gun was the final proof they needed.

"Would you like another cup of tea? You look as if you could use it," Cathy said gently. "This is as much of a shock to you as waking up in 1863 was to us." She refilled his cup. "We spent the better part of an entire morning convincing ourselves of the time jump, and we have been adjusting to it ever since."

"Are you here," Eldon began, and choked on a sip of tea. "Oh, pardon me. It's difficult." He coughed and started again. "Are you here permanently?"

"We cannot say for certain. We have assumed that we are here for a purpose, and hope that once we have fulfilled that purpose, we shall be returned to our own place and time." John realized that anything more was unnecessary.

"I know, and fully appreciate, how confusing this is for you." Cathy smiled at the Pinkerton man. "I saw your reaction when I was struggling with Mr. Reissen – a woman of this era would not have done what I did. Mr. Lincoln even joked about the fact that I didn't swoon. I hope you can accept my actions more readily now."

"You are quite right, Miss Howell. I was puzzled with the way you handled the situation."

"I must ask for your word of honor that you will inform no one of what we have told you, either of our being from a different time or our knowledge of your future," John said firmly. "The smallest leak could spell disaster for our world and existence."

"Please be at ease in your mind regarding that," Eldon hastened to assure them. "I carry quite a few secrets, and I shall let this be one more. Besides, I doubt I would be believed."

"Thank you." John noted that his reaction was the one they had gotten from General Buford. "Now, let us get to the reason for your visit. To begin, does General Stoneman know you are bandying his name about?"

"I do hold the military rank of Major, and I asked the general, who does want to meet you both, by the way, if I could act as his aide," Eldon said with a smile. "I had related the full incident at the White House to him, and when I received your latest letter I had a conference with him. The general has the highest regard for John Buford's opinions, as they are close friends. Has any progress been made about this new conspiracy plot?"

"President Lincoln is to be assassinated." John made it a flat statement. "I cannot dissuade the two men who are behind this that it will do no good towards ending the war, and might, in fact, serve to extend it." He took a deep breath.

"I am listening."

"I have a plan in mind; however the details must wait until certain events have taken place," John concluded after a half-hour of discussion. "I am going to put myself forth as the man for the job, and as Cathy indicated, if all else does fail, I shall miss my shot. I would suggest, therefore, that she and I visit General Stoneman sometime next week."

"Agreed." Eldon leaned forward in his chair, his grey eyes on John. "Can you give me any idea as to what your plan involves?"

"It has to be in confidence, as some of the circumstances haven't fallen into place as of today."

Eldon thought about it, and repeated, "Agreed."

"I am going to assume that you, and by extension, Mr. Nicolay, are aware of the proposal to create a national military cemetery here on part of the battlefield" John began.

"Yes. President Lincoln has given approval, and Mr. David Wills has been in to see him. The tentative date set for the dedication is Thursday, the 22nd of October. Mr. Wills has, I believe, asked Edward Everett to deliver the main address."

"That was Mr. Wills' date. The date will be changed, if it hasn't been already, by Governor Everett, to Thursday, the 19th of November. Governor Everett will state he cannot possibly prepare an address of this importance in any less time," John stated quietly.

"You are therefore suggesting that the assassination attempt be made here in Gettysburg," Cathy said softly. "Can you get the men involved to accept that?"

"Better away from Washington and here on ground we know where he has less protection. At least that is the way I intend to put it. Once I am accepted as the shooter, I shall simply reject any and all other suggestions." John paused for a moment, and added, "It is imperative for President Lincoln to attend the ceremony."

"You will keep me apprised of developments." Eldon was not asking.

"You have my word. This is going to be difficult enough with your assistance. Without you I doubt I could attempt it." Brown eyes stared into grey eyes as John regarded him with a tight smile. "There is the devil to pay, sir, but be assured I'm on your side regardless of how it is going to appear."

"You are playing a dangerous, double game, Major," Eldon said as he rose. "I shall do everything I can to help. You have chosen a hard path indeed, and I do not envy you."

Monday, 7 September

John woke up with a sense of expectation. At church the day before, he had announced that, with everyone's permission, he and Cathy would not be coming into town until late morning. He had refused to explain to Cathy, even privately. She finally gave up badgering him about it.

John got up to do some preparations, and when she arose, he was standing with towels and her robe at the cabin door.

"Dr. Howell," he told her with an impish grin, "your hot shower awaits!"

When she came back to the cabin, she was singing, "*you know that somewhere the sun is shining and so the right thing to do is let it shine for you....*"

Saturday, 12 September

Cathy was in her garden picking green beans when James Weston rode up to the cabin. Tethering his horse to the corral, he petted Dizzy, and crossing to the garden, bade her a good morning.

"Dizzy looks very content." He gave her a warm smile. "Is John around? I told him last evening that I would be stopping by."

"He's inside," she replied, nodding. "I came out to do some weeding, and thought I'd pick some beans for our dinner."

"You have managed so well out here," he told her. "John seems completely healed."

"Thanks to be to God," she said fervently. "That wound was downright nasty. Now that his ordeal is over, I confess there were times I was not certain of the outcome. Go in, I'll be along directly."

She was putting the hoe away when Scovel rode up. After exchanging greetings, she murmured softly, "So it is James. I wasn't sure until now, but it doesn't surprise me."

"He's one of the two. Will you be all right? James will be around a lot from now on," he told her in a low voice. "I told John I was concerned, but he seems to think you can handle it."

"I shall be fine," she replied, putting her hand on his arm. "My concern is for you as you are far more open and honest. Can you hold out until this is over? He is not a fool and he is very dangerous."

"I take courage from John's confidence and your conviction that he is right," Scovel said wryly. "In point of truth, I doubt I have a choice. I am in it, and have to see it through to completion."

"As do we all. Let us go in." As she entered, she said, "John, Bartholomew is here. What mischief are you men planning?"

"Miss Cathy, these two are determined to have me decide which of them is the better shot," Weston explained.

"A competition! May I be a witness?"

"James, I told you she would want to see it," John commented with a chuckle. "Cathy, since I am not altogether certain for whom you would cheer, I believe you should stay here. If you cheer me on, I might laugh and miss the target, and should you choose to cheer for Bartholomew, he might blush and do the same."

Cathy noted that while Scovel did blush, Weston visibly bristled.

"John, you are incorrigible," she retorted with a smile. "Please, regard Bartholomew. It is not I who made him blush, dear brother, but you." *Not to mention angering Weston in the process.* "However, since my company is evidently not desired, I shall stay home and console the loser on your return."

John, who barely kept from laughing, caught her eye as they left and winked. He had seen Weston's reaction to his jest about Scovel.

Less than an hour later, Cathy was repairing a tear in a blouse, something which had happened moving a large crate at the store, when the three men returned. John's grin, which was almost ear to ear, told her all she needed to know.

"Gentlemen, you certainly did not take long! Would any of you care for a cup of tea? There is also some warm spiced bread." She put her mending to one side to fix the snack.

"Aren't you going to inquire which of them won?" Weston inquired with a smile.

"I suppose I should, although Johnny's face is giving it away."

"Your brother bested me four out of five shots," Scovel reported good-naturedly. "I have been supplanted as the best shot in Adams County."

"If we keep it our secret," John said, "no one else need know. After all, this was strictly between the three of us."

The men chatted about inconsequential things for a while, which Cathy took to be for her benefit.

"Well then," Weston said, standing up, "I shall see you both this evening at the Globe. Miss Cathy, we agreed that the winner would buy a glass of ale for the three of us."

"I shall be there," John promised. "At seven?"

The other men agreed and left.

"Whew! I'm glad that's over. James now agrees that I should take on the job." Noting her lack of surprise, he asked, "When did you tumble to his identity?"

"About two weeks ago, but it wasn't until he rode up today talking about this contest of yours that it became more than an educated guess. Who's the other hothead?"

"Benjamin Blakeley."

"That quiet, mousey, fussy little man?" Cathy knew Blakely from the store. Only two inches taller than she was, he was soft spoken, appeared deferential to anyone who spoke to him, and had a tendency to be overly picky about the smallest details. She couldn't imagine anyone so drab and obsequious being anything other than a follower.

"Yeah, I know. He doesn't look the type, and he lets James do the talking, but he's the idea man I have been trying to hold in check. He has a grudge against the president."

"Seriously?"

"When Mr. Lincoln was a lawyer, he got a member of Blakely's family into some deep trouble. He's also a snob who considers Abraham Lincoln to be an uneducated clod who should never have been elected." John sighed. "Don't underestimate him, Catie. It's him I have to convince of all this."

"You're still trying to hold it off until the dedication?"

"It will be the easiest to sell. James is inclined to go along with me – I suspect in hopes of winning my permission to court you. By the way, we may need his support to stall it all off. You may have to warm up to him a bit."

"Crap."

"I know. The jealousy angle, which stuck out today like a thorn on a rose stem, may be something we can use to keep him distracted. Don't even try to tell me you didn't spot that."

"Yep, I did. I'm not sure how strong it is, and I'm even less certain I want to find out." She sighed. "So what's next? Is this all-fellows-well-met tonight social or is it going to be a meeting of the dark side?"

"To be honest, I'm not certain."

"Wonderful. What plans have been announced for the dedication? I keep hearing things, but it all seems to be rumors."

"Publicly? The date has been changed, I did hear that much. Behind the scenes, David Wills has everything moving fairly well." John brightened. "I met him yesterday. He came into the Commission to speak to someone, and I was introduced."

"Mary pointed him out to me about three weeks ago. That's one hell of a project."

"He's quite the organizer. This town plays host to thousands of people, too, and that is going to be one of my selling points. Crowds are easy to get lost in."

"You aren't going to suggest you try to shoot the president on the platform as he gives the speech. I've seen photos of it – you'd never be able to pick him out, I don't care how good you are. You'd need a telescopic long-range sniper rifle to have a chance!"

"I realize that, and no, that's not the idea. I can think of several other times that would be easier. The only drawback is Blakely might insist on having others ready in case I don't get the job done."

"When do we get all this to Mr. Eldon?"

"I sent him an update on Wednesday. We'll be taking another trip into Washington as soon as he sets up a few things, but he knows about the contest today. I'll let you know more tonight when I get home."

***

Later that evening, Cathy was trying to read her Nero Wolfe omnibus, one of two books John had presented to her as a "thanks for sharing the adventure" of the re-enactment they had been attending before they were snatched up into the past. Archie Goodwin's predicaments, usually so enthralling, were not as absorbing as what was going on around her, Cathy realized after reading the same page three times. She put the Wolfe volume away, and not bothering to see if the Poirot anthology of short stories would be more riveting, took out a deck of cards. She was shuffling for her third game of solitaire when she heard a horse approaching. Since John had the carriage cart, she waited – hand in her pocket on the faithful Beretta she now always wore – until she saw who her visitor was.

"Cathy?" John Scott called as he knocked.

She ran to the door, praying he wasn't there to report John had been shot in a duel or something. One look at his face told her she really needed to curb her imagination. *Cripes, Howell, steady it out – you don't need to borrow trouble, there's enough to go around as it is.*

"Come in, Mr. John," she said, trying to appear calm.

"You may tell me this is none of my business, Cathy," he started. "I talked it over with Martha and Mary, and we agreed you should know. Since I had to come out here with a telegram," he said, handing one over to her, "we agreed that now is as good a time as any."

"Mr. John, please come in and sit down. I'm afraid you're not making much sense." She got a glass of water and offered it to him. When he shook his head, she kept it for herself. She looked at the telegram envelope, addressed to John. "John isn't here right now. He's in town."

"Yes, I know. Martha asked me to get her some ale – she really loves that recipe of yours, you know. I may never get anything else," Scott commented with a smile. "I walked to the Globe to get some, and while I was there I saw John with about five men. Bartholomew Scovel is a good man, but I have doubts about some of the others. There has been talk, more like rumors of gossip, that a group of men in town want to bring about the end of this war in whatever way they can. I have heard these whispers and Benjamin Blakeley's name is usually part of them. He was one of the ones with John tonight."

"I do appreciate your concern, Mr. John, truly I do. John has also heard these whispers. I am not completely certain what, if anything, he intends to do about it, and I am even less certain that his turn in town tonight has anything to do with it. He was invited by Bartholomew and James Weston, I believe."

"I know you both to be honorable and loyal to the Union, Cathy, but these are perilous times. I do not wish to interfere, yet I wanted to ensure that John is aware of the company he has been keeping. It could be dangerous."

"I will relay your concerns when he gets home," she assured him.

"Mary, Martha, and I feel you two are part of our family now," he said sincerely. "I would do no less for them as I have done for you. I hope I have not offended you."

"I would never take offense at genuinely offered concern," she assured him. "You are welcome to wait to see him, if that would ease your mind."

"No, thank you. I have said my piece for tonight. Perhaps we shall see you in church tomorrow."

"We are planning on it," she said, hoping she was being more reassuring than she felt. "Until then, please, try not to worry."

Alone with her cards, Cathy laid out her game but her thoughts were far from the table. She was still sitting with the untouched game in front of her when John returned. He took one look at the table and her face.

"What happened?"

"John Scott brought a telegram out and stayed to leave a message." She related what he had said and handed him the telegram.

"Cripes. I knew things were leaking, but I think I can turn this to our advantage." He opened the telegram. "Yes! Oh, this is great!"

"Johnny, you're supposed to let me in on things now. Yes, what is great?"

"Okay, okay. I have been telling the group for the last couple of weeks that people are getting concerned, even suspicious, about the meetings so we are going to lie low for a while. Tonight it was agreed to let me plan what comes next." John smiled, relieved. "The telegram is from Eldon. He wants us in Washington on the seventeenth. It's all coming together."

"It's all coming together? From where I'm sitting, it looks like it's all coming apart!"

"I am juggling the appearance of cooperation with behind-the-scenes activity to stop it. To a great extent, you are too. Mr. John's warning couldn't have come at a better time – it's going to give me the backing I need to tell the men to cool it if they don't want to be discovered. It's also a real way to stall and buy some time. Mr. Eldon wants us to meet his people so we can fully plan how to avoid disaster and nail the bad guys." He looked at her face. "Follow all that?"

"I think so. Where do I fit in?"

"Catie, I'd like to keep you out of this," he began slowly.

"You can't," she interrupted. Her jaw was set – he knew that meant no arguments.

"Yeah, I thought so. Can I finish?" At her nod, he continued. "Eldon has accepted you as part of the effort to stop this, so you are my backup. Can you handle it? Think about it – you may have to act as courier, and possibly a shooter if I get sidelined."

"I told Bartholomew that we're all in this until it's over, Johnny, and I meant it." Cathy sighed. "Oh, I told Mr. John we'd be in church tomorrow. Frankly, I think I need it."

John stood behind her and reached down to massage her shoulders. "I do too, lady. We're fighting against the devil and we need all the help we can get."

"The devil to pay? You should use that as a code name."

"Well, I want to see his paycheck bounce, but that's an interesting thought." John looked at her cards. "Red queen on the black king."

Sunday, 13 September

The service at the Christ Lutheran Church on Chambersburg Street was full. John and Cathy were greeted warmly and made welcome; their acceptance was complete. Cathy found solace, as she never had at any church 'back home', and it surprised her. Weston was there, and made a point of handing her into the carriage cart.

"I really did need that, rituals and all," Cathy sighed on the way home.

"Somehow it does seem more relevant here," he agreed. "Maybe because we went through the fire of war, directly, dodging bullets on our own soil so to speak. Plus, what we're facing is daunting."

"I think the scariest part is knowing James believes, fervently, that what he wants to do is right." Cathy frowned. "He's not a bad man, Johnny."

"No, but it's no use trying to tell him that eliminating Lincoln is not going to end the war. Stanton is far more adamant about crushing the South than Lincoln ever dreamed of being, and Hamlin would never be able to stand against Stanton."

"You tried?"

"I tried." John replied flatly.

"Mr. John is still worried. I wish we could tell them what we told Mr. Eldon," she sighed, "but I know we can't. Two people already know."

"I may pull Mr. John to one side and explain that I know what's going on, but can't tell him what I'm doing about it," John mused. "Yet even that would be risk."

"Lonely is the life of a spy," Cathy said.

"Very. At least we have each other. Another silver lining…."

Tuesday, 15 September

Cathy was walking across the street from the store to the Scott home when she heard her name called.

"Miss Cathy!" Weston hailed her from horseback.

She stopped in front of the Scott home while he swung down out of the saddle.

"James," she greeted him. *Remember to be nice – you're a diversion in this mess.* "Good morning. I'll be back in the store shortly – I have a message from Mary to Miss Martha. If you came to see me, why don't you go over there and wait for me?"

"I shall wait here and see you across."

Cathy nodded and went into the house. Martha met her in the front parlor, took a look at Cathy's face, and peered out of the curtains.

"You appear to have an escort," she observed.

"Unsolicited, I assure you," Cathy replied, sighing. "Mary sent me over to ask if you need anything from stock, and he came up while I was crossing the street. I am going to have to do something about this, but I have no idea what."

"Tell Mary I can use some potatoes and about a pound of bacon," Martha said. "On second thought, we shall go across together, so I can choose the bacon myself." She was smiling broadly. "That ought to help."

"Miss Martha, is it possible you have you been around me too long?" Cathy asked. "I believe you are becoming more devious by the day, but thank you!"

Laughing, the two women left the house, and sure enough, Weston was waiting. Momentarily taken aback seeing Martha with Cathy, he settled for following them at their invitation. Mary, watching from her shop window, chuckled – her sister dealt with him almost as tidily as she had the two soldiers over a berry pie she had made the first day of the battle.

"Miss Cathy, I was wondering…." Weston began as they entered the store. He stopped, realizing the two sisters were paying close attention.

"Please, James," Cathy said, "I do not wish to embarrass you, but I have been honest with you, have I not?"

"Yes, you have," he replied earnestly, "yet I have wanted to call on you since the first time I walked in here and saw you. I have never made a secret of that."

"No, you have not." Cathy sighed. "At the moment, however, I must remind you I am working. This is not the appropriate time or place to discuss anything of a personal nature."

"May I call at the cabin?"

"I would ask you to arrange that with my brother, so as to be assured he would also be present."

"Of course," Weston smiled. "I would not want anything improper."

"Nor would I."

"Thank you, Miss Cathy. I shall find John and discuss this with him." Weston wished the sisters a good day and left the store.

"Cathy, are you sure?" Martha's tone said much more than her words.

"Mary, have you got some paper? I must send Johnny a note," Cathy stated, swearing up a storm in her thoughts.

"You feel this is the only way to get rid of him?" Mary asked, handing Cathy paper and pencil.

"If he makes a formal declaration, maybe a formal refusal will work." Cathy's frustration was evident. "I have no wish to hurt him, but he has yet to take heed of anything else." She quickly jotted her message on the paper and folded it. "Knowing James, he went straight to see John. I can't run this down to him, nor can either of you. Is Mr. John..?" She stopped as the door opened.

Bartholomew Scovel came in and started to greet her, but she interrupted.

"Bartholomew, will you take this note to John? Please, I need to get this to him as soon as possible, and I cannot deliver it myself." Cathy's voice underlined the urgency in her eyes.

He held out his hand, took the folded note, and left.

"I wish I could be what Bartholomew thinks I am," Cathy murmured as she watched him cross the street. "He truly deserves the best."

"What an odd thing to say!" Mary said.

"Bartholomew Scovel is one of the most gentle, kind, and honest men I have ever met," Cathy told her. "His wife must have been a very special woman."

"Amy Scovel was sweet, kind, and giving. Her death crushed him," Martha explained. "We thought we would never again see him laugh."

"I hope I have shown him that life can go on," Cathy replied. "He would make a wonderful father, and he should be given that chance."

"Not with you?" Martha asked.

"No, not with me. I'm past that. Besides, John and I will not be here forever. Once the university re-opens, we shall return to our jobs."

Cathy was sweeping the floor when John pulled up in the carriage cart with Scovel.

He was barely through the door, Scovel immediately behind him, when he burst out, "Catie, have you taken leave of your reason?" He strode over to her and put his hands on her shoulders so forcibly she dropped the broom. "I ask again: have you completely lost your reason?"

Mary and Martha looked from one to the other, and then to Scovel, who shrugged. "I have no idea," he explained quietly. "I delivered the note, and found myself in the carriage cart on my way back. He never said a word."

"Johnny, James is determined to call on me, and I thought if we let him do it, the situation might resolve itself." Cathy explained with a shrug. "Nothing else has worked so far. He's intractable. You have tried to discourage him,

I have tried to discourage him, and yet he is now s more determined than ever. The only thing left is to let him call on me and see if the glow of his ardor will fade. It shall at least prove to be a diversion, if you wish to look at it thusly." She gazed into his eyes – normally dark brown, they were almost black, which was never a good sign. *Damn it, Johnny, come on. Pick up on what I'm not saying.*

"I see," John murmured finally. He dropped his hands. "I apologize, dear sister. You are undoubtedly correct."

"John," said Scovel, his voice full of mischief, "perhaps the four of us could get together, and spend time away from town." He looked at Cathy and smiled.

Relieved that the larger man had caught on, she smiled and turned to John. "I do not believe we have much choice, John."

"Mary," Martha began, "are you as confused as I am?"

"I may see Cathy's point," Mary began slowly, "but she is braver than I would be under similar circumstances."

"Mary, why do you think I made sure Johnny would always be present? If Bartholomew is also there," Cathy said with a big smile at Scovel, "so much the better."

"You mean that nothing cools ardor like a crowd?" Martha asked.

"Something akin to that." Cathy chuckled. "You and I even did it crossing the street. My note obviously caught John off-guard. What did you tell James?"

"You told me to arrange it for Friday, so he'll be calling Friday evening. He told me – oh!" John paused for a moment. "Pardon me. James told me this was more important to him than having a glass of ale with the men." He looked at Scovel. "You'll come?"

"Try and stop me!" Scovel laughed.

"I had best be getting back to the Commission – I left in a bit of a hurry," John said sheepishly. "Cathy, I'll be back at closing."

"Now, Miss Mary," said Scovel, "I do need a couple of things, if you will see to it? It seems I got a tad sidetracked delivering a message."

Thursday, 17 September: Washington, District of Columbia
Arriving at the White House over an hour later than planned, John and Cathy hurried to Nicolay's office.

"Good afternoon," Nicolay greeted them. "I was afraid you were not coming."

"One of the trains was delayed," John reported, grimacing. "Apparently a section of track fell away during the rainstorm you had yesterday."

"You are here which is what matters. General Stoneman is with President Lincoln. I am to let them know of your arrival." Nicolay took in that John, once again in uniform, was walking without any assistance. "Major, I am heartened to see you are fully recovered." The men shook hands as John thanked him.

"Mr. Nicolay, is there any chance we could get a glass of water or cup of tea?" Cathy asked, straightening her bonnet and skirts. She was wearing the first day dress Mary had given her, which was of a heavier weight than the one she had worn during her last White House visit. "Please forgive my boldness, but with all the fuss of the delays, I must confess I am parched."

"Miss Howell, I shall arrange for tea to be brought into the president's office," Nicolay said with his beautiful Teutonic accent and a smile. "I assure you it will be no trouble. I shall return shortly."

John and Cathy exchanged glances.

"Tea at the White House with President Lincoln and General Stoneman!" Cathy gulped. "Oh my God! Johnny! I can't believe it!"

"And no camera at hand," he moaned. "Or did you bring the phone and the battery?"

"I did, but I don't think I have the nerve to use it." She held up her small reticule. "Want them?"

"I might." John heard footsteps. "Here he comes."

Nicolay escorted them into the president's office, which Cathy noted wryly, was next door. She idly wondered if the extra door in Nicolay's office connected the two.

"Major Andrews and Miss Howell, sir," Nicolay announced. He stood to one side to let them enter, and performed introductions. John came to attention and snapped his salute while Cathy dropped into the deepest curtsey she had ever done. General Stoneman, replete with his full, bushy beard, returned the salute and came forward to shake John's hand while Cathy found herself being raised by the President, who ushered her to a chair.

"It's good to see you both again," Lincoln greeted them, smiling warmly. "Major, you appear to be completely recovered from your wounds. I am heartily glad."

"Yes, sir," John smiled. "I believe I informed you that Miss Howell is the best nurse in Missouri."

"You are not rejoining your unit?"

"No, Mr. President. That decision was taken out of my hands when General Buford recommended my discharge." *What the hell, I didn't ask for the damned discharge.* He saw that Cathy was getting nervous.

"Mr. President," interjected General Stoneman, "I authorized his discharge based on his time of service. I also took into consideration the work he is currently coordinating with Major Eldon of our military intelligence unit. Between Major Eldon and General Buford, I am quite familiar with Major Andrews' exemplary record."

"It was a simple question, General. I certainly did not mean to imply there was anything amiss. Major Andrews and Miss Howell each demonstrated considerable courage the last time they were here." Lincoln's craggy face broke into a smile. "You missed that fracas."

There was a knock on the door. Nicolay opened it and admitted a servant with a tea cart.

"Let's keep this informal," Lincoln suggested. "Miss Howell, would you do the honors?"

"It would be my privilege, Mr. President," Cathy beamed. "Hopefully, my hands won't shake this time."

"This is my least favorite tea service," Lincoln confided as he accepted a cup. "Rest assured I shall say nothing if anything happens to break."

"General?" Cathy called softly as she chuckled.

"Miss Howell, thank you," he said, accepting his cup and refusing sugar and milk.

After Nicolay and John had their cups, she poured one for herself, and was crushed to realize that her hands shook.

"Relax, Miss Howell," Lincoln commanded, low enough for her alone. "It's a simple afternoon tea. There's no need to be nervous."

"Mr. Lincoln, maybe that is the case for you, but I cannot recall ever sitting down with the President of the United States for tea," she replied, "much less pouring out. I suspect if I had, I would remember it."

"When you put it that way, it's a wonder you haven't dropped a cup," he observed, smiling.

"Sir, we are not yet finished," she pointed out with a low laugh. "Give me time!"

Lincoln laughed out loud. "As the French say, 'touché!'"

Apparently, she reflected as the men deposited their cups on the cart after some small talk, it was just that – a simple afternoon tea. Yet as they prepared to leave his office, the president expressed his thanks.

"These days, it is refreshing to have visitors who are not demanding the moon with a star or two tossed in," he reflected with a sad smile. "You will see them to Major Eldon's office, John?"

"Yes, sir."

"After that, please return here. We have work ahead of us."

General Stoneman accompanied the trio downstairs to Eldon's office, stating he would wait for them there. "I do have questions, but they will wait until after the briefing."

"Briefing?" John queried as they proceeded down the corridor with Eldon. "You are going to brief your men, and you want me there?"

"Not precisely," Eldon replied with a chuckle. "*You* are going to brief my men and you want *me* there."

John stopped for a moment, his mouth hanging open.

"Johnny, you'll look more impressive with your mouth closed," Cathy whispered as she tugged on his arm to get him moving again. "Major, I believe you caught him out."

"I started the briefing by giving them some basic information," Eldon stated, bemused. "You can take it from there."

Inside the conference room, five agents stood as they entered. Eldon introduced John to George Baker, Abel Martinson, James Albright, Samuel Morgan, and Michael Addison individually, and after shaking hands with each man, John presented Cathy to the group as a whole as his sister. Eldon took a seat at the foot of the table with Cathy to his immediate right.

"Major Eldon has informed me he has given you the purpose of our mission and the general plan," John began, standing at the head of the conference table. Falling into lecture mode, he continued, "I am not prepared to divulge details, as many of them are not yet in place. I do want you to know that there may be other men in Gettysburg who will step in ready to proceed when I fail. If you can arrive in Gettysburg on the evening of the seventeenth of November, we will provide names and either I or my sister will point them out to you."

"Sir, you say you have volunteered to be the primary shooter?" asked Baker. The oldest agent present, he had black hair liberally sprinkled with grey, and sideburns.

"Mr. Baker, I have no intention of actually taking that shot, but it seemed logical that if I am the designated marksman, I can maintain control over much of the situation."

"Major Andrews, if you know the intentions of these men, why not arrest them now?" Addison, the smallest man in the group asked, and added, "Why wait?" Addison was under John's height, with light brown hair and dark brown eyes.

"Mr. Addison, we are two months and two days away from the dedication. I am hoping I can yet forestall the entire conspiracy; if I cannot, others may join the dissident group. We do not want to give these men a chance to reorganize and try again."

"The president has not yet said he will attend," pointed out Martinson. By far the tallest man in the room, he reminded Cathy of Lincoln's gangly frame.

"Mr. Martinson, I have been assured by Major Eldon and Mr. Nicolay that they will do everything in their power to convince Mr. Lincoln that he should attend."

"And should they fail to do so?" Morgan, a brown-haired man with a very slim, wiry frame, continued. "All this will go for nothing." His blue eyes seemed to penetrate whoever fell under his gaze.

"If Mr. Lincoln is not in Gettysburg, Mr. Morgan," John replied, "I cannot be reasonably expected to shoot him." There were some chuckles at this. John added, "However, you would then be armed with knowledge of the dissidents, the ability to identify them by face, and have a greater chance of foiling any further attempts. Correct?"

Morgan nodded, smiling. "I see your point, sir."

John looked at Albright, the redhead in the room. "Any comments or questions, Mr. Albright?"

"One." Albright, whose green eyes were almost as distinctive as Cathy's, directed his gaze at her. "Why is Miss Howell here?"

"Miss Howell is to be treated as my deputy at all times. If you cannot reach me, go to her with anything for my eyes or ears. She will see I receive it."

"She is a woman," the red-head stated.

"Well-spotted," Cathy murmured with a smile.

"With all due respect, Miss Howell," Albright persisted, "I do not understand why you have been included."

"Perhaps I can clarify this, Major," Eldon stood and moved around the table to stand beside John at its head. "You recall I briefed you about the explosive device we managed to find and disarm on the eleventh of August." All five heads nodded. "It was brought here by one Jake Reissen, who was apprehended." He paused while all five heads nodded again. "Miss Howell apprehended him, taking him to the ground and incapacitating him by herself."

All five heads turned towards her in unison. Cathy did her best, but felt herself blushing.

"Gentlemen, I assure you Miss Howell has my complete confidence to handle any circumstance you are likely to encounter," Eldon said with calm but forceful tones. "Indeed, should any of you sustains a wound in the course of this mission, seek her out. She is an excellent nurse."

Once again, the five heads swung in her direction. Cathy happened to look at John, who winked at her. As soon as the heads turned back to him, she stuck her tongue out, which startled Eldon into smiling.

"We know that President Lincoln tends to ignore the issue of his personal safety," Eldon said seriously, "and we have never had the luxury of this much time to prepare for a threat. I felt it was imperative for you all to meet."

"Major Eldon, Major Andrews," Cathy began, "may I make a suggestion?"

"Certainly," John said as Eldon nodded.

"In view of the time we do have to prepare, perhaps it might be wise to have your men come to Gettysburg, one or two at a time, in order to familiarize themselves with the town's layout."

"A most appropriate suggestion," John nodded approvingly. "Major?"

"Agreed. I shall inform you when to expect the teams. For your reference, Major Andrews volunteers at the Sanitary Commission in town, and Miss Howell works at the McAllister store. Both are easy to locate."

"Gettysburg has become somewhat of a tourist attraction since the battle," Cathy added. "No elaborate cover should be needed. You may also claim to be surveying the work being done by the Commission."

Albright, who had started to raise his hand to speak, quickly lowered it again.

"Did you have another question, Mr. Albright?" John asked, recognizing the aborted gesture from his class lectures.

"Miss Howell answered one of them, sir, but I do have another one, a little more personal." At John's nod, he asked, "May we know what you did in civilian life, sir? You both seem more than adept briefing and speaking."

Cathy laughed and came forward to stand beside John.

"We each taught at the University of Missouri prior to the school's closing," she replied. "We have found it more than handy, when dealing with a group of students, to be able to put names and faces together in quick order."

"If that's all," John said, with a pause long enough to be contradicted, "I believe we are finished for today."

Moments later, they found General Stoneman waiting, as promised, in Eldon's office.

"It went well, sir," Eldon reported as he sat behind his desk. He offered his hand to the pair. "Thank you. I believe we can now afford to wait for any other developments. Keep me advised?"

"Assuredly," John confirmed.

"Now, if you will excuse me, I shall let you continue with General Stoneman for the remainder of your stay."

"I would like you both to accompany me to Mr. Nicolay's office, which I have arranged to borrow in his absence," General Stoneman requested with the barest ghost of a smile.

Upon arriving there, they found Mr. Nicolay's office occupied – by President Lincoln.

"Miss Howell, Major Andrews, please come in," he said, rising. "Mr. Nicolay regrets he cannot be here as he is attending to some tasks I set for him. General, please join us."

As the three found seats, Lincoln quietly told Cathy, "relax, Miss Howell, there are no teacups in sight."

"I'll pause while you add the word 'yet', Mr. President," she responded, just as quietly. "I never knew teacups could provide such insight into one's emotional state." She sighed as he chuckled.

"Major, I wanted to keep this informal, which is why we are not meeting in my office. I have been told that you two are at the heart of a counter-conspiracy to save my life," the president said to John and Cathy. "Is this so?"

John nodded. "Yes, sir. I don't know what, if any, details you have been given, but I have confirmed there is a plot to take your life and we mean to thwart it."

"One plot foiled wasn't enough for you, then?" Lincoln queried with a gentle smile.

"It was more than enough for me, Mr. President," he assured the tall, awkward-looking man. "However, it has not seemed to satisfy the men who planned it. They are insisting on trying another one."

"Your tone, like mine, Major, appears to be in jest although I know you're serious. I fear General Stoneman and Major Eldon fail to understand why I take a light-hearted attitude towards my own possible demise."

"Frankly, sir," said General Stoneman, "I do not."

"Perhaps, General, Mr. Lincoln is attempting to remove some of the terror out of the notion that someone is determined to end his life," Cathy responded. "Humor in dark situations is often misunderstood. Personally, I have found that when I lose the ability to laugh at myself, I also lose the ability to think logically."

"Miss Howell, you are uncommonly sensible for a woman of such attractive appearance," the president commented. "You'd best be careful – it could scare most men."

"I sincerely hope so, sir," Cathy dipped her head, returning his smile. "It is my severest test."

"I've also been told that I should attend the dedication of the soldier's cemetery in Gettysburg," Lincoln continued. "This could be a stumbling block. I'm readying a major proposal for Congress in between my other duties, and I may not be able to avail myself of the opportunity."

"I understand the constraints on your time, Mr. President, yet I would urge you to make the effort. As the commander-in-chief of the men who gave their lives, you should be there if at all possible," John said quietly.

"You framed that from the point of view of the soldiers."

"Of course, sir," John replied. "As I was waiting to be removed from the field after I was wounded, it did occur to me that I might be joining the men who fatally fell around me."

"Johnny," Cathy murmured. "I didn't know."

"Catie, I was not sure I would be able to get to you," he told her with a sad, gentle smile. "I admit this is a somewhat limited viewpoint, Mr. President, and quite possibly selfish, but no other has crossed my mind."

"Major, the invitation I received to the dedication was undoubtedly issued as an after-thought prompted by political wisdom," the president replied with a wry smile, "assuming, of course, there is such a thing. I must admit I prefer your reasoning, which I find very persuasive. Few people can marshal words that well."

"Thank you, sir."

"Mr. President," said Stoneman, looking at his watch, "there is something I need to discuss with Major Eldon, if I may be excused. When you are finished, perhaps Major Andrews and Miss Howell can meet me there." At

Lincoln's nod, he left the office.

"You are correct, of course, to put this in terms of military loyalty. I sent those men out by declaring war." Lincoln rose to his feet. "I shall do my best to be there, barring any crisis at the time." He turned to Cathy, who also stood. "Miss Howell, I'm almost as proud of your brother as you are. Yet I find there is something odd about you two."

"Odd, sir?" John inquired, standing and hoping he appeared more innocent than he felt. "If I may ask, in what way do we seem odd to you?"

"Well, there's nothing in your appearance, to be sure, or in your speech. It's a more subjective and subtle feeling." Lincoln paused, considering the two in front of him. "Merely an undercurrent, an attitude that lends the impression you know what is going to happen."

"I have heard you are perceptive, Mr. President, but this observation is more than astute."

Cathy looked at John, and extended her small bag. "Well?"

"Yes," he said thoughtfully, "I agree." He took the bag, pulled out the phone and battery, and put them together. "Mr. President, you are correct, although I believe I would prefer the word 'different' to 'odd'. I know as the chief executive officer of the United States, you are accustomed to secrets. If we offer you one more, will you keep it?"

"As long as you do not try to convince me you are from the moon or Mars, Major, I believe I could accept about anything else."

"No, sir, nothing quite like that." John grinned mischievously. "We truly are from Missouri."

"So the secret is not where you are from." Lincoln thought for a moment. "There have been several mythologies in history and fictional stories in the early part of this century that center on the concept of time." He looked at the pair. "Am I getting close?"

"That's amazing, sir," John admitted. "Yes, you are."

"Anyone else around here know?"

"If you will forgive me, I would really rather not say. The whole of time can be altered by the simplest slip, which is what we are risking now, in fact." John held up the phone and grinned again. "This device emits a flash of light and takes a photograph. I would like to demonstrate if you would stand next to Catie."

"Absolutely fascinating," Lincoln murmured. "Of course. How long do I need to stand still?"

"Not long at all. Mr. President, may I take your arm?" Cathy asked shyly. He crooked it, and she continued, "Look at John, please? And please, sir, smile." She hoped John would realize that he was going to have to work to get them both in the frame. She felt like a midget next to the tall man beside her.

The light flashed twice. John looked at it, and gave Cathy a smile.

As John and Cathy traded places, Lincoln looked puzzled. "That was it? Not exactly overwhelming," he commented, chuckling. "It really took my photograph?"

"Yes, sir," John replied, still smiling as if he'd won a lottery.

"Gentlemen, shake hands, please, and look at me as you do it," Cathy instructed. She took two shots and checked them. Nodding to John, she asked, "Would you care to see it, Mr. President?" She held the phone up.

"It's in color – and I'm smiling!" He was amazed. "No one would believe this, no one!"

John took the phone and removed the battery, putting both back into Cathy's bag. As she took the bag, she cocked her head to one side. "General Stoneman is returning."

"Are you also telling me you have eyes in the back of your head that see through walls?" the president asked curiously.

"No, Mr. President," John explained, with a chuckle. "She has extraordinarily good hearing, even for *when* we call home."

"Sir, are you all right with this?" Cathy asked. "No fuss or confusion?"

"I could not claim that with total honesty, and I must admit it is only with considerable effort of will that I am curbing my curiosity," Lincoln replied. "Your secret is safe, you have my word. Who would believe me anyway? Besides, you never did elaborate." He kissed Cathy's hand, and shook John's. "Ah, General," he greeted Stoneman, "you are just in time, so to speak. Please see our guests out safely, unless there is something else we need to discuss."

"Mr. President, I shall take them out the front entrance. They did come here to see me, and I should be seen escorting them to the station." Stoneman gestured them to the corridor. "I only have one matter of a more personal nature to discuss."

"It has been our privilege, sir," Cathy said. She curtseyed while John snapped a salute.

The president went down the central corridor, past his office and the library. Stoneman indicated they should take the nearest staircase. Cathy recognized it as the one she had dashed down on her first visit. *One more trip and I'd know how to get lost efficiently.*

"Sir, have you any word from General Buford or the 9th New York?" John asked as they exited the building and entered a waiting carriage. Stoneman gave the driver instructions to proceed to the train station.

"The 9th New York is fine, still under Colonel Devin. General Buford, on the other hand, has been given another leave," he sighed. "If we had not done that I would have been forced to report him for insubordination."

"May I speak as a trooper who served under General Buford?"

"Please do."

"Sir, I do not pretend to know the circumstances, but I have never met an officer who cared more about his men than John Buford. His troopers would follow him into the very mouth of hell because they know he would fight for them just as fiercely as he would battle the devil himself. If he felt his men were being placed in jeopardy through the actions – or inactions – of commanders higher up, he would undoubtedly speak his mind quite plainly." John took a deep breath. "When you communicate with him, please give him our kindest regards, and assure him I have recovered."

"Thank you, Major, for your observations; you have saved me the trouble of asking for them. I shall certainly pass on your words to John." He paused. "This conspiracy you and the Major are working against – can you prevent it?"

"We are going to prevent its success, General. As General Buford would say, there is the devil to pay, and I mean to see he's paid in full."

"Well put," Stoneman replied. "John Buford would also add, 'God keep you safe.'"

The carriage halted at the station. John got out, and handed Cathy down.

"General Stoneman, thank you." He saluted, and Stoneman returned it. "Go with God, sir."

On the train, John looked at Cathy, gently shaking his head. "I have no words," John murmured. "But you can now say you've been in the Lincoln bedroom at the White House."

"What?"

"President Lincoln's office, where we had tea today, becomes the Lincoln bedroom once the west wing is added to the White House."

"Really? Interesting." She thought about that. "Well, I am going to savor the memories," she said as she tucked her arm through his. "It was too lovely. Maybe we can talk about it tomorrow. Can I tell Mary and Miss Martha we had tea with him?"

John laughed. "Sure – just make it seem routine."

"I'll have to work on it – that's going to be a stretch."

Friday, 18 September

At the store the next afternoon, Mary declared a break from work. She and Cathy had been cleaning and scrubbing every shelf, rearranging things as they went.

"We've done enough for a while. Martha said she would bring tea across, and stay to visit." With a sigh, she sat at the small table to the side of the main counter. Cathy tossed her damp rag behind the counter and did the same. "We both want to hear about your trip to Washington."

The shop door opened and Martha appeared with a tray. "Am I late?" she asked, seeing the other women already seated.

"No," Cathy replied with a smile. "We quit early!"

"Well, Cathy," Martha began, handing Cathy a cup of tea and taking the napkin off a plate of sliced cake, "did you meet General Stoneman?"

"Ladies, yesterday about this time, John and I were having tea with General Stoneman," Cathy confided. "You will never guess who else was there."

"Mrs. Lincoln?" Martha ventured.

"Not precisely," Cathy teased. "It was her husband."

"Cathy! You met President Lincoln?" Mary was astounded.

"We were quite late getting to Washington – one stretch of rail track had been washed out by a severe rainstorm and our train out of Baltimore was delayed," Cathy related and went on according to what she and John had agreed on. "The General had an appointment with Mr. Lincoln, and invited us to join them for tea."

"My goodness," Martha fussed, "imagine having tea with the president! Weren't you nervous?"

"Oh, most assuredly – my hands were shaking! I was asked to pour out, and I was terrified I would drop and break a cup or saucer."

"What is Mr. Lincoln like?" Mary asked eagerly.

"He didn't pay a lot of attention to me," Cathy replied, sticking to their narrative. "Of course, I was far too nervous to say much at all! It was not a formal meeting and nothing official was said." She chuckled. "We each had a cup of tea and then left. No cakes, no bread – jut tea."

"What about General Stoneman?" Martha queried.

"Did you see Major Eldon while you were there?" Mary asked.

"After tea, we spent time with General Stoneman, who was very polite, and complimentary to John. He's a good friend of General Buford's and was curious to meet us. Somehow, I managed to impress General Buford," Cathy smiled. "I suspect General Stoneman wanted to find out why."

"Maybe he heard from Major Keogh. We know you impressed him," Mary commented with a sly grin.

"We did see Major Eldon. He is trying to sort out something with regard to John's back pay. General Stoneman fussed about his discharge – even asking if he wanted to rejoin. Johnny was polite yet firmly declined."

"Now, what are your plans for this evening? James Weston is going to call on you?" Mary asked.

"Yes, he is. It will be interesting to see how he reacts when he discovers that Bartholomew is also calling," Cathy replied with a sly grin.

"Well, it's not quite the usual thing to have two suitors call at the same time," Martha observed.

"Still," Mary pointed out, "at least Cathy is not attempting to hide one from the other!"

The three women laughed.

CHAPTER SIX:
OCTOBER, 1863

Sunday, 4 October

Cathy, chafing under the pressure from Weston to do his courting without the presence of his rival, agreed to let him escort her to the church service. Afterwards, as John had predicted, he wanted to see her back to the cabin.

"James, I am so sorry – we are not going back right away. John and I have been invited to spend the afternoon with the Scotts." She gave him a hesitant smile. "I would ask you to call this evening, but you told me you are to be on duty beginning at six o'clock."

"We shall make it another time," he said as he bowed over her hand, obviously disappointed. "Thank you for attending service with me."

As she watched him leave, she managed to cue John that they should head for the Scotts. Sunday dinner after church had become a standing invitation any time they wanted to stay in town. She made a note to ask John if she was doing enough to keep Weston occupied for the time John needed to set up the mission.

When they arrived at the Scott home, Mr. John handed John a telegram from Major Eldon. Although Scott was curious about the contents, he kept quiet. John was able, in a private moment, to tell Cathy that the first two of Eldon's agents were going to visit Gettysburg the following day.

Monday, 5 October

George Baker and James Albright arrived at the Commission at nine in the morning, posing as men interested in seeing how the Commission worked so they might set up a church mission after other battles. John spotted the redhead as the two were brought to his cubbyhole by one of the senior officials, and was told to take them on a tour. After showing them around the Commission, he escorted them outside.

"Gentlemen, I should like to show you the town and the proposed site for the soldiers' cemetery," John said, "if you would be interested."

Both agents regarded the carriage cart and Dizzy with curiosity. The few townspeople around them, who were used to the odd-looking vehicle, smiled knowingly.

"Dizzy is my small, steady horse," he explained, "and she now regards the carriage cart as hers. I did try to hitch another animal to it once, and she got quite upset." Chuckling, he looked at his team members and added in a lowered voice, "You really need to relax a bit. Laugh, smile, and give the appearance of enjoyment, or you will draw attention to yourselves." Raising his voice again, he continued, "Dizzy is now one of the characters of Gettysburg."

Albright laughed aloud and commented, "Dizzy must have been one of the few horses left in town after the battle."

"Yes, and I am grateful no soldier on either side decided she was worth more than derision," John replied.

The three men got into the carriage cart, and John set off. "Much better, Mr. Albright."

Baker informed him that Major Eldon wanted to give their mission a name, which could be used as an identification code. "He suggested we consult you on the matter."

"I have adopted a saying I heard General Buford use when things got tense," John replied wryly. "When General Reynolds came up to scout for himself on the first day of the battle, he asked General Buford how things were going. Buford replied, 'there's the devil to pay.' I always took that to mean the situation was dangerous, and that he was going to pay the devil by giving him hell. I believe I used that in a conversation with Major Eldon, as well."

"'*The devil to pay*'. The Major mentioned the phrase as a possibility," Albright admitted.

"I do not quite see how it would be used," stated Baker.

"We keep it simple," John explained. "If you see someone and wish to determine if he's part of our mission team, ask how things are going. If the answer includes, 'the devil to pay', you are talking to a team member. We cannot overuse the phrase, however, as we do not want people to begin to use it randomly."

"Agreed." Baker was silent for a moment. "I think it will do nicely. We shall report this to the major."

John took them to the cemetery site, encompassing seventeen acres along the Baltimore Pike and extending down to Taneytown Road. John pointed out Cemetery Hill, which is where the central monument was to be placed and explained that the project for body reburials was currently up for bid with a deadline of the 22nd of October. He then showed them the two Round Tops, the cabin's general location, and took them back through town along Chambersburg Street, stopping at the McAllister store.

"I thought you might like to meet my sister, who so ably tended me after I fell during the first day's fighting," he explained for the benefit of passers-by.

"Miss Mary? Cathy?" he called out as he entered. "I have some visitors with me." As Cathy came from behind the counter, Mary appeared in the storeroom doorway. "Would it be possible to get some refreshments?"

"Certainly, Major," Mary said promptly. "I have a small stove and water is always hot for tea. Cathy, dear, would you slice some of the cinnamon bread you brought this morning?"

John introduced the two men to Mary, while Cathy, smothering a smile, made tea and put bread slices on a plate. Mary disappeared back into the storeroom as Cathy brought the refreshments to the small table.

"Miss Cathy, thank you – this is unexpected." Baker reached for a piece of warm, buttered cinnamon bread.

"This is delicious," Albright said after sampling it.

"Gentlemen, you are most welcome," she said, and murmured, "just because I took down a would-be assassin, Mr. Albright, does not mean I am incapable of baking." She smiled at the red-head.

"Cathy, we're going to use General Buford's phrase for identification," John informed her, trying not to look at Albright as he blushed. "How goes it with you?"

Cathy looked around – there was no one else in the store. "John, there's the devil to pay." She smiled at the agents' reactions. She said softly, "I believe I got it right, but we should use it sparingly."

"I have proposed taking my guests to see the first day's battlefield, and it occurred to me that I have yet to show you the location. Would you care to accompany us?"

"I would indeed. Let me ask leave to join you." The men stood as Cathy gathered up the tea tray and took it to the storeroom. Returning a few moments later, she had donned her shawl and her day bonnet.

As they drove west on Chambersburg Pike, John turned north and informed his guests that it had been along this stretch, between the Chambersburg Pike and the Mummasburg Road along McPherson's Ridge, that he and his troopers of the 9th New York Cavalry had helped hold the lines. Cathy watched John's face as he stood off on his own for a while. She knew he was remembering the chaos.

Coming back, John asked if they had any questions that needed to be asked openly. "We are remote enough here. It's your opportunity."

"Sir, I thought we were to meet, or at least see, some of the men we need to be able to identify," Baker pointed out as Albright nodded.

"Weston should be at the Globe at noon. He and Blakeley often meet there. I can take you in, as we will not be sitting with them. Cathy, can you describe them, so I only have to nod?"

Cathy quickly did so, and the agents took notes, voicing the confidence that they would be able to spot the two with a guiding nod. John then gave three additional names: Robert Adelmann, Nicholas Caine, and Hans Baumgarten.

"These men have recently decided to become active under Weston's guidance," he stated, watching Cathy's jaw drop open.

She had barely gotten over the first shock when Baker turned to her and asked for additional descriptions.

"Robert Adelmann is of medium build and height, with dark hair, dark eyes, and a dark curly beard. Nicholas Caine is slight of build and about three inches more than my height, with sandy hair and blue eyes, and a simple mustache. Hans Baumgarten is tall, about two inches above John's height, with short silver hair, a broad face, grey eyes, and a silver trimmed beard." Cathy paused as they made additional notes. "I confess I am quite surprised to learn Mr. Baumgarten has begun to actively participate. He made a remark in passing to me last week that he was happy to hear of the latest Union victory."

"As head of the actual planning, I can seek him out – perhaps one of the others has pressured him in some fashion." John frowned. "If I can find a way to help him stand down, it would give us less to watch."

"As it is," Albright commented, "we are four agents to five conspirators. I would prefer more balanced numbers."

"There is one other man involved," John stated. "Bartholomew Scovel. He was the man who alerted me to the plans in hopes I could prevent its success. I shall introduce you to him if I can see an opportunity. You are to treat him as one of the conspirators, although he is utterly loyal to the Union."

"Description?" Baker had his pencil poised.

John gave it to them.

"Perhaps Mr. Baker and Mr. Albright can impress upon Major Eldon the need for his presence at the proper time," Cathy suggested. "Also, gentlemen, do not count me out. I may be able to perform tasks which you may not, because I'm a woman, as Mr. Albright so accurately observed the last time we met."

"True," agreed the redhead with a smile. "I shall never undervalue you again."

"Drop me off at the store on your way to the Globe," Cathy requested as they returned to the carriage cart. "Oh, before we depart, I want to mention, in case John has yet to do so, that the telegraph office in town is located across the street from the McAllister store. John Scott, Mary McAllister's brother-in-law, is the telegrapher. He's reliable, discreet, and loyal to the Union."

"That is good to know," Albright said as he noted it. "Thank you."

***

John was waiting with Dizzy when Cathy came out of the store carrying her bag.

"Did you make the trade?"

"Of course," she replied, handing the bag to him. "This morning we had some radishes and spinach. Now we have potatoes. Mary was quite impressed with the notion of planting a second round of the cool crops for a late harvest, but it has been fairly warm."

"I don't think this will fracture the timeline any more than the beer bread did," John teased. "I'm betting that beer bread is something which gets invented every century or so, strictly out of need."

"How'd it go with Mr. Baker and the redhead?"

"Fine. I sent word to Eldon that I expect him up here with the others. Speaking of others, Addison will be here for his orientation in about ten days, and the final two will arrive at the end of the month."

"Want to bet that Eldon comes with Addison?"

"Nope – no bet." John inhaled sharply as they approached the clearing. "Uh-oh – were we expecting company?" he asked as he spotted Weston and Blakeley.

"Crap, no," Cathy lowered her voice as she waved. "James keeps asking me questions about what Lincoln is like. It's bordering on obsession."

"Could be coming from Blakeley. Thanks for the tip - we did see them at the Globe today." He pulled Dizzy up to the corral, and mumbled, "And here we go." He began to unhitch the horse. "James! Ben! This is a surprise!" he called out as Cathy jumped down before anyone could assist her, and with a look to John that said, 'you're on your own', disappeared into the cabin.

Weston patted the horse. "Dizzy looks good."

"I think Cathy is beginning to worry about cold weather at night. She has become quite attached to this little horse. I promised I would pick up some horse blankets in town." John finished and came out of the enclosure. "Was there something specific we needed to discuss?"

"We were a mite curious about the men we saw with you today," Blakeley said slowly. "Looked like strangers."

"Yes, they were. The head of the Commission brought them to me and asked me to show them around. They said they wanted to study the way the Commission was set up so their relief group could better serve other areas after a battle." John sighed.

"What did they think of Gettysburg?" Blakeley asked.

"Overall, I believe they thought we were doing well considering what happened here. I explained that the town had been caught square in the middle of the fight." John sat on the bench and stretched out his legs. "Of course, they also wanted to see some of the battlefield. Frankly, I believe that is why I was handed the task. I did take the opportunity to ask Cathy if she wanted to ride out to the area where I was felled – she had not seen it before."

"Had you been out there since you were hit?" Weston asked, concerned. "Miss Cathy told me you were still having some trouble remembering what happened."

"No, I hadn't been there since that day, and she watched me pretty closely out there." John shuddered. "It did not seem to help my memory. Cathy has told me that sometimes a bad shock can do that, though." He lowered his voice. "I think it is time to meet – maybe just the seven of us."

"I was going to suggest that," Blakeley muttered, irritated that John did it first.

"How about a week from Thursday? I also thought it might be better if we met during the day, if possible. It might look less suspicious that way. We cannot keep meeting at the tavern and then disappearing together."

"John, can you take the time?" demanded Blakeley.

"I wouldn't have suggested it unless I could, Ben," John replied evenly. "My duties are not as heavy as they once were, allowing me time to do things like the tour with the visitors today. I do not believe I shall have any difficulty."

"I can arrange my schedule so I am not on the rails that day," Weston said. "I shall notify the others. I would like to suggest we meet at my place."

"Fine." John got up, and looked at Weston. "I would ask you to come inside, but I do not believe Cathy is feeling quite herself today."

"I am sorry to hear that," he replied. "Maybe I can stop at the store tomorrow to pay my respects."

"I am sure she would appreciate that," John told him. "Thank you for coming out." He watched them ride off.

"Gone?" Cathy inquired from the doorway.

"Oh yeah. I guess I should have expected that," he reflected, once inside at the table. "They wanted to know who the strangers were and why were they here. That sort of thing. Oh, we're meeting on the fifteenth at James' place, during the day. I saw it coming and brought it up before they did."

"Thanks for heading James off. I didn't want the hassle tonight."

"I told him you weren't feeling quite yourself. He said he'll stop by the store tomorrow. Be prepared to be better."

"Gee, thanks." She grimaced. "Any message for Bartholomew if he shows up?" she asked as she set the table.

"If James isn't around at the time, invite him for a game of cribbage."

"Only if you promise to relax when we play."

"We can relax around Bartholomew – he probably needs it, too. These last six weeks are going to be tense, Catie. We're really playing that double-game Eldon mentioned."

"I vote we read some Poirot after supper," she suggested, putting food on the table. "It's been a while."

"Okay," John agreed with a grin, "we'll let the Belgian do the thinking for a bit. His little grey cells must need exercise!"

Wednesday, 14 October

John came into the store at eleven, looking smug.

"Cathy, your brother is here, and if he was a cat, he would have a bird feather stuck on the end of his nose," Mary called out.

John laughed as Cathy came around the counter, took one look, and replied, "You are entirely correct, Mary. He does look remarkably pleased with himself!"

"I am," he said. He held out a letter. "It's addressed to Cathy, but I opened it."

"Who on earth is it from?" Cathy wondered as she took the envelope. "General Stoneman! Writing to me?"

"I would advise you to sit down, Catie. Seriously." He took her arm to steer her to the small table. "Sit."

"Do be quick, Cathy – now I am all curious," Mary stated. She looked at John. "Tea?"

"Wonderful thought," he replied, watching Cathy and waiting until she hit the big line.

"Johnny!" Cathy sounded elated and sad at the same time. "Oh, my."

"Good news?" Mary set the tray on the table. "I'll pour. You're shaking."

"Good news, with a dose of bad, I'm afraid." Cathy used both hands to pick up her cup. "General Stoneman writes that General Buford is up for his second star, but adds that he has fallen ill. General Buford is going to be staying with General Stoneman, and we have been invited to visit."

"I've had a letter, as well," John informed them, "not nearly so emotional, but every bit as welcome."

"Do not simply sit there, Johnny, give over!"

"My letter is from Myles Keogh. He writes that he will be accompanying General Buford to Washington, and asks if he may come up here to see us."

Cathy's thoughts raced as she looked at John's face, knowing they would have to wait until later to discuss some of the implications. One notion stuck out. "Do you think Myles would be willing to assist in saving me from James?"

"It was one of my first three thoughts," he replied with a wry smile. "I shall answer his letter and bring that up along with a few other things."

Thursday, 15 October
Weston's Place

Weston welcomed his friends as they arrived at the house he had on the edge of his small farm. He had asked Scovel and John to help with some refreshments. Scovel's mother Ida had complied, and John had brought some of Cathy's bread along with pickles she had made with her cucumbers. The men sat around a table in the main room drinking ale and lunching on hard sausage, cheese, bread, and the pickles.

"I have some news," John began as they ate. "I have been informed that President Lincoln has tentatively agreed to attend the cemetery dedication here in Gettysburg on the 19th of November."

"How did you hear this? Last week David Wills mentioned to me that the president," Blakely made the word sound dirty, "had all but decided he was not going to have the time because he was trying to put together his proposal for reconstruction." The mousy-appearing little man, dressed in drab brown as usual, took a sip of ale as if to wash a bad taste from his mouth.

"I received a letter yesterday from General Stoneman. The General, who apparently has not yet given up on enticing me to rejoin the army, mentioned that Lincoln is discussing possible travel arrangements, which I took to mean he will be here."

"General Stoneman? You went to see him in Washington," Scovel stated accusingly, as he and John had planned. "Twice."

"General Stoneman, at General Buford's urging, put through my promotion and back pay," John pointed out, totally at ease. "I have expressed my thanks in person, and while I do not feel I owe him anything further, I am not about to alienate him as he is proving a valuable source of information."

"So what is your plan?" Adelmann wanted to know. "It has been weeks since we met, and we need to know."

"I want to wait until the cemetery dedication," John informed them.

As he had predicted to Scovel and Weston two nights before at the cabin, that statement touched off a series of arguments from the others. John waited patiently for about two minutes.

"Please, gentlemen, please," he said as he stood up, "I understand the need to rid our country of the man, sooner rather than later. However, we must also be practical."

"I am just as eager as you are to have this done and over," said Scovel, the only man in the room - other than John - who was liked by everyone. "John, James, and I discussed this two nights ago."

"Why were we not invited to that meeting?" Blakeley demanded crossly.

"You have put me in charge of the mission, Ben. I figured that if I could not convince them of my reasons, I would have to rethink the entire operation," John replied smoothly. "They called on my sister and I took the opportunity."

"I know they are both besotted with Miss Cathy," Blakeley said with some disdain, "although not entirely without reason. Still, John, it is not fair to the rest of us." He strode to the window and looked out.

"I admit I was not convinced at first," Weston stated, "but I am now. John gave us his reasons. His plan is sound." He rose to refill one of the plates.

"We are still waiting to hear it," Nicholas Caine said sourly. "Frankly, I'm losing patience with all these delays."

"Please, gentlemen, I let me explain. Once I am finished, I shall answer any questions you may have." John waited until the others had resumed their seats and sat.

"My reasons for choosing to wait until the president is in Gettysburg are threefold," John began. "First, in Washington, he is well-guarded. I have seen the office area in the White House – his is on the second floor. Lincoln's office is adjacent to that of one of his secretaries with the other one across the hall. None of these are far from the man who commands the men assigned to protect him. This was undoubtedly what Jake ran into – the men are at hand and it only requires a shout to bring people running to his assistance." *Okay, Eldon's office was down two flights, but what the hell.*

John turned to Scovel. "You brought up the fact that I have been to Washington twice, both times, I may add, with my sister. Although I went to discuss my military service, I was able to do the scouting I needed to decide that further attempts should not be made there."

Scovel nodded, as if chastened, although inwardly he was pleased that their ploy had worked.

"My second reason is simple. One of the first rules of military strategy is to know your ground," John stated. Standing again, he put his hands on the table and leaned forward. "Gentlemen, we know this area very well: streets, alleys, back roads, buildings that are empty, and so forth. This gives us a tremendous advantage – we can choose our locations, and getting away will be easier than trying to work our way around Washington." He waited until he saw thoughtful nods from Hans Baumgarten, Robert Adelmann, James Weston, and Bartholomew Scovel. *Four out of six – time for the hard sell.*

"My third reason combines two thoughts," he continued as he settled into his chair again. "This town is going to be crowded. One editor is estimating there could be fifty thousand people here for the dedication, which is an exaggeration but salient. It is much easier to get lost in a crowd than it is to run out of a building alerted to your presence. The main point is this: while he is here, Lincoln will be on show, out in the open. Riding in a procession, on a stoop to greet a crowd, even giving a speech, he will be vulnerable."

"All sound reasons," Caine agreed. "You still haven't told us what you plan to do."

"I have formulated two possible times during the dedication when Lincoln would be least guarded. One is the night before. I am not about to give you details at this time — it's too early and I may decide otherwise. Lincoln will be staying at Wills' house, and his movements will be public knowledge."

"Why not wait for the dedication itself? It would send a clear message to the rest of the country if he was felled trying to justify his actions in starting this war," Blakeley pointed out.

"In my work at the Commission, I have been hearing most of the plans for the ceremony. There will be a platform full of dignitaries, and a huge audience. A large crowd to cover an escape or in which to hide after the fact is one thing. Trying to take out a lone target among so many would be too risky."

"You said you have selected two possible opportunities," Blakeley persisted. "If not the dedication, when?"

John smiled. "Lincoln will be riding with the others in a procession to the cemetery site for the dedication and it will be a slow-moving line. Think on that," he concluded, leaning back in his chair. "The route will be known, as the visitors will want to glimpse him. It should be easy to find a vantage point along the route."

John gave them time to think, and quietly took a slow, deep breath. Cathy had recommended he do his presentation seated, and although he had made one point standing, it had helped, mostly to hide shaky legs.

"Any questions?" he asked, reaching for his glass.

"I think we should have a more active part," Adelmann said bluntly. "We can back you up."

"I would remind you that we have already agreed that Bartholomew is to act as the back-up shooter," John responded, "and I have a few thoughts I would ask you to consider. First, the more men we have out on the streets, so to speak, the easier it will be to have confusion and contradictions among ourselves. Second, if anything goes wrong, if for some reason I fail and Bartholomew cannot act in my stead, we may need the rest of you to assist in our escape. Third, if everything completely falls apart and the two of us are taken, the five of you can start over." *Damn, Catie called that one right on the money.*

Weston stood up. "Friends, I think our efforts were blessed when John joined our group. We were foolish to let Jake run off on his own without someone to assist him in case of trouble, but that is not the situation here. I realize I have had more time to think about John's plan than you have, but I also had a chance to ask my questions. I believe it is well thought out, and stands as our best chance of success."

"I agree," said Scovel as he stood. "I am honored that I have been chosen as John's assistant for this important and vital task. Once the final plans for the dedication are made public, I intend to let him decide where we shall place ourselves."

"Gentlemen," Hans Baumgarten said as he rose, "I hope we are all in agreement behind John."

Caine and Adelmann rose slowly, each stating his agreement. Everyone looked at Blakeley.

"Ben," said John to the only other man still seated, "do you have any questions?"

"Will we be told where you will be when you make the attempt?"

"No," John returned bluntly. "Ben, I shall be honest with you. I did not want to share this much with all of you. The success of the mission, as well as my life, is now in your collective hands."

Blakeley, still bristling at John's blunt 'no', snapped out, "Meaning?"

"If there is a leak and I am caught in the act of trying to shoot Lincoln, I will be arrested for treason. The penalty for that is death," John reminded him. "The more people who know the details, the greater are the risks of discovery. If one word or idea is overheard, the whole operation could be broken and everyone around this table could be taken prisoner and charged with treason." John smiled, and it was cold. "You cannot divulge something you do not know."

"That changes the perspective," Blakeley murmured softly after a moment of reflection. "I had not considered it from that viewpoint." He stood and said stiffly, "Then I agree. Forgive me, John, you are quite correct. You are bearing the weight of our demands and you deserve our full support."

John stood and put his hand out to the center of the table. Weston and Scovel did the same, clasping John's hand. The other men joined their hands with no hesitation.

"So be it," said Weston. "It has been decided."

"Thank you, gentlemen. I am humbled by your trust." John paused before continuing. "I have one last thing to say before we depart. I do not believe we should meet again. If anything changes, it may be passed along individually."

"I agree," said Weston. "It would be easy enough to meet up in town in the normal course of things. Is this acceptable to the rest of you?"

All the men agreed.

John checked his pocket watch. "I am afraid I need to leave. I told Edward Fahnestock I would not be two hours, and although it has not been near that, I do not wish to raise any questions."

***

Back in Gettysburg, John went immediately to the Commission. At his desk, he wrote out a note to Cathy, and stepped to his doorway.

"Dan!" he called out.

"Major?" Skelly appeared almost immediately.

"I would like you to take a message to my sister at McAllister's. If you see anyone there other than Bartholomew Scovel, take it instead to Mrs. Scott and request that she deliver it later." John smiled. "I know this is an odd request, but would you do this for me?"

"Right away, sir!"

The teen made his way over to Chambersburg Street, and saw two horses out in front of the store. Recognizing them as belonging to Scovel and Weston, he went straight to the Scott home and explained his errand to Martha when she answered his knock. Returning to Fahnestock's, he reported what he had seen and done to John.

"Thank you, Dan, I appreciate it," John said with a smile, handing him a couple of coins.

"My pleasure, Major," replied the youngster. "It is not necessary to tip."

"Take it anyway," John smiled. "You saved me from having to do it!"

***

Late in the day, Cathy was arranging items on shelves when Martha came across the street.

"Young Dan Skelly brought this to me earlier to deliver to you," Martha told Cathy, handing over the note. "The Major told him to bring it to me if there was anyone here besides Mr. Scovel. He recognized the two horses, and decided to skip coming in here at all." She watched as Cathy opened and read the note.

"Miss Martha, John has asked me to inquire if we may take supper with you this evening," Cathy said with a smile. "I am not altogether sure why he wishes to stay in town; however I have not seen him all day."

"We have often told you that you are most welcome any time," Martha stated firmly. "I shall set two extra places. My John will be delighted. I think he has been itching for a game of cribbage." She went home.

"Cathy, forgive me for being blunt, but it is obvious something is going on," Mary observed. "I do hope you and John know what you are doing."

"Believe me, Mary," Cathy said with a sigh, "so do I."

Just before closing, the store's door opened to admit Weston.

"Miss Cathy? I was wondering if I might see you home this evening."

"Oh, James, I am so sorry," Cathy replied. *So that's the reason – thank you, Johnny.* "We won't be going home until later. The Scotts have asked us to take supper with them, and John. has been challenged to a cribbage game thereafter." She smiled up at him. "This is the second time I have had to ask your forgiveness. We shall make it another time, I promise."

"Certainly," he acknowledged somewhat reluctantly, "until then." He left, heading in the general direction of his home.

Less than ten minutes later, John pulled the carriage cart into the Scott's yard and came across the street.

"Good afternoon," he greeted the two women.

"I see you assumed the plan worked," Cathy teased as Mary locked up.

"Did someone come a-calling?" he asked with all the appearance of innocence.

"James was here about ten minutes ago," Cathy explained as they proceeded to the Scotts'. "He wanted to see me home."

"You knew he would come by?" inquired Mary.

"Let's assume I had a hunch he would, and figured that Cathy would appreciate a supper she did not have to cook more than being escorted home by James," he responded with a chuckle.

After supper and two games of cribbage, John guessed it was safe to go home. Dizzy picked her way along in the darkness as John filled Cathy in on the meeting.

"You were right when you predicted that someone would ask to keep an eye on us," he finished. "Thanks – if you hadn't brought it up I might not have been prepared."

"Blakeley finally bought it all?"

"Only after I pointed out that he could be arrested for treason. He agreed but it was begrudging."

"That was big of him. Still, someone had to fuss. I swear that word should be his middle name."

"What did Bartholomew and James want? I sent the note by Dan, and he told me he saw their horses at the store," John explained. "Good thing he's an observant kid."

"They stopped in to see me," she sighed. "I was dying to ask Bartholomew how the meeting had gone, and he was probably just as eager to tell me, but we couldn't get rid of James. The best he could do was to nod and grin when James' back was turned, which I took to mean all was well."

"Speaking of James' interest, I did get a letter off to Myles explaining that we would like to see him if Buford can spare him. I did not go into details, but his presence – and I trust him completely – would give me one more set of eyes at the dedication."

"Yep, and one more man around me. James is not going to take this kindly, but I did meet Myles first. Maybe he needs to come in civvies."

"We'll get to that later. Remember, there will be a strong military presence here." John was quiet for a moment. "Catie, I would like to put one man of ours on each of the five conspirators. Myles would balance the numbers."

"What about me?" Cathy saw what John was going to say and cut him off. "*NO!* I will not, repeat, *not* stay in the cabin with my head down. Not again. Waiting to find out what was going on during the battle was horrible. I *refuse* go through that again. So don't even think about it."

"Okay, okay," he placated her. "I'll work on it."

Monday, 26 October

John looked up as Robert Eldon and Michael Addison approached his work area, noting that Eldon had forsaken his uniform to once again become the grey man he and Cathy had first met.

"You do not seem surprised," commented Eldon as they left the Commission building in the carriage cart.

"It struck me that you would see this as a good opportunity to acquaint yourself with other areas of the town, and exchange any needed information between us," John stated.

Addison looked startled at this.

"Is there something wrong, Mr. Addison?" John asked. "You seem perplexed."

"No, sir, it's just that you gave the same reasons as Mr. Eldon did, in almost the same words."

"Have you never heard that great minds often think alike?" Eldon asked.

"Yes, sir, but rarely so succinctly."

"I would suggest you become accustomed to these notions," John said with a chuckle. "My sister and I have been asked if we can communicate between our minds without words, which," he continued for Eldon's benefit, "we cannot."

As they set out, he explained some of the work taking place.

"The reburials and landscaping have been started in preparation for the dedication. We also had a flag-raising ceremony at the Round Tops last week." John added that with their agreement, he was going to follow the same route he had used when Baker and Albright had visited.

"Yes, please," replied Eldon, "with one additional stop. I have been asked to see the location where John Reynolds fell. There is a dignitary who may want to visit the spot should the opportunity present itself."

"I understand they were friends," John said with a knowing smile. "I shall also include a stop at the McAllister store, for refreshments."

"You are becoming quite the tourist guide," commented Addison after the pair had been taken to the cemetery site. "The dedication will take place in less than a month."

"Yes, it is scheduled for the nineteenth of next month," John acknowledged. "Most of the city is going to be involved."

He pulled up at the store, noting Weston's cart. Cathy, who had been watching on the sly, greeted them at the door.

"John – I am glad you're here! Oh, I see we have more visitors. I was just going across the street. Mary has not yet come over and James wanted to know if Miss Martha has baked any bread. Bartholomew's mother is feeling poorly, and he sent word with James asking if we could help. You know where the kettle is if you want some tea," she called over her shoulder.

John ushered in his tourists as Cathy continued across to the Scotts'. He introduced the men to Weston, hoping like hell the latter didn't catch on to Addison's nervousness.

"I am sorry to hear that Miss Ida is feeling poorly," he began, primarily to keep Weston's attention on him. "Bartholomew must be concerned."

"I was hoping Miss Cathy could ride out there with me," Weston replied, "but Miss Mary is not here. Miss Cathy said she has not been here this morning. I hope she is not also feeling under the weather."

"Cathy will find out – for now, it seems I have to be host," John muttered with a grimace.

Weston chuckled. "It is good for you – I had my turn!"

Cathy returned as John was getting mugs of tea. She was holding a wrapped loaf of bread. "We are in luck – Miss Martha made some bread this morning." She put the bread in the bundle for Weston to deliver, along with some loose tea and carefully wrapped tea cookies she had made. "Please relay my regards to Miss Ida. I have put in some extra tidbits for them."

Weston thanked her for her kindness, and John walked him outside.

"More tourists?"

"Yes, we are becoming quite the attraction. These are business associates of the last two, and asked for me specifically." John rolled his eyes. "They thought the flag-raising was today, apparently."

"Now, be nice," the taller man teased. "You're getting good at this."

"That is not exactly what I need to hear," John groaned as Weston laughed.

John stayed outside until Weston turned the corner. Going back inside, he found Cathy on the stool behind the counter.

"That was fun," she murmured to him. Aloud she added, "Did you have any trouble?"

"All is well. He even teased me about being a good tourist guide," John informed them. "Where is Miss Mary?"

"She is at home. She had gone across right before James arrived, so she was not here when he came in," Cathy let out a sigh. "I think she saw him pull up and decided to stay there."

"Miss Howell, why the charade?" asked Eldon.

"I knew John was going to be stopping here with you and Mr. Addison," she explained. "When James Weston arrived, I wanted to stall him long enough for you to get here, while at the same time giving him a good reason to leave shortly afterwards."

Addison looked from John to Cathy and back again, while Eldon stared at Cathy for a moment before looking accusingly at John.

"No," said John firmly to the two men in response to the implied question, "I did not tell her Mr. Eldon was here – I did not have the chance." He turned to Addison with a smile, "I did warn you that we thought alike. She assumed, as I did, that Mr. Eldon would accompany you."

"When James walked in, I confess I had a moment of panic," Cathy said with a grimace.

"I sincerely doubt that," Eldon commented dryly. "So, that was one of the prime conspirators."

"In the flesh," John confirmed. "The other one is Blakeley."

The store door opened, and John Scott entered. "Mary sent me to let you know she will stay at home for the rest of the day, in case James returns. She told me that if I wanted an explanation, I was to ask you."

John introduced him to the visitors, adding that he was the telegrapher. "Mr. John, do you want an explanation?"

"I surmised that this was, at least in part, a ploy to make sure Cathy did not have to ride out to Scovels' with James," he said. "If I need more than that, I am confident you will let me know when I need to know it."

"Tell Mary I appreciate her caution, and thank you," Cathy told him as he left.

"Gentlemen, I suggest we continue our tour," John said as another customer entered the store. "Cathy, I shall see you later."

As they approached the area of the first day's battle, Addison commented, "Major Andrews, you and your sister seem to take all this in your stride. While teaching may explain your ease at lecturing and briefing, it does not begin to encompass how you both are staying two steps ahead of the conspirators."

"Well put, Michael," Eldon affirmed. "I was wondering along those lines myself. No amount of teaching could prepare you for the improvisation we just witnessed."

"I beg to differ," John protested mildly. "I teach engineering, and although it is regarded as a dry and pedantic pursuit, it is generally a matter of a logical expression of steps, each building on the one before. Cathy, as you know, is a highly qualified nurse, and medicine requires logical thought plus the ability to make adjustments on the fly." John chuckled. "I do, however, admit that what we are doing, and our success so far, has often surprised us!"

"So you're not trained agents?" Addison asked outright.

John laughed out loud. "Absolutely not! Back home we are exactly what we have represented ourselves to be: a civil engineer and a medical professional, both of whom teach our respective fields." *Nice to tell the truth, as far as it goes. Maybe the hours watching Mission: Impossible, the Bourne films, and all the mysteries have warped our thinking enough to survive this!*

As he drove to the field where John Reynolds was shot, John had a few moments to reflect that Cathy had been right in her assessment of their situation shortly after their arrival in 1863. *We have the tools and skills to do what has to be done, and it's taking both of us. But never, ever did I dream I'd be up to my ears in a counter-plot to save Abraham Lincoln. We'd better not fail!*

He stopped the cart, and gestured across the field towards the west. "John Reynolds was placing his men here, when he was struck in the head by a bullet from a rifle. There is debate whether it was an overshot from a volley from the Confederate side or whether it was a shooter aiming at him deliberately. The general died before he hit the ground."

"Were you here at the time?" Eldon asked.

"No, sir. This was the center of General Buford's line. I was on the right flank and from what I understand, I had been hit shortly before General Reynolds arrived with his troops."

The three men looked around the now-quiet area, each imagining the battle. For John, it was starting to become too vivid, too close. He cleared his throat, and coughed.

"Mr. Eldon? Mr. Addison? Was there anything else you wanted to see?"

"No, Major. I do want to know what plans you have told your group and how you intend to counter them," Eldon replied, aware that John was uneasy on the battlefield. "Is there somewhere we could talk quietly?"

"Let us go to the Globe for refreshment, and see if any others of the seven are taking lunch. From there, we can proceed to my cabin."

***

Later in the afternoon, John dropped his two visitors off at the train station and realizing he had time, he took Dizzy back to her corral, unhitched her, and made a big fuss over how good she had been as he groomed her. Hearing a horse coming up to the cabin, he turned and gaped.

"Major Andrews! Is that a large pony?" called Myles Keogh as he dismounted and walked over.

"Major Keogh, Dizzy is a small horse, and she is very sensitive – she resents being called a pony," John called back, laughing.

"Then I shall tender my apologies for even suggesting such a thing," Keogh replied as he and John shook hands. Turning to Dizzy, he noted that the small animal was well-proportioned and healthy. Petting her, he reached into his pocket for a sugar lump. "There you are, me beauty. Apology accepted, I hope."

"Myles, it is good to see you. Where's General Buford? How is he?"

"I left him in Edward's care in Baltimore. The campaign in Bristoe has taken his last strength, and although he is still in command, he is on his way to Washington where he will stay with General Stoneman. He sent me up here to find out, in his words, 'what in tarnation is going on?' Rumors are flying, John, little of it good."

John grinned. "To reply in kind, 'there's the devil to pay.' How long can you stay? Do you have civilian clothes? And do you have your cot?"

"So, you are up to your ears in trouble. I am here for at least two days,

114

after which I shall report back to the General. If you need me, I feel certain he will order me to return," Keogh grinned, "especially if his Miss Catie is in need of me. I have my regular togs. As for a cot, surely we can find one." The Irishman regarded his friend and former comrade in arms. "Your leg is fully healed. Your sister did remarkably well."

"She was amazing – she nursed me night and day, bullied me when she had to, coddled me when she could."

"And now she has two suitors? Shall I throw my hat in her ring?" Keogh's grin widened.

"I shall get to that," John realized he was grinning again, mostly from relief at the presence of the Irishman. "Since I have just finished grooming Dizzy, let us take a walk back to town." John checked his watch. "Change into civilian clothes, and we can get Catie at the store. She will be glad to see you. As for what is going on," he shrugged, "we are not just up to our ears, Myles. We are both in up to our eyeballs. If I am misplacing my trust telling you all, heaven must help us because the devil himself will come down on us."

On their leisurely walk to town, John laid out the conspiracy and the counter-plot to the former member of the Company of Saint Patrick and Vatican guard. They sat on the half-way log while Keogh digested what his friend had told him.

"General Stoneman mentioned a bomb plot that you two foiled in a letter to the general," he told John, "but he did not say Miss Catie – beggin' your pardon, I am used to hearing the General refer to her that way – was responsible for taking the man down." He gave it some thought. "I doubt it would surprise him."

"No, probably not," John agreed. "I know both you and he gave us sterling recommendations or we would never have gotten the letter from General Stoneman, which is what got us to John Nicolay and Robert Eldon."

"What shall I do now?" Keogh asked as the two men resumed their walk to town, adding with a mischievous grin, "You know we Irish are known for our theatrical talents."

"I always suspected you were a master of the blarney, Myles, however little will be needed for what I have in mind," John teased. "Catie has two suitors at the moment, Bartholomew Scovel and James Weston."

"Weston is a conspirator, and Scovel, like you, is a double player."

John nodded. "We have been trying to keep Weston off-balance and if you present yourself as another interested man, it may help."

"May it not also chase him from the field?" Keogh inquired doubtfully.

"I do not believe so. She has been playing James a bit, and Bartholomew knows she is not interested in a real courtship," John explained. "That brings me to a very pertinent point – Catie is her own woman, and not interested in courtship or marriage. I do not need you getting all soft and gooey, deciding you are the one to carry her off, so to speak."

"Ah, Johnny me lad, rest assured no woman is going to set her collar on me, not even the delectable Miss Catie," Myles responded with a deep brogue. "I shall simply enjoy tweaking the other fellow's nose. If it keeps him off-kilter, the task will fairly be done. But if I'm to stay at the cabin, would it not be damaging to her reputation?"

"I am not certain – we shall have to play that as it comes. One night will not, as I shall also be there. On your return, if you can come back in a couple of weeks when I have everything else arranged, I might have Catie stay with the Scotts for the final week."

"You'll not be stayin' after this conspiracy is over," Keogh observed.

"I see General Buford has been talking to you," John said with a smile. "Yes. At first we stayed because Catie wanted me to heal completely before doing any major traveling. When I uncovered the bomb plot, she insisted on coming with me – I was still using a crutch. When the foiled plot did not stop these men, I felt it my duty to intervene. Once this is over, we do hope to return home."

"A concept to which poor Mr. Weston refuses to subscribe," Keogh nodded, his blue eyes dancing. "I shall greet the lady with my most charming bow."

"You do that," John agreed, laughing. "God bless you, Myles – it is good to have you here. It will not be all fun and games, though."

"Of that I am aware – yet we must take our frolics where we can," the Irishman observed philosophically.

"The store is on Chambersburg Street between the Globe and the Eagle," John told him once they reached Gettysburg proper. "The Scotts live across from the store, and John Scott is the telegrapher – very discrete man, totally loyal."

Keogh nodded. "The town is much more at ease than the last time I was here," he stated as he looked around.

"The lack of a battle raging through it does help," John replied with a chuckle. Suddenly he stopped, and grabbed the other man's arm. "Hold a moment. There is a horse and cart in front of the McAllister store. It's Weston's."

"Johnny me lad, the fates are with us today," Keogh stated firmly. "Shall I be entering yon establishment on my own?"

"I doubt I could hold you back," John grinned, "and I shall follow shortly. You can tell Catie you found me at the cabin, and I am checking on Miss Mary across the street. If you call her Miss Catie, it will let her know we have spoken."

"Will it be also annoying Weston?"

"Most assuredly."

Keogh grinned, and it was full of mischief.

***

Cathy was trying to finish her day's work while Weston was pressing her to come out to the Scovel place with him. She knew John would be returning to get her after work. *I'm running out of small talk and stall tactics, not to mention patience. Johnny – hurry up!* When the store door opened, she fully expected it to be John and turned with a 'what kept you' look she knew he'd understand. She was not prepared for the man she saw.

"Myles!" Cathy, surprised and delighted, forgot to be formal as she approached him.

"Miss Catie," he replied with a huge smile. "You are the sight I have missed the most from my time in this town," he continued, giving her the bow he had promised John and kissing her extended hand. "I found Johnny at the cabin, and we walked in together. He told me to let you know he will be here shortly, as he is across the street seeing how Miss McAllister is faring."

"Major, may I present Mr. James Weston?" Cathy drew Myles by the hand to where the latter was staring. "James, this is Major Myles Keogh. He and John served together under General Buford."

"Mr. Weston, a pleasure," Keogh said, offering his hand.

Weston shook it. "Mine as well, sir."

"General Buford is on his way to Washington," Keogh told Cathy. "When we arrived in Baltimore, he sent me north to see if you and John were well. You know the General has a great regard for you both."

"I shall always remember the general's kindness when John was wounded," Cathy murmured. She turned to Weston. "I do not believe we have told you, James. John fell in battle the first day, and General Buford honored a promise he made to me the afternoon before – he had Myles bring John to the cabin to me, on the General's own Grey Eagle."

"That would be the General's horse." Keogh smiled down at Cathy. "It was then I met Miss Catie. I couldn't understand why, until I saw her, the General had insisted John be brought to her." He looked at Weston. "I helped her carry the man into the cabin and watched as she removed the cloth I had put on torn flesh of his leg. She never flinched, which was better than I did when I first laid eyes on it. Most ladies would have fainted dead away, but she packed me off saying she could manage on her own."

"She is a strong-willed woman, I have learned that much," Weston commented, also smiling down at her. "Ah, here's John."

"Cathy, Miss Martha would like you to see Miss Mary, as she's afraid her sister may be taking a bad fever," John said, taking in the body language of the two men on either side of Cathy. "I am to close up." He turned to Weston. "I hope you bring good news about Miss Ida?"

"She is much improved," Weston replied. "I was going to suggest Miss Cathy visit, but if Miss McAllister is taking sick, I shall find my way home. I am certain Bartholomew will come by tomorrow and thank you himself, but Miss Ida did request I relay her thanks for you kindness. She enjoyed the tea cakes."

"I'm glad," Cathy said truthfully as she walked out with him. She saw him on his way, and went to the Scott home.

Moments later, when she was in the kitchen with Mary getting a cup of tea, Martha called from the front parlor.

"Cathy — whoever is that with John?"

"That, Miss Martha, is Major Myles Keogh, General Buford's aide. Are they heading here?"

"Yes." Martha came back to the kitchen. "Mary, let's set another extra place for supper."

"Thank you!" Cathy smiled at Mary. "Be prepared to be overwhelmed by Irish charm!"

***

Back at the cabin for the night, John and Cathy went through all the details John didn't have time to go over with Keogh on their walk. John recommended that he make contact with General Stoneman and ask to be introduced to Robert Eldon. It took them until well after dark.

"Your presence will make my team of agents complete," John sighed with relief.

"To my way of thinking, you are having to watch too much in too many directions," Keogh observed. "When I come back, maybe we can divide this up a wee bit."

"Myles, when will you be back?" Cathy asked. "I know General Buford needs you. If, as you say, rumors are flying, I hope he doesn't worry unduly."

"I do not intend to burden him so I shall not inform him about this new conspiracy," Keogh paused thoughtfully. "However, since you say General Stoneman is aware of most the plot, I should be able to work with him and Mr. Eldon. When are the last of your Pinkerton men coming up?"

"I should know in another week," John informed him. "If you consult with Eldon, who is actually Major Eldon, by the way, you may know before I do."

Cathy yawned. "Pardon me. I think my day was longer than I had anticipated. Myles, if you accompany me to the store tomorrow, I can almost guarantee you will meet Bartholomew Scovel, and he can take you down to the Globe and point out the others."

"'Tis a grand suggestion indeed," Keogh agreed with a yawn of his own.

Cathy cleared the mugs, and set up her bedroll by the stove claiming she wanted to be warm and the men could have the cooler bedroom. "Now, if you gentlemen would be kind enough to leave my bedroom," she ordered with a chuckle, "I shall retire for the night."

CHAPTER SEVEN:
NOVEMBER, 1863

Saturday, 14 November

Cathy found herself sitting on an early morning train to Baltimore, heading to Washington on her own. It had taken a heated discussion with John and Bartholomew Scovel to get them to agree to let her go solo, but after she flatly stated that it would risk John's standing with his conspiracy group if he were to see General Stoneman again, John saw her point. It was then a matter of convincing Scovel that she could manage on her own; she insisted he didn't need the risk either. Her final argument was that she hoped to bring Myles Keogh back with her.

The last two Pinkerton agents, Able Martinson and Samuel Morgan, had had their orientation to Gettysburg on the ninth of November. They had reported to John that General Buford was already in Washington, although it wasn't generally known so he could keep his command status.

She reflected on the letter which had prompted the trip; it was in her bag. General Stoneman had written to her openly, asking her to visit General Buford at the latter's request. He had suggested the earliest train possible as the general seemed stronger in the morning than in the afternoon. Major Eldon had written to John in a separate letter enclosed in Stoneman's, informing him that the president was balking at attending the cemetery's dedication, currently less than a week away. Faced with both situations, John decided to send Cathy to Washington, to see John Buford and hopefully convince Lincoln to commit to the event. They had carefully discussed how she should present the case to the president, and she was armed for it.

Knowing John Scott was trustworthy, John had finally convinced Stoneman and Eldon that telegrams were a safe mode of communication. Cathy had telegraphed General Stoneman of her expected arrival. When she stepped off the train in Baltimore, ready to find her way to the train she needed for Washington, she spotted, with significant relief, the tall figure of Major Myles Keogh striding towards her.

"Miss Catie, I have been ordered by no less than two generals to ensure your safe travel," he greeted her with his characteristic charm. "I dared not disobey."

"Indeed not," she responded with a laugh, taking his offered arm. "Far be it for me to argue with either of them."

The short trip passed quickly as Keogh filled her in on Buford's condition.

"From what you are describing," Cathy said, frowning, "it would appear that his earlier wounds and his rheumatics have been complicated by hard campaigning under less-than-gentle conditions."

"That is the conclusion the doctors in Washington have given us," Keogh observed. "I wonder at how well you summarized it."

"I have seen much as a nurse," she told him, "and chronic conditions take their toll on a body. I had only to see the general dismount Grey Eagle the afternoon we met to recognize the signs of advanced rheumatics. The constant pain renders true rest impossible and is more of a factor than most would realize." Cathy sighed. "My father, who is a doctor and responsible for much of my training, has a theory that intense stress of the mind might also weaken the body. I know the general has lost family this summer. No parent should have to bury a child."

"I am hoping that your visit might help raise his spirits. He is looking forward to seeing you."

"No more than I. It is so sad to know such a wonderful man will probably be soon lost to us."

"The other general has arranged for you to meet with another honorable gentleman after you see General Buford."

***

Cathy was escorted to the parlor where John Buford was resting. She looked into the kind, pained eyes and smiled.

"General, I bring Johnny's wishes for a speedy recovery to add to my own," she told him as she seated herself in a chair next to the chaise.

"Miss Catie, you are a sight for sore eyes," he replied. "I fear your wishes are in vain, however." Buford waved his black servant Edward and Keogh out of the room. "Tell me, as I know you have knowledge of what is to come. Am I to meet my Maker before the year is out? Be honest with me now, please."

"John," Cathy countered, dropping all formality, "you are seeking information I do not wish to impart."

"Catie, if there is good to go with the bad, I can bear the bad." Buford smiled warmly. "I promise I shall not tell anyone. If delirium sets in, it will be brushed off as the ravings of illness." The smile briefly became a grin.

"The president will give a speech next week that will be long remembered as one of the best in the nation's history. You will be granted your second star, becoming a major general, in about a month. Mr. Lincoln will be re-elected next year, and the war will end in a Union victory in April of 1865." She paused, watching him carefully as he took in her words. "That is the good of it."

"I won't live to see the New Year."

"No, you will not," she replied sadly. "If I had here everything I would have back home, it might be a different story. I'm so sorry, John."

There was a knock on the door and Buford called come in.

"I have heard rumors about a conspiracy against the life of the president, in which you were mentioned." He chuckled as Keogh came in with a tea cart. "From what I understand, you single-handedly took down the man responsible. I always said you were not one to cross."

After a cup of tea and small talk, including the fact that John's leg had healed completely, Buford instructed Keogh to take the tea things away and give them a few moments before showing in General Stoneman.

"Catie, I thank you for your honesty," he said, taking her hand. "I now know I will see my father and my child in heaven, and I shall wait to greet you when your time comes. May God keep you safe until we meet there."

"May God take you into His care without pain, John." Tears filling her eyes, she stood as another knock sounded on the door.

"No tears, Catie." Buford stated softly even as his own eyes watered. "Thank you for coming. I cannot tell you how much this has meant me. Tell Major Andrews to take as good care of you as you did of him, or he will have to answer to me." He smiled, totally at ease.

"I shall, General," she responded, trying to smile as General Stoneman entered.

"My apologies, John, for interrupting. Miss Howell has another appointment."

"No apologies are necessary, George," said Buford, sank back against the lounge, obviously exhausted.

"Rest easy, General," Cathy said gently.

"I believe I shall, Catie." His eyes closed, but a smile played on his face as Stoneman closed the door.

"Thank you, Miss Howell. Your visit meant so much to him," Stoneman commented as he ushered her outside to a waiting carriage.

"General, I assure you it meant every bit as much to me," she admitted, fishing in her bag for a handkerchief with which to dry her eyes. "May I assume we are headed to the White House?"

"Yes. Major Eldon has asked to see you, and then you will be meeting with the president."

"I wish to thank you, sir, for the courtesy of having Major Keogh meet me in Baltimore. My brother was very concerned about my traveling alone."

"Miss Howell, John Buford made the request. I simply followed it," Stoneman said. "John has the oddest mix of perceptions about you – one moment, he believes you capable of dealing with anything while in the next he wants you protected like the daintiest flower."

Cathy laughed aloud. "That sounds remarkably like the attitude I get from my brother."

"Speaking of Major Andrews, please relay my thanks regarding John's promotion. It is in hand." Stoneman paused. "As for the current situation, although I do not know the particulars of what is being planned, Major Eldon is determined to see that the president attends the cemetery dedication."

"Sir, we feel the president's presence is vital, if for no other reason than protocol."

"Edward Everett, former governor of Massachusetts is to give the key-note address. The president has only been asked, as he related it, to make a few appropriate remarks of dedication."

"I understand, yet history would be terribly harsh in condemning any commander-in-chief who was not present at the dedication of a cemetery solely for soldiers who died in a war he ordered." Cathy smiled. "At least that is the way my brother has phrased it."

"You should be aware that the president's young son is very ill," Stoneman confided. "I believe that is why he is hesitating."

"After losing Willie, I can understand why it would be a concern. I shall see what he says," Cathy murmured. "However, first I must see Major Eldon."

"I have cleared Major Keogh to return to Gettysburg with you," Stoneman informed her. "Frankly, I do not believe we could stop him."

"Thank you. I shall be glad of the company. Even I would hesitate to travel alone after dark," she said, smiling. "Shall I return to your home once I finish my meetings?"

"That won't be necessary. I plan to have the major waiting here." Stoneman descended from the carriage and offered Cathy his hand. "Miss Howell, it has been an honor to meet you. I had my doubts that you were as John Buford first described you."

"I sincerely hope I do not disappoint you," she said.

"Ma'am, if anything, I have discovered he underplayed his words. It is a long-standing habit of his," he replied with a smile as they walked to Eldon's office. "If I do not see you again, Miss Howell, may God keep you safe."

***

Cathy's meeting with Eldon consisted mainly of filling him in on the new developments of John's plans.

"I find it amazing that your brother has never been in the military. This entire operation is based on classic strategy. If you two do find yourselves marooned in our time, please come to me for employment."

Cathy laughed. "Coming from you, sir, that is the ultimate compliment. Be assured I shall relay your precise words to John. May I tell him you will be with us in Gettysburg?"

"Yes. As to your other meeting, I should inform you that two things have come up at the same time which the president sees as precluding his attendance in Gettysburg."

"I have been informed that his son Tad is ill, and I can understand his concern, especially seeing he and Mrs. Lincoln have already lost two sons. What is the other thing?"

"According to John Nicolay, the president is working on his proposal for the reconstruction of the South. He feels that his time would be better put to use on that task rather than an event where he is not the major speaker. He has also confided to Nicolay that he would rather not write the remarks he would have to deliver on the occasion."

"I believe I have my work cut out for me."

"You are not discouraged?"

"Not in the least." Cathy lowered her voice. "It is imperative – absolutely essential – he attend. Between us, let me assure you that his 'few appropriate remarks of dedication' will be long remembered as one of the greatest speeches of all time."

"You are serious."

Cathy nodded. "He has to be there because he has always been there. That may not make sense, but it appears to fall to me to convince him to go." She rose. "I am ready if he is."

Major Eldon escorted her to John Nicolay's office. Nicolay received her warmly, and assured her President Lincoln would see her shortly. Major Eldon bowed, and left. Cathy sank into a chair and sighed.

"I am beginning to feel like a parcel or a report everyone wants to see," she commented with a small grimace, "as I am being passed from hand to hand."

Nicolay chuckled, and asked her if she wanted some refreshment.

"Perhaps a glass of water. I did a significant amount of talking with Major Eldon, and I'm afraid my mouth is quite dry."

"I'll see to it," Nicolay offered, rising. He stopped, looking past her.

"Is my guest here?" Lincoln's voice sounded behind her.

"Yes, Mr. President. Miss Howell and I were just discussing how parched one's mouth can get from doing a fair amount of talking."

"Miss Howell, I believe we can take care of this in my office if John will see to it," Lincoln said.

"Certainly, sir."

As Lincoln escorted her to his office, he asked if she had seen John Buford and inquired how he was.

"Not well at all, sir. I am very much afraid he will leave us before the year is out," Cathy replied honestly.

The president nodded. "His promotion seems to be stuck on a desk somewhere."

"The battle in Gettysburg would have had a totally different outcome without his contributions," Cathy asserted. "You have my apologies, sir, if I speak out of turn. I am not well-versed in military matters so perhaps I should have said nothing on our first meeting."

"I shall see that it happens."

As Cathy nodded her thanks, Nicolay came in with a tray of a carafe of water and glasses, and placed it on a table. Nodding to Cathy, who smiled, Nicolay withdrew.

"Let me relieve your mind, Miss Howell," Lincoln said, getting up. "I believe I shall pour this time."

"I sincerely appreciate it, sir," she said, with a low laugh.

"I thought you might, after all your experiences with teacups around here," he chuckled, handing her a glass. "Now, as to the matter of the dedication in Gettysburg. I know you and your brother have said my attendance is imperative, but circumstances seem to be against it." Lincoln pulled a chair closer to hers. "I asked to see you in the hope you can convince me otherwise."

"I believe I can, Mr. President." Taking a sip of water, she put her glass to one side. "First, let me relieve your mind. Your son Tad will recover from his illness."

Lincoln's face visibly relaxed. "Thanks be to God. After losing Eddy and Willie, I do not believe Mrs. Lincoln would survive losing Taddie."

"Your reconstruction plan is going to be completed in time for you to properly present it."

"Fair enough." Lincoln regarded her closely. "You are remarkably well informed."

"Mr. President, I have spent time today with General Buford, General Stoneman, Major Eldon, and Major Keogh. I listen." Cathy shrugged. "Listening is one of the great secrets of the world."

"I agree. Besides listening, have you come to any other philosophical conclusions?" he asked out of curiosity.

"Well, sir, as I pointed out to Mr. Nicolay, after being passed from one meeting to another for most of the day, I have a reasonably good idea as to what it must feel like to be a confidential report."

Lincoln laughed and slapped his thigh. "You are a breath of fresh air, Miss Howell." He became serious. "What reasons can you give me to attend?"

"Sir, my brother gave you the soldier's viewpoint. The commander-in-chief should be at the dedication of a national military cemetery to honor all the men who fought, especially the men who gave their last full measure, under what are ultimately his orders. You said yourself it was the most persuasive argument you had heard, and it still stands."

"I am not denying it."

"As for the appropriate remarks themselves," Cathy looked Lincoln in the eye, "have you received a copy of Governor Everett's oration yet?"

"I know you did not hear *that* from any of the men to whom you have been passed this day," Lincoln commented, startled. "Yes, it arrived not long ago. What do you know about it?"

"It is long."

"You condensed that down better than he did. It's quite long," Lincoln admitted. "Miss Howell, I know you and your brother are involved in preventing another attempt on my life, yet here you are urging me to put myself in that danger. Why?"

"It is interesting that you should phrase it that way at this juncture," Cathy replied. "It is a fair question, though."

"I await your answer."

"Mr. President, if I thought there was any chance we could not thwart the attempt and apprehend those responsible, I would be the first to tell you to stay home and read to Tad in his sickroom. I once told John Buford something that applies to you: you are an honorable man, sir, and the world needs honorable men to save it from its own follies." Cathy paused for a moment. "John has planned the assassination attempt *and* he is coordinating the counter-plot to block it. My brother is a very thorough man." She smiled as she added, "even Major Eldon is impressed. If something untoward occurs and we feel you would be in real danger, you will be informed immediately. As of this morning, I know you will be safe."

"Say I grant you all of that. Why should I take what amounts to two days out of my schedule to make a few appropriate remarks?"

"Your remarks become known as the Gettysburg Address. It is one of the most important speeches in the history of this country, quite possibly the world."

The tall man sat back in his chair. "You are serious."

"Time is flexible, but certain events are fixed." Cathy leaned forward. "Mr. President, I first learned of you through the remarks you will make five days from now."

"You are truly serious," he repeated. "I have yet to commit anything to paper."

"You will start it today, and put the final touches to it in Gettysburg."

Cathy smiled warmly. "You already have the first line in mind, sir."

"You cannot *possibly* know that."

"Are you saying you have not been toying with any phrases?" she queried, raising an eyebrow skeptically.

"Well, possibly."

Cathy sat up straight, folded her hands in her lap, took a deep breath, and recited: "Four score and seven years ago, our fathers brought forth on this continent a new nation, conceived in liberty and dedicated to the proposition that all men...."

"...are created equal." Lincoln stared at her. "If I did not believe you before, I surely do now. But how can you possibly know these words?"

"When I was in school, my history class had to memorize it."

"You still remember it?"

"Mr. President, it is possibly the most succinct, understandable, and meaningful speech ever given. I remember each word, because they describe the rebirth of the nation's purpose." She reached into her bag and pulled out a sheet of paper. "If nothing else, I would ask you to sign this. I wrote it last night from memory."

He took the paper and read the words twice. "These are my thoughts! This is everything I have been pondering. The phrases, the meanings, everything. It is as if someone has gone into my mind, pulled them out, and written them down." He looked up at her. "How can this be?"

Cathy smiled. "It is your speech in your words; it expresses the whole meaning of the day in two hundred and seventy-three words far better than Mr. Everett's oration."

Lincoln took the page to his desk, wrote something on it, and signed it. He then folded it and brought it back to Cathy. "I do not wish to keep it."

"No, but with your permission I shall." She gave him a smile as she tucked it back in her bag. "You asked me for reasons to attend the dedication. This is the best I could offer, but it had to be to you alone. These words define your cause of uniting the country torn apart by states' rights and slavery."

"Miss Howell, I am humbled by your arguments," Lincoln told her. "I hope I shall see you and Major Andrews in Gettysburg."

"I shall see what we can do about meeting. We have not been invited to any of the receptions, but John should be able to think of something."

"I have another appointment," he said, rising, "and I must prepare for it." He opened his office door and called for Nicolay.

"Thank you for your time, Mr. President," Cathy stated as she curtseyed.

"No, Miss Howell, it is I who thank you – for everything." He reached and took her hand as she stood, and kissed it.

Nicolay took her to the entrance where, as promised, Myles Keogh was waiting with a carriage.

"Mr. Nicolay, I hope to see you in Gettysburg next week," Cathy said with a warm smile. "Please, take care of yourself, and do not let President Lincoln work you too hard."

"Miss Howell, it would be a pleasure to see you there, and I thank you for your kind thoughts," he replied, smiling back. "Major Keogh, please see her safely to her brother."

"Rest assured, sir, I shall." Keogh handed her into the carriage, gave the driver instructions, and climbed in after her. "All is as it should be?"

"All is well," Cathy replied with a sigh. "Now all we have to do is prevent an assassination and apprehend the culprits."

"'Tis hardly a matter worthy of concern," he commented wryly.

They looked at each other and burst out laughing.

***

John met them at the station with Scovel.

"Welcome back." John's statement was flat and he was scowling.

"What's wrong?" Cathy demanded.

"Nothing you need be concerned about, dear sister," he replied abruptly.

"John," began Keogh, but Cathy put her hand on his arm and shook her head.

"Not here - back at the cabin," she suggested.

After they were inside with mugs of tea, Cathy looked at John questioningly.

"Hans Baumgarten was found dead shortly after you left," he informed her bluntly.

"*Damn it!*" Cathy took a deep breath and looked at the other two men. "Forgive me, gentlemen. What happened?"

"My theory is he took his own life." John took a swallow of his tea. "Either that or he was killed. My hunch is he couldn't take the pressure of knowing what he knew."

"If I examine the body, I might be able to tell more," Cathy murmured to John alone.

"I'm not sure it would be worth it," he responded.

"We suspected he had been forced to join the plot," Scovel explained to Keogh, "however we could not prove it. We were unable to convince him to tell us who applied the pressure – we each tried."

"He was a good man," Cathy said softly. "He was always polite, worked hard, and kept to himself. What a waste."

"Is this going to cause problems next week?" Keogh asked.

"Hopefully not," replied John. "I should ask if the exercise on. Without the man's presence, things could get very interesting." He regarded Cathy with a raised eyebrow.

"All is as it should be. President Lincoln confirmed to me that he will be here."

"That is what I heard at the Commission late this afternoon. Mr. Wills came in to see me." John suddenly smiled. "We have been invited to the luncheon and reception after the dedication. Mr. Wills came by to issue the invitation in person. He said he has been hearing of my service, both in the battle and at the Commission, and specifically requested that I bring my sister. What have you been up to?"

"She has been charming everyone from the president down to his secretary, with a couple of generals and two majors in between," explained Keogh, "all the while claiming to feel like delivery package."

The four of them laughed. John checked his watch. "Weston will be here this evening. He asked if he could come by, and I explained that I had to pick you two up at the station. He said he would stop by after we got back."

"What does he want?" Cathy asked. "With Myles here, it cannot be the conspiracy."

"Maybe he found out something more about Hans' death," suggested Scovel.

"Catie, in all this fuss, I forgot to ask if you two have had anything to eat," John said. "I can put out some cheese and sausage, with bread."

"That would be lovely, Johnny. Since you brought it up, I'll not offer to help."

The snack had been eaten when they heard a horse pull up outside. John went to the door.

"James! Come and join us."

"Is Bartholomew here?"

"Yes, he is, along with Major Keogh."

"May I have a word with you and Bartholomew outside?"

"Of course. Give me a moment." John came to the table as Cathy stood with her hand in her pocket. He put out his hand and took the Beretta, hiding it so it wouldn't scream modern, and clicked the safety off. "Bartholomew? He seems more agitated than he was earlier. Join us?"

The larger man rose, and they went outside.

Cathy started pacing after five minutes.

"Catie lass, settle down, please," Keogh encouraged. "Johnny can handle himself."

"Myles, the tension – the real tension – has been building for about two weeks," she relayed, perching on the edge of her chair. "We have all our pieces in place, but according to Johnny, the group has started to come apart. Hans' death may be the first sign they are cracking open."

"That would be to the good, would it not?"

"Not necessarily," John stated as he and Scovel came back in. "These are zealots, not professionals. When the pressure is turned up, they tend to become unpredictable." He sat down. "Weston informed us that Ben Blakely killed Hans because he feared the man was going to tell the authorities. Caine was with him."

"Heavens above," Cathy groaned. "Blakely has gone insane."

"It gets worse," John stated. "Both Blakely and Caine have disappeared."

"What about Robert Adelmann?" Keogh asked.

"Adelmann managed to convince Blakeley he is bowing out but swore he can be trusted to keep mum," Scovel informed them. "Caine is a close friend of his, so he probably is safe."

"This puts you and Bartholomew in danger," Cathy whispered.

"Not so. James came to let us know that he wants us to carry on as planned. We need to keep an eye out for Blakeley and Caine," Scovel stated.

"And what happens now?" Keogh inquired.

"We act as we were planning to. We can't arrest Blakeley and Caine on suspicion of murder without giving everything away." John sighed. "If possible we could confine Blakeley and Caine, but I don't see how that might work. I have an idea, but I want to sleep on it. For the moment, I suggest we all make an early night of it."

"Major, how long will you be staying?" Scovel asked the Irishman.

"Bartholomew, please call me Myles. I shall send telegrams to Washington tomorrow, requesting General Stoneman put me on leave until this is over. I shall also suggest he encourage Major Eldon and the others to definitely plan their arrival for the seventeenth."

"Thank the Lord," the stocky man breathed. "Myles, you strike me as a good man to have around during troubled times." He rose. "I'll head home and see you tomorrow."

"Thanks, Bartholomew," John said. "You are not a bad man to have around yourself!"

Tuesday, 17 November

Scovel galloped up to the cabin, dismounted, and banged on the door.

"Myles! I know I am supposed to be following John, but I came to warn you. There's the devil to pay!"

"Trouble?" the Irishman asked, shrugging into his jacket in the open doorway.

"Weston rousted me early to tell me that he met with Blakeley last night. They see John as a traitor and it's now up to me to carry out the assassination. Weston is working with Blakeley and Caine to go after John. I am worried about Cathy. I think James may go after her to get to John."

"Lord Almighty! Catie stayed in town with the Scotts last night." Keogh stepped into the cabin to grab his belt and pistol. "You go after John. See that he doesn't come to harm and tell him I shall go into town and stay with her."

***

John was taking his time going into town, letting Dizzy choose her own pace along the familiar pathway. His thoughts were focused on the plot, and he was uneasy. *Blakeley was behaving more and more oddly, missing most of his usual activities while avoiding face-to-face confrontations. Definitely not good.* Suddenly alert, he heard a horse behind him coming at a gallop. Instinctively he pulled off to the side and dropped off the carriage cart. He sprinted for the woods and had no sooner stepped behind a tree than he saw Weston dismount.

"John Andrews!" Weston roared. "Come out and fight, you traitor!"

John drew the Beretta Cathy had insisted he keep on the grounds it was a more accurate weapon. He noted that Weston wore a gun at his side but hadn't drawn it. Staying in the shadows of the trees, he carefully and quietly worked his way around to a better vantage point back towards the other man.

"You traitor! You coward!" the man screamed. "Ben is going for Miss Cathy to tell her you are dead – by the time he gets to town you will be! Make your peace with God and face me!"

John heard a second horse coming up.

"James!" Scovel called out. "Do you have him yet?"

"Bartholomew! Thank God. No, we are going to have to flush him out," Weston snarled savagely. "The coward will not stand and fight. I sent Ben and Nicholas to town."

Scovel, seeing Weston focused on one area of the woods and knowing John wouldn't be there, looked in the area between him and Weston. John stepped ever so slightly to the side of the tree and caught his friend's eye. They exchanged nods. John replaced the small handgun into his inside coat pocket.

"There he is!" Scovel cried, pointing to a spot in the woods in front of Weston, well away from John.

Weston drew and hesitated. John tossed a rock to the area where Scovel had pointed. As Weston fired, John jumped out and landed a solid punch on the man's jaw, putting his whole weight behind it. Weston went down.

"You saved my life," John said, rubbing his hand. "Thank you."

Scovel sighed with relief. "My apologies for being late. I went by the cabin to warn Myles there was the devil to pay."

"Catie! She's in danger!" John moved to the driver's seat.

"Relax, John. I sent Myles to her," Scovel assured him as he put a hand on his friend's arm. "He will be more than a match for those two. Now let us get James tied up and into the carriage cart. Then we can head to town." He got a length of rope off his saddle. "Weston gave me this earlier. It was supposed to be your noose."

"All the more fitting to use it to tie him up," John commented wryly. "Thank you again, my friend."

"My pleasure." Scovel made it the work of a moment. "I guess Blakeley and Caine figured they could handle a woman. I shall tell you what I know on the way."

***

It was ten o'clock when Mary and Cathy heard the door of the store bang open. They stared as Keogh entered solemn-faced; he handed Mary a note.

"Miss Mary, casually make your way to your home and stay there. Have Mr. John send this at once."

"Of course, Myles. What about Cathy?"

"As much as I would prefer her to be goin' with you, she is to stay here with me. I promise to take good care of her." Keogh smiled at Mary. "There's the devil to pay. Go."

"Be careful," Mary replied. As she opened the door, she called back, "I believe I shall take a break, Cathy. If you need me, I shall be at home helping Martha."

"Now there is an intelligent woman," observed Myles. "'Tis a pleasure to regard her. All is quiet here?" he asked calmly.

"Myles, if you don't tell me what is going on, I shall start using language you have never heard before," Cathy threatened, one hand on her hip.

"As educational and entertaining that would be, Catie me darlin'," he responded, his brogue thickening, "I shall be filling ye in as soon as ye step away from yon window." As she complied, Keogh moved one of the chairs so he could observe the street. "James told Bartholomew early this morning that he believes John is a traitor to the conspiracy. Blakeley, Caine, and Weston are now gunning for him, and Bartholomew wondered if any of the three would come after you to get to John, so I volunteered to come here. Bartholomew went to help John."

"Myles, how much do you know about us?"

"Back in July, when he told me to visit you the night I was not there, General Buford hinted there was more to you both than appeared. I confess I have done a lot of guessing since, particularly after I heard about how you took down Reissen, which by the way, was something that impressed Major Eldon mightily."

"So you haven't been specifically told?"

"No, ma'am," the Irishman smiled, "and I'll kindly be asking ye not to."

"I wasn't planning to," Cathy replied with a smile.

"Johnny told me you are thirty-five. Is it true? I suspect he was trying to convince me to leave well enough alone without actually telling me so," he responded, changing the subject, "something about me not being old enough for you."

"We both are," she affirmed. "Myles, are you trying to distract me?"

132

"I'm simply killin' me time with small talk. Wherever you call home is kinder to aging looks than this climate. I thought we Irish were well preserved," he commented absently, gazing out to the street. "Ah, so much for a peaceful, pleasant morning. Here comes yon trouble."

"Who?"

"Little man. Wait now, there be two of them, one only an inch or so taller than the other."

"Blakeley and Caine." Cathy stepped behind the counter. "I guess James is trying to take on John while these two quell a woman."

"Which one of yon pair would you like?" he inquired courteously.

"Whichever one you spare," she returned. She put her broom in easy reach, wishing she still had the Beretta. John had kept it on the grounds that it was smaller than his officer's pistol. "If they do not see you immediately, it may be an advantage."

"Yes, ma'am." He stepped to the wall next to the door, pistol drawn. "'Tis surely a shame I canna bring meself to shoot a man in the back." He sighed regretfully.

The door opened.

Blakeley entered and approached the counter, with Caine two paces behind him. "I regret to inform you, Miss Howell, that your brother is dead. Please come out from behind the counter." He pulled a derringer out of his pocket. "I have no wish to harm you."

Caine's attention was also on her; Cathy watched Keogh slowly advance behind him. Cathy waited for his nod before she started to move as Blakeley requested, her hands at her side. Keogh hit Caine with his pistol, and when Blakeley began to turn at the sound, Cathy lunged. She tried for the hand holding the tiny weapon, and fell against him with enough force to spin them both around. The derringer went off in the struggle and flew out of his hand.

At the same moment, Cathy felt a searing pain in her upper left arm. She and Blakely wrestled, each struggling to master the other; they were too close together for Keogh to intervene. As the Irishman hovered near them, trying to find a vantage point, Cathy lost her temper.

"Shit!" She grabbed Blakeley's arm, turned into him, and forcibly drove the tip of her right elbow back into his chest just below his sternum. Badly winded, he bent over. Whirling to face him, she backed up one step, and brought her arm up horizontally under his chin, knocking him backwards into the counter. His head hit the corner edge of the counter and he slowly slumped to the floor.

The store door slammed open; Keogh spun around, his gun raised to meet the new threat.

John stood in the doorway.

"Johnny, 'tis a grand sight to see you alive and in one piece," the Irishman said, lowering his weapon with a sigh of relief. "Yon miscreant told Catie you were dead."

"Not a scratch on me. James, however, has been trussed up by an expert in the rope that was supposed to be used for my noose. He is currently housed in the Scott's cellar under Bartholomew's watchful eye while Mr. John sends for Major Eldon and his men to come immediately. I thought I would see what I could do here, but you appear to have it under control." John looked at Cathy. "You are bleeding."

"No, really?" she retorted. "Blakeley shot me with a derringer."

"Is he breathing?"

"Frankly, my dear, I don't give a damn," Cathy muttered as she leaned over the prostrate figure and pulled a clean handkerchief out of the man's pocket. Putting it to her upper arm, she took Blakely's pulse. "He is alive, but he won't be for long. I think the corner of the counter got his brainstem." She stood up as the fluttering pulse stopped. "He is gone."

"Then it is over, and thanks to God we won." John took a deep breath. "Myles, get a towel from the storeroom. Miss Mary keeps a stack of them near the tea kettle. Catie, sit down." John took the handkerchief from her and tore the sleeve of her blouse open.

"Catie lass, where in the name of heaven did you learn those moves?" Keogh inquired with a grin, handing John a towel. "More importantly, can you teach them to me? That was sheer poetry, it was."

"Myles, can you tote Caine to Bartholomew? You have never seen such a master with ropes. I learned a lot just watching." John lifted the towel to check on the wound. "I shall stay here."

Scovel entered at a run. "How can I help? Mr. John is watching James."

"Cathy!" Mary exclaimed in dismay from behind Scovel.

"Mary, I assure you, I shall be fine," Cathy said. "It is merely a graze."

"Bartholomew, let us take this sorry sod across the street and you can give me lessons on tying ropes," Keogh suggested. The men picked up the unresisting Caine and hustled him out the door.

"Sorry, Catie, you are better at this than I am," John apologized as the first bandage slipped off.

"Let me see if I can help. We have also sent for the constable," Mary continued, as she tied a bandage around Cathy's upper arm.

"Mary, I do apologize for bleeding all over your floor."

"No matter - this has been exciting! Please, however, do not tell Martha I said so. She believes I shouldn't enjoy events such as these."

"After all the planning, this seems almost too easy a way to end the trouble," Cathy observed.

"Don't argue with success. And will you please sit still?" John demanded as Cathy started to get up. "You will loosen the bandage."

"I want the derringer," Cathy stated crossly. "It's cute."

"I shall task Myles with the search for it. Stay put." John commanded impatiently. "Please?"

"Constable Hardy will want to see you, Cathy," Mary cautioned.

"The constable can make do with me," Keogh stated as he came back in. "Johnny, you were correct – watching Bartholomew work with rope is indeed a true education. Miss Mary, ma'am, since I was here, I can explain all to the constable."

"You can?" Mary asked. "Suppose you tell me first."

"Blakeley was insane, babbling about how Catie here was keeping all his friends on a string. He called her a whore of the devil." Keogh shrugged. "Blakeley raised a small pistol at her, it went off as they struggled, and she knocked him backwards. He was killed when he hit his head. The constable does not need to be burdened with anything more."

"What about Nicholas Caine and James Weston? Mind you, I am not criticizing, you understand," she added, "simply curious."

"Major Eldon will be here later and he will take care of any loose ends," John told her.

"Miss Mary, I am telling ye there was no one else here but Catie and myself," the Irishman said with a smile. "If there had been, I would have seen them, would I not?"

"I believe I understand," she admitted, "and I do thank you for clearing that up."

"Now, Johnny, what is it I'm supposed to find for Catie?"

***

"I cannot believe Benjamin Blakeley wanted to kill me," Cathy said later to the constable, shuddering for effect. "I did not even see the gun until he had it in front of me. I do apologize – I do not suppose I am being much help." She was sitting with John's arm around her shoulders in the Scott's front parlor, still in her bloody skirt and blouse. Her arm was still bandaged in the tea towel.

"Miss Howell, you and your brother are well-known as honorable people. I simply needed your version of the events. I have Major Keogh's account," the constable informed her gently. "I saw Mr. Adelmann and Mr. Scovel earlier. They both confirm Mr. Blakeley has been acting oddly for over a week."

"Constable, my sister has been through a terrible ordeal and needs to rest. Have you finished?" John wanted the man out of the way before Eldon and his men arrived.

"Of course." The constable folded up his notebook and stood. "I trust you will be feeling better soon, Miss Howell."

"John, dear," Martha cut in firmly once the law was gone, "Cathy should stay here at least overnight. We have room for both of you."

"Miss Martha, I thank you for your offer. Myles and I should stay until

Major Eldon arrives. If Cathy can rest here, we shall decide more once we have seen him."

Cathy moved her arm and winced. "It's bleeding. Again."

"Is that going to need stitches?" John asked, frowning.

"I fear so. Every time I move it, the bleeding starts afresh. Miss Martha, do you have a hand mirror?"

"Yes, and we have some whiskey. Shall I boil a length of silk on a small needle? You will also need cloth squares and a pair of small scissors." Martha smiled serenely as Cathy nodded, recalling the two sisters had helped her attend injured soldiers after the battle. "I shall set it up in the kitchen."

"Will you bring me an extra threaded needle? No need to boil it."

"You are going to stitch up your own arm?" John asked incredulously.

"No, Johnny, you are." Cathy laughed at his stunned expression. "I am simply going to show you how."

While Keogh held her arm steady John, assisted by Martha, performed admirably. Once it was done, Cathy leaned back against the chair. "Johnny, you did well but please do not give up engineering for medicine. Before we fashion a sling, I would like to clean up." She surveyed her clothing, now thoroughly splattered with blood.

"Catie lass, please allow us to find you a whole new outfit," Keogh said with a gallant bow. "'Tis the least we can do. Do you not agree, Johnny?"

"I do indeed. I know where the emporium is, and you deserve it, Catie." John saw a question in her eyes. "We shall also stop at the cabin for a few things, as well." He knew exactly where the med bag and phone were kept. "We shall not be long."

On their way to the cabin, John suggested to Keogh that they should locate and detain Adelmann, to make their set complete.

***

Major Eldon arrived at the store before one o'clock, having broken all speed records getting there. Mary McAllister, relaxing after scrubbing her floors, told him he would find John, Catie, and answers in her front parlor, adding he needn't bother to knock as he was expected.

"Major Andrews!" Eldon snapped out as he opened the front door.

"Major Eldon!" John snapped back without necessarily meaning to. "My apologies, sir. We have had an interesting morning."

"So I gathered. Where is Miss Howell?"

"She is in the kitchen with Martha Scott, getting cleaned up and changing into fresh clothes. She adamantly refused to wear the torn, bloody ones a moment longer."

"*Bloody?*"

"Yes, sir. Benjamin Blakeley, the mastermind of the plot, shot her about three hours ago - a flesh wound in her arm."

"Major Eldon!" Keogh came in slowly, supporting Cathy as she walked to the divan. "Meet the heroine of the day."

"Miss Howell, would you please tell me what, exactly, you have been doing today?"

"Major Eldon, I had a struggle with Benjamin Blakeley; he hit his head on the counter at the store. He is dead." Cathy sat, carefully cradling her arm.

"I am pleased to report that the remaining three conspirators are in custody in the cellar. Your men can act as guards tomorrow and Thursday; however, it is over," John informed him.

"It is over?" Eldon's tone held awe. "The conspiracy?"

"Yes. Please assure the president he may safely come to the dedication."

Wednesday, 18 November
Late Evening
John Scott came into his front parlor carrying a telegram.

"Cathy, I believe this is the one you have been expecting," he reported with a smile. "I hereby authorize you and Major Andrews to deliver it."

Minutes later, John and Cathy were in the carriage cart heading for the Wills house. John, once more back in uniform, escorted Cathy to the front door. Back in the first day dress Mary had given her, the only thing that spoiled her appearance was the sling. When the butler answered the door, John gave their names and asked to speak to David Wills or John Nicolay. Both came to the door; the sounds of the large dinner party drifted past them.

"Major Andrews! Miss Howell!" Nicolay's pleasure was obvious. "What may I do for you?" His eyes fell on Cathy's sling.

"Mr. Nicolay," she replied with a beautiful smile, "we have been asked by John Scott to deliver a telegram to President Lincoln."

"Right this way," Nicolay told her, holding his curiosity in check. "He will be delighted to see you."

"Go ahead, Catie," John smiled. "You have earned it. I shall await you here."

"Major, dinner has concluded and you would be most welcome inside," Wills informed him. "I have been hearing whispers about events in town yesterday. It even half of them are true, you deserve a drink."

***

"Mr. President?" Nicolay wound his way through the guests with practiced ease. "Miss Howell is here to see you, sir. Major Andrews is here as well."

"Miss Howell!" Lincoln greeted her warmly. "You saved me the trouble of finding you."

"I do not wish to interrupt your evening, sir."

"Nonsense." He regarded her. "You are injured."

"A scratch, nothing more. The sling is a ploy for sympathy."

Lincoln chuckled. "It makes a great hiding place, too, I see," he commented as she pulled the telegram out.

"Excuse us, please," he said to Secretary Seward, who turned to another guest. Lincoln pulled out his spectacles and sat as he opened the envelope. "Please, Miss Howell, be seated."

"You will find it good news," she informed him softly, "as I once mentioned."

"Yes," he confirmed, taking off his spectacles and wiping his eyes. "Indeed. Thank you. I was just going up to my room to work on my speech for tomorrow. Would you care to see it?" He winked at her and handed her two sheets of paper he had in his pocket.

"I would be honored, sir." Cathy read the familiar words in the man's own hand and felt a shiver of wonder. "It is almost perfect," she told him in a low voice. "Add, 'under God' to the last phrase so it reads, 'that this nation, under God, shall have a new birth of freedom....'"

"I shall," he promised. "I would be willing to wager your injury had something to do with the matter we spoke of in Washington. I would like to know."

Wills brought John over to where they were sitting.

"Good evening, Mr. President," John saluted. Not seeing another chair, he knelt at Cathy's side.

"Major Andrews, your dear sister won't say anything about her injury," Lincoln complained in a mocking tone. "Would you shed some light on this?"

"I can only relate the generalities," John confessed, "I was not present at the time. She was shot."

"Mr. President, I was shot by a madman," Cathy cut in, stating it flatly. "I managed to get the better of the situation."

"I doubt that even begins to cover the events," Lincoln told her. He glanced around for Wills, who was standing nearby. "Mr. Wills, have my guests been invited to the festivities?"

"I have invited them for the dedication and the luncheon reception following, sir."

"Good." Lincoln turned his gaze to John. "Major, I believe you are familiar with the battlefield overall."

"He has become quite the tour guide, Mr. President," Cathy put in slyly.

"I should like to see the area where John Reynolds fell," Lincoln explained. "Would you be available to show it to me early in the morning? Mr. Seward and my Canadian guest, Mr. William McDougall would be with me, and of course, Miss Howell would also be most welcome."

"I believe this is one time Catie will not object if I speak for her," John replied with a chuckle. "It would be our pleasure, sir."

"Mr. Wills, if you would arrange for a carriage for eight o'clock," Lincoln said, rising, "we shall consider this a plan."

***

Thursday, 19 November

One Minute after Midnight

Cathy woke with a start, feeling tingly. She looked at her window in the Scott home and saw a branch hitting the window, but could not hear it. Unable to move, it took her a moment to recognize what was happening.

"The time is right for coming full circle." The deep voice sounded in her mind.

I am injured. I can't go back yet. Please.

"Acknowledged. The days are two." The rich tones echoed through her mind.

Two days – we have only two days? Damn!

"You have done well. In three days, you will come full circle." The warm voice enveloped her.

Thank you – this is important to us.

"Understood. Now sleep." The voice faded and she slept.

***

John came into her room at dawn.

"Catie?"

Her eyes flew open. "Johnny, I had a weird dream."

"We have three days."

"Yep, that was it." She got out of bed – a much nicer one than theirs at the cabin – and started to get dressed. "Damn it, this hurts."

"Acetaminophen coming up. Turnabout is fun – me handing out the meds," he teased. "Do you need the antibiotic?"

"I don't think so. Between the bleeding and the whiskey, it should be clean. I'll know by today." She lifted her arm carefully. "Crap, I'm going to need help. It's stiff and I don't want to tear the stitches."

"I'll send Miss Martha up after I get the tablet." He left and was back in a flash. "Here."

"Thanks. I want to wear the new dress you bought."

Footsteps sounded on the stairs as Martha called out, "Cathy! John!"

"We are both up," John called back. "Cathy needs assistance."

"That, John, is why I am here."

***

At eight on the dot, John and Cathy were standing outside the Wills home next to the arranged carriage, having walked over after a hasty breakfast.

"Johnny, we get to see it all happen!"

"We've done well. The Voice even said so." John smiled down at her. "I'm sorry you were shot."

"For this it was worth it. By the way, Myles found the derringer. I'm adding it to our souvenirs."

"I invited him to stand with us at the dedication. Do you have the phone?"

"You betcha." She grinned. "Here comes President Lincoln with Secretary Seward and Mr. McDougall."

Cathy managed a curtsey as she was introduced to the Secretary of State and William McDougall. John was about to help her rise when Lincoln the honors. John handed her into the rear of the carriage while Lincoln took the seat beside him.

John explained the first day's fighting, and showed them the area around McPherson's Ridge, as well as the cupola at the Seminary where Buford had awaited Reynolds' relief.

"I was to the north with the 9th New York, with only the 17th Pennsylvania to our right flank, between the Chambersburg Pike and Mummasburg Road," John gestured to his right, "generally speaking, over that way."

"How were you hit?" Seward asked.

"I was trying to bolster our lines, which were starting to buckle during a push by the Confederates. I had just argued with General Buford to get him away from the front of the line when a sudden push about broke through. It's still blurry, but I caught a bullet in my upper leg."

"And John Reynolds?" Lincoln asked.

"General Reynolds had brought his First Corps up to relieve us, sir. He was placing the Iron Brigade when a bullet struck him in the head." John paused and pointed to a line of trees in front of them. "Sir, it is believed that he was dead before he hit the ground."

"Thank you, Major," Seward said, as Lincoln got out and strolled towards the spot. "You have been very informative. While we have you on our own, may I ask what took place two days ago?"

"Sir, there was a group of conspirators planning to assassinate President Lincoln. I managed to infiltrate the group, gain their trust, and eventually volunteer to act as the shooter so I could thwart the plans."

"Johnny, I believe I will take a walk and see if the President needs anything," Cathy said. "Will you hand me down?"

As she walked off, John continued his summary. Since she knew it, she focused on the tall, lonely-looking man staring out across the field, his unkempt hair blowing in a light breeze.

"Mr. President?" Cathy called softly.

"Miss Howell."

"Johnny is telling Mr. Seward about the conspiracy so I thought I would see if you needed anything."

"I am glad for the company," Lincoln said softly. "The man who shot you was part of the conspiracy?"

"Yes, he was the instigator."

"Did he survive?"

"No, sir. I knocked him over and he was killed when his head hit the corner edge of a counter." Cathy sighed. "I did not set out to kill him. I am trained to preserve life, not take it."

"Will you and your brother be at the dedication later this morning?"

"I do not believe we could be stopped, sir."

Lincoln chuckled. "I do not doubt that for a moment." Still gazing across the battlefield, he said, "I wish to ask you a question yet I hesitate because I am not certain I want to know the answer."

"Ask, and trust me to tell you as much as I think you need to know," she responded. Hearing a cough, she turned and looked back at the carriage. "John is coming out to us, but Secretary Seward and Mr. McDougall have stayed with the carriage."

Lincoln turned as John joined them. "Your sister has offered to listen to a question of mine and tell me what she believes I need to know. Do you concur, Major?"

"Mr. President, I disagree with Catie only when I find it is absolutely necessary. I trust her judgment implicitly, as I believe she does mine."

He nodded. "I understand." With a hint of hesitation, Lincoln continued, "Does the country survive this?"

"Yes, sir. The Union prevails, and the country is reunited," Cathy stated firmly. "A lot of blood will be spilled before the war is over, but the United States of America survives."

"It goes from being referred to as plural states to being referred to as a single country. We now say, 'the United States is' rather than using the plural form 'the United States are.' If I'm making sense," John explained.

"You are. Thank you for that," Lincoln acknowledged thoughtfully.

"Is your next question whether you live to see this war end?" Cathy asked gently.

"Yes," he whispered.

"You are re-elected next year — the people don't wish to change horses in the middle of the stream," John informed the commander-in-chief.

"If what we know as history remains intact," Cathy added, "you shall live to see the end of the war. We suspect part of the reason we were put here was to help ensure that outcome."

They watched the great man take it in. Cathy saw his tears welling even as her own vision blurred.

John cleared his throat. "We had best be getting back, Mr. President.

Secretary Seward is looking at his watch."

"Thank you both so very much, for everything," Lincoln said simply. He offered his arm to Cathy and they walked in silence.

***

After the procession, music, prayers, more music, Everett's two-hour oration, and more music, Abraham Lincoln rose and began the speech he had memorized. John and Cathy, together with Myles Keogh, were close enough to hear the words that would eventually grace the Lincoln Memorial in Washington, D.C.

"Fourscore and seven years ago our fathers brought forth on this continent a new nation, conceived in liberty, and dedicated to the proposition that all men are created equal. Now we are engaged in a great civil war, testing whether that nation, or any nation so conceived and so dedicated, can long endure. We are met on a great battle-field of that war. We have come to dedicate a portion of that field, as a final resting-place for those who here gave their lives that that nation might live. It is altogether fitting and proper that we should do this. But, in a larger sense, we cannot dedicate - we cannot consecrate - we cannot hallow - this ground.

"The brave men, living and dead, who struggled here have consecrated it, far above our poor power to add or detract. The world will little note, nor long remember, what we say here, but it can never forget what they did here. It is for us the living, rather, to be dedicated here to the unfinished work which they who fought here have thus far so nobly advanced. It is rather for us to be here dedicated to the great task remaining before us - that from these honored dead we take increased devotion to that cause for which they gave the last full measure of devotion - that we here highly resolve that these dead shall not have died in vain - that this nation, under God, shall have a new birth of freedom - and that government of the people, by the people, for the people, shall not perish from the earth."

John noted applause had interrupted the speech several times, and more followed the conclusion lasting over a minute, and three cheers for the President were offered after that. *So much for the doubters who said it wasn't a success.* John glanced at Cathy – tears were falling down her cheeks unnoticed. He had wiped a few away himself. *Damn, I still have goose bumps.* His arm ached from holding up the phone as unobtrusively as he could, but he had gotten the whole speech; he had even sneaked a photo of Keogh standing with Cathy. He got the battery out and handed the two items to Cathy.

Cathy tucked them into her sling. Their memories of history would keep, and they wouldn't pull out the phone again until they got back to their own time. She leaned against John, and smiled at Keogh who was guarding her bad side from being jostled by the crowd as they left the field. The cavalryman smiled back at her and nodded.

Only after the crowd had disbursed and they found a quiet patch of ground did they speak.

"I shall attempt to describe this to General Buford," Keogh said. "Thank you for the opportunity of hearing his speech. It will surely go down as great."

"Thank you, Myles, for all your assistance." John held out his hand. "If you look back on our times together and it seems an unlikely dream, just shrug."

"Myles?" Cathy reached up with her good arm and put it around his neck. "You will be one of my fondest memories of Gettysburg. Let thoughts of me be the smile on your face that no one understands." She kissed his cheek.

"This is goodbye, then," the irrepressible Irishman said. "I know I must report to Major Eldon before I leave, but I had hoped to see you both again."

"We must get back to our home in Missouri," John told him honestly. "We shall only be here another day or two."

"Long goodbyes are for romance novels," the Irishman replied. "May God keep you safe wherever your journeys take you." He saluted John and kissed Cathy on the cheek.

"May God keep you in His care," she whispered, knowing that after the war he would join Custer's cavalry.

They watched as he strode off toward the Scott home, and made their way to the Wills home. Cathy asked John for the time and was startled to hear it was approaching three in the afternoon.

David Wills greeted them, and although Mrs. Wills never did seem certain why they had been invited, she graciously seated them at table. Cathy noted they were both too caught up in events to eat much. Lincoln was far too busy to pay them any attention, which they thought appropriate. Later, in the receiving line, though, they were stopped.

"Major Andrews, Miss Howell!" Lincoln greeted them warmly, startling more than a few of the assemblage. "I am pleased you could attend." He leaned down as he kissed Cathy's hand and asked her, "Was it all right?"

Laughing, she told him he should have known by the three cheers that he gave it splendidly.

Chuckling, and still holding her hand, he turned to John. "Major, is this goodbye?"

"Yes, sir." John stepped back and snapped a salute. "We do need to get back home."

"May God keep you in His care," Cathy murmured. "It has been an honor."

Lincoln nodded and smiled. "Take care of each other." He gave Cathy's hand a light squeeze and turned to the next person in line.

***

They slowly walked to the Scott house. Bartholomew Scovel was waiting, having brought Dizzy and the carriage cart from the cabin.

"I heard the speech. I was off to the side."

"Bartholomew, we thought you were not going to attend," Cathy scolded. "We asked you to stand with us!"

Scovel grinned. "I was not planning on it, truly – I am not overly fond of crowds."

The door opened and Martha called out, "Will you three please come inside?"

"Yes, Ma'am!" they said in unison.

"How was it?" Scott wanted to know. "I have been running telegrams over to David and they all seem good."

"President Lincoln's speech was very well-received," John reported. "He was interrupted five times by applause and received more applause and three cheers after finishing."

"What about the great orator? How was he received?"

"Fair." John grinned. "It was, as Cathy observed, long. The man was exhausted after speaking for two hours."

"*Two* hours?" Martha gasped. "No wonder it all took so long."

The door opened and Mary entered. "The crowds have finally died down, so I closed."

Martha got up and announced she had prepared a light supper, if anyone cared to partake of it.

The meal was shared with lively conversations and much laughter. Even Bartholomew Scovel joined in, proving that he was not the solemn fellow most thought him to be.

Martha brought out an apple pie for dessert and John asked her to relate the story of the berry pie. It took her a moment to recall the incident, but she told the tale of outwitting two Confederates who insisted she eat a piece first and who suspected it had been poisoned when she wouldn't.

"Their loss," Mary commented while the rest chuckled. "It really was delicious."

Later, in the parlor, Mary regarded the siblings. "You two seem totally at ease for the first time since we have known you."

"The battle was won. Johnny is healed, has been discharged, and no longer needs to fight. President Lincoln is safe. We heard him give one of the best speeches any president has ever made," Cathy recited with a satisfied smile.

"The only thing remaining to us is going to hurt almost as much as being shot," John commented quietly.

The room fell silent.

"We must go back home," Cathy added sadly. "I must return to the hospital, and Johnny has private clients who need him."

"The only reason we stayed this long," John added, picking up where she left off, "is because we became involved in preventing a threat to the president. With that done, we no longer have an excuse to remain."

"Bartholomew, we would like you to have Dizzy and the cart," Cathy told him. "We cannot take her with us and she likes you. We want to be sure she has a good home."

"I would be honored of course," the big man said. "I have always known this moment would come, but I guess it snuck up on me."

"Miss Martha, once we have left, please help yourselves to anything we leave behind in the cabin," John continued. "Cathy put up some canned goods and they should not go to waste."

"We shall be glad to, of course, but you need to take your things with you," Martha stated. "Do not even consider leaving your clothes, Cathy Howell."

"Drats," Cathy gave her a mock scowl. "I guess that plan is not going to work."

"I would not mind having the bench," Mary spoke up, "and I'm sure Martha would not mind having the tables. When will you be leaving?"

"Probably early Saturday morning, unless we can get everything organized tonight," John replied.

"I would be honored to take you to the station, John," Scovel offered.

"That is most kind of you, but I believe we want to leave town about the same way we came in," John replied with a chuckle. "You did not know us then, but Cathy and I arrived on foot with two duffel bags, two knapsacks, and my tent."

"Really?" The shy man stared from one to the other.

"I have not thought about that in a while," Mary commented. "Cathy was dressed like a thirteen year-old boy!"

"Mary was the first person we met," Cathy confirmed. "She offered us a cup of coffee and some bread." She smiled. "We could not believe how lucky we were."

"We still feel that way." John rose. "We should get back to the cabin. We would take a ride out there now, Bartholomew."

Cathy hugged her friends. "When you look back and remember this, think of it as a waking dream."

"You act as if we shall never hear from you again." Martha was thoughtful. "If that is indeed the case, there is something I wish you to have." She disappeared into the kitchen.

"Mary, what is she doing?" Cathy asked, puzzled, watching Martha go up the stairs, then back into the kitchen.

"I have no idea," Mary replied. "She is becoming as mysterious as you two are."

Martha came back into the parlor, carrying a large carpetbag and holding a box. "Cathy, this is a tea set we never use because it only has two cups. Please accept it to remember us by."

Cathy, tears falling down her face, took the box. "I shall treasure this."

"Major, I believe you will find this of use," Martha continued, wiping her own eyes. "Your wardrobes have grown and you will need the room."

"You have touched our lives in ways I am certain we shall not appreciate until we are home," John said, hugging each of the sisters in turn. He held out his hand to Scott. "Sir, I am proud to call you friend."

"I speak for all of us when I say we were blessed when you two joined our family, even if it was only for a short time," the older man returned.

"Major, I do not have your gift for words," Mary added. "We shall miss you – life with you around has never been dull!"

As they all laughed, Cathy and John left the now-familiar parlor. Scovel pulled Dizzy around in front, and they set off for the cabin.

***

At the cabin, Bartholomew Scovel simply held out an arm to Cathy, and she put her free arm around his neck as he carefully gave her a hug.

"Do not assume life has passed you by because Amy was taken too soon," she whispered. "You have a lot to offer the right woman."

"For a while I thought you were she," he replied, smiling. "Now I know you are not. If she's out there, I shall find her."

"Bartholomew, I could not have asked for a better partner in that conspiracy. I am proud to know you," John told him as they shook hands.

Cathy went over to Dizzy, and petted the small animal. "Be a good girl for your new master."

With as little fuss as they expected, Scovel took his leave.

***

Cathy looked around the bedroom. The clothes had been rolled and packed into the carpet bag. After Cathy had peeked into the box – the tea set was Blue Willow – John had carefully packed it in their midst. Their souvenirs, including the zip lock bag with the bullet and bone fragment, their letters and special papers, and the little derringer, were just as carefully bundled in Cathy's backpack. Her phone and battery were in an outer pocket of her med bag, which had been unpacked, sorted, and repacked. John had, under Cathy's instructions, wrapped an elastic bandage around her wound.

John went outside to take his tent panels down from around the sink, using the lamp for light. He and Cathy both had the impression they would be drop-kicked back to their own time as soon as they were ready, rather than having the three promised days. Time probably didn't mean to the entity what it did to them.

"Catie," he commented, "I may never be able to put this together as again as a tent."

"Did you grab the extra canvas and the rope I used for laundry?" she asked, coming into the main room.

"Oh, yeah. It's all here." He spread the panels out on the floor and bundled them, tying it up with her laundry line.

"Johnny, are we ready?" Cathy yawned. "Oh, crap! I forgot to stick the clock in my bag." She took care of that, pulled her watch out and put it on. It was eleven-thirty.

John carried the canvas bundle into the bedroom.

"Catie, I've been thinking. We were transported in time but not in place, and we arrived in our intact tent with all our things. Maybe if we lie down on the floor on the sleeping bags with our bags around us, we'll go back the same way."

"Your logical, engineer's mind can be a joy to watch," she observed. "You get to do the work. I'm wounded."

"Yeah, right - I saw how much it's bothering you when you were packing your clothes," he teased. "Are we going to have to make excuses when we get back?"

"Have acetaminophen, will work," she quipped. "But I'm taking half a pain pill now."

He spread the double bag out, made a line of their bags and satchels, and stretched out on the bedroll.

"My God, Catie, I can't believe you slept like this for weeks! Ugh." He motioned her down next to him. "Cuddle up as best you can."

"I wonder where we'll end up," she murmured.

***

"The time to come full circle is here."

John heard the voice as he struggled to stay awake, but no go. He was vaguely conscious of flickering light, and instinctively held Cathy tighter, still able to feel the bags behind him. The flickering faded and he slept.

"The time to come full circle is here."

The odd, deep voice sounded in Cathy's dreams. She tried to think something profound, but nothing came to mind except, *please, not the Wal-Mart parking lot.*

She heard a chuckle. *"You need not worry. Sleep now."*

She slept.

PART THREE:
BACK FROM THE PAST

CHAPTER EIGHT:
SUNDAY, 28 JUNE 2015

Dawn came early bringing warm air and birds chattering.

John stirred, conscious of Cathy still cuddled up to him.

"Are we there yet?" she mumbled. "I haven't looked."

"Neither have I. I was going to ask you," he murmured. "On a count of three, we'll open our eyes."

"Together: One, two, *three.*"

No cabin, just sky – and a *contrail!*

"Johnny, look!" She pointed to the long white plume in the barely lightened sky. She sat up.

Smiling, John rose and saw that all the bags were where he had placed them. "Everything made it!"

"So where are we?" she questioned, getting up carefully. "All I see is woods."

"Well, we're not in the Wal-Mart parking lot, at least. What time is it?"

"Shortly after five o'clock in the morning." Cathy frowned. "Wait a minute. That may not be right. It may be after six."

"Get your cell out," he suggested, "and put the battery in. I'll roll up the sleeping bags."

She got the phone and battery out. The instant she turned it on, it rang.

"Hello?" she said, hitting the speaker button.

"Cathy! This is Randy Thomas. Where the hell are you? Your tent is gone, and I can't find John."

"Randy," John said, "I think we were the victims of a practical joke. We seem to be in some woods, and I honestly have no idea where. We are going to start walking, but I'm in uniform and Cathy is in period costume."

"Can you see the fire tower?"

"Not from where I'm standing."

"Does Cathy have GPS? Give me the coordinates and I'll send someone for you. You're both needed."

"Let me call you back once we get sorted out."

"Make it quick, buddy," the re-enactment coordinator ordered.

John disconnected the call, looked at Cathy and they burst out laughing.

"So it's Sunday, the 28th of June, 2015, a bit after six. Let's walk the way we would if we were going from the cabin to town. We need to be closer to a road or the story dies."

"Wait a minute, Johnny," she replied thoughtfully. "I want to see something."

He watched, curious, as she made her way from the bedroom through the main room, out the door, and around the cabin to behind it, as if the walls were still there. She bent over and dug around a bit. "It's still here!"

"Hold on." He dug to the bottom of his re-enactment bag and pulled out a water bottle. "We have to get going, but fill this." He walked directly to her and flinched as he went through the wall that wasn't there. "I have the coordinates here," he told her, making a note on his pad of paper. "Let's go."

Cathy tucked the water bottle in her med bag, picked it and the carpet bag up. "Can you manage the others?"

"Yeah." He thought for a moment. "Using your method of pretending the cabin is still here, let's head to town. At least part of the shortcut should be a real road by now."

A while later they hit a paved road which they followed it to a larger one, and proceeded to follow that one towards Gettysburg. A sign told them that if they had turned the other way it would lead to a community college.

John took coordinates, but Thomas called back before he dialed.

"Are you *that* lost?"

"Calm down. We're on the approach road to the community college just northeast of town."

"That's clear the other side of the city! How in bloody hell did you get there?"

"I have no idea, but we're attracting attention," John replied as a car pulled up. "I'll see if we can get a ride. Stand by."

"May I help you?" a man's voice asked as the window lowered.

Cathy leaned down to look and gasped. Recovering quickly, she said, "Sir, we are part of the re-enactment out to the southwest of town, and it seems someone played a joke on us last night."

The man chuckled. "I'd be happy to run you down there – I'd love to get a glimpse of it. I've always wanted to join one of the units, but didn't know how."

"We'd be very grateful," Cathy assured him. She turned to John. "We have a ride. Tell Randy that for a quick tour of the re-enactment camp, he's off the hook."

John relayed the message. He started to offer his thanks as the man got out of the car to open his trunk but stopped in mid-word. Gulping, John extended his hand. "I'm John Andrews, and this is Cathy Howell. We surely do appreciate this, and our coordinator sends his thanks. He'll be happy to give you a tour for returning his two lost lambs."

"I'm Bart Scovel, and I'm really tickled about this. I was heading to the college to grade some assignments, but believe me, they'll wait." They got the assorted bags and bundles into the trunk.

"You're an early riser. Are you from around here?" Cathy inquired as the car turned around and headed in the opposite direction.

"My family has lived in the area for over five generations."

"Did any of them fight in the Civil War?" John questioned cautiously.

"No – but my great-grandfather Bartholomew told my great-grandmother Abigail that he heard Abraham Lincoln give the Gettysburg Address. I was named after Great-grandfather but I prefer Bart." He sighed. "I can't even begin to imagine what it would have been like to hear Lincoln himself say those words."

"Yeah," John murmured. "That would be a real goose bumps moment."

"Bart? Could we stop for something to eat? Maybe a drive-through?" Cathy asked. "Oh, never mind. I keep forgetting – in period clothes, I don't have pockets." *And I have no idea where my wallet got stashed.*

"That's okay – it's on me," said Scovel, a dead ringer for his ancestor.

"We appreciate your kindness," John commented honestly. "Thank you. Did your great-grandfather keep any kind of a diary?"

"No, and it wasn't until after his death that Abigail told any of his stories. He claimed to have been involved in saving Lincoln's life at the cemetery dedication, and made her promise not to tell anything until after he had passed on."

"Those must have been some stories. Did you ever see a picture of him?" Cathy asked.

"Abigail told my mother she had to about hog-tie him to get their wedding picture taken. She was the one who insisted I be named after him, and my folks finally gave in."

"Any particular reason why?" John asked.

"My mom said Abigail took one look at me in the nursery and told anyone who would listen that I was the spitting image of her Bartholomew." He grinned as he pulled into the drive-thru line. "She was one-hundred years old, and died right after I was born, so I don't remember her. According to that wedding photo, though, she was correct about me looking like him."

"It sounds like your great-grandfather was a good man," Cathy said quietly.

"Yes, he was, a real character, too. Abigail was much younger, and it was his second marriage. His first wife died of a fever, and he thought he'd never marry again. Abigail once told my mother that it wasn't until after a friend convinced him that his life wasn't over that he even considered marrying again."

"Bart, I'll have scrambled eggs with biscuits on the side, with coffee," John said. "I believe that Cathy will as well."

The order was placed, paid for, and collected; they were on their way again.

Cathy's phone rang. John looked at the battery level as he answered it. "Randy, we grabbed something to eat, and we're almost there. Don't call again - the battery is almost dead." He took the battery out again. "We're going to have to charge this."

"I'll plug it in when I get to the medical tent," Cathy said.

"This coffee is good, but I've had better biscuits," John commented to Cathy. "Is your breakfast acceptable?"

"Completely – I didn't have to cook it," Cathy grinned. "Does Randy panic this way often?"

"It's probably over you more than me. You head the medical team," John teased.

"We're coming to your site," Scovel stated. "Where do I park?"

John gave directions to their rental, and Scovel found a spot near it. John dug out the keys and put the canvas bundle into the trunk. Cathy suggested he get his cell phone out of the glove compartment while they were there.

"Anything else we can leave here?"

"Not at the moment," she replied. "If we do think of something, we can come back."

"Yeah, it's not like it's going to vanish or anything," John mumbled.

"Let me help with those," Bart offered. "You're hurt."

"Ooooh – thanks. I need to dump the sling." Cathy removed it and stashed it in the carpet bag. "I have a cut that's healing, but I'll be blasted if I'll walk into the med tent looking wounded."

***

"John! Cathy! It's about time. Is this your rescuer?" Randy Thomas's relief was obvious. "*Wait a minute!* When the hell did you become a major?"

Cathy, who had just taken a large sip of coffee, did a perfect spit take all over the ground, and, trying desperately to stifle laughter, turned to John. "Oops?"

"Yeah – oops." John coughed. "I'll check in with my unit. Oh, Randy, my tent is unusable. Find out if someone has a spare we can borrow. I'll see you later."

Cathy introduced their new friend to Thomas. "Bart's family is local and goes way back. He's never had the chance to go behind the scenes, and we promised him you'd take him on a tour."

"Happy to, but first I've gotta ask – what the hell happened to you two? I saw you go into your tent last night, but when I looked this morning, there was nothing there but grass."

"John's theory is someone moved us during the night as a joke. Was anyone else missing this morning?"

"Not that I've heard. I tried calling. Your radio unit didn't answer, I left a message on John's phone, and got nothing on yours."

"The unit was off, you left a message in the glove box of our rental, and I had the battery out of my phone." Cathy shrugged, and regretted it. "Frankly, I believe this should come under the heading of all's well that ends well." She put the battery back into her phone. "Speaking of my phone, here's the charger and the phone – can you plug it in for me?"

"Do you have your radio unit?"

"Yep, it's in here." She pulled it out of her smaller bag with its holster and turned it on. "Sort of ruins the lines of the costume. Randy, take Bart and show him around while I get things organized here. He says he's always wanted to be a re-enactor – he's a willing recruit, so recruit him!"

Cathy sank onto a stool and took a deep breath. Her sutures itched, and they needed to be checked. She looked around and spotted Gail Collins, the nurse she had left in charge last night, about five months ago. Checking her watch, she saw it was not yet eight. "Gail?"

"Yes, Cathy?"

"Can you keep a secret?"

"Sure."

"Before we get swamped, I have a favor to ask. How are you at stitches?"

"Embroidery or medical? I do both." Gail was a sturdy, no-nonsense woman who had been a great help at sorting the real patients from the men who were just plain exhausted. Like Cathy, she was in period garb.

"Medical." Cathy removed her blouse and slipped on a patient gown. She turned so Gail could see the elastic bandage. "I'm not going to answer any questions about how or why, but there's a gash under this with stitches about four days old." *Sounds better than a century and a half plus four days old.* "I'd like you to look and see if we need to do anything else."

"Ooooh – I love conspiracies!" Gail responded, grinning. "Say, who was that with Randy Thomas? Is he local?"

"Yep, from a long line of locals. He teaches at Harrisburg Area Community College," Cathy replied as the nurse got down to the bandages. "Do we have a mirror? I'd like to see this thing. You're from around here, aren't you? You said you work at a clinic in Gettysburg, if I'm remembering right."

"Yes, I do. If he's single, I want to meet him." Gail used peroxide to soak the bandage off, and whistled. "You said medical stitches, but I've used that color thread on Christmas stuff," she said. "If you aren't answering questions, I won't ask them, but Cathy, that's a lovely stitching job." She held a compact mirror for Cathy.

"No swelling, no signs of infection." Cathy sighed with relief. "I got lucky."

"Catie?" A voice called from the tent opening.

"Behind the screen, Johnny. Come ahead."

John's head came around the corner of the screen and he was grinning broadly. "I'm keeping my brevet rank," he announced. "It's driving Randy crazy because he can't figure out how I got it. How's your arm?"

"It looks good to me," Gail answered. "I'm not asking questions because she isn't going to answer any, but this is a decent job of stitching. Yours?"

"That's a question, but yes. With her instructions, of course. No infection?"

"Nope." Cathy smiled. "Oh, Gail was wondering who Bart is. I think they need to meet."

"Randy is about to induct him into his unit," John said. "I'm sure we can figure out something. Got to run – we're doing some stuff with Buford's forces today."

"Can the stitches come out?" Cathy asked, trying not to think about Buford.

"I'd leave them in for another day or so," Gail advised, soaking sterile gauze with peroxide to clean the wound. "Is this cotton thread?"

"Nope – it's silk, and it was boiled. Do you think we should replace them?'

"Not if they're silk. I'm ready to dress it. Do you want anything on it?"

"How about antibiotic ointment and a telfa pad? You can use some gauze and reuse the elastic wrap. It gave me more freedom of movement than Kerlix would have."

***

Later in the day, Cathy took the opportunity to do a fast sponge bath. She had just put her blouse back on – the one Mary had given her – when she heard someone come into the tent. "I'll be with you in a moment."

She came around the screen and froze. John Buford was standing next to John. She gulped and fought back tears.

"Wow. I know you're an actor, but wow," she stated, coming forward. "I thought Sam Elliot was close, but you have bested him. You are amazingly like him."

"I want to be as authentic as possible," the man, introduced as Brad Worthington, said. "John thought you might be able to help."

"One thing you want to bear in mind is John Buford had advanced rheumatoid arthritis, and it was very painful," Cathy began as Thomas and associate producer David Steiner walked in. "Don't stride and stay mounted when you can. Buford needed assistance to get on and off his horse. You should stoop slightly, and walk carefully. Also, the pain undoubtedly prevented restful sleep, so feel free to look tired."

"May I ask how you know?" Steiner asked. "I mean, you couldn't have met him."

"I didn't need to," she replied evenly. "There's a picture of him with his staff – John showed it to me. I'm a doctor, and the signs are obvious."

"Anyone else you can profile?"

"Mr. Steiner, you don't want to get her started," John cut in with a smile. "She's worse than Sherlock Holmes for observations."

Worthington thanked her, and left for his scene.

Steiner asked why they had been late that morning. "Randy told me what you told him, but I want to hear it from you."

"Mr. Steiner, I'm sorry – we have no explanation. We went to bed here, woke up across town, and made our way back." *With one hundred and fifty plus years in between.* Cathy let her exasperation show.

"You misunderstand me, Dr. Howell. I'm concerned that someone played a nasty prank on you, and I want to find out who's responsible."

"Please, then, do accept my apologies for the sharp response," she replied. "I would suggest that you leave it be, as I doubt it will recur." *Damn, my language hasn't completely arrived back in the twenty-first century. At least I didn't curtsey.*

"We're going to run a couple more scenes and break for the day," Steiner told Thomas. "We have one more day with your people, correct?"

"That's correct." Thomas turned to John. "Okay, you're a budding technical advisor now. Are you coming?"

"I want a word with Cathy and I'll follow you." He waited until the men left before continuing. "You're having trouble, too, I see."

"I'm sorry, Johnny. I feel as if I've got one foot in each era. I almost curtseyed to Steiner just now."

"It would have seemed perfectly normal, even here. Has Randy made any comments about your blouse?"

"No, he hasn't. Oh, crap, I forgot – this is the skirt you gave me our first night here, but it's Mary's blouse. I can't wear the other one - Martha burned it and the skirt I was wearing when I was shot."

"Cripes," John sighed, "it's still complicated. Somehow, I thought that once we got back everything would be okay with no hassles."

"Face it, we're not that lucky." Cathy sat on her stool. "I'm glad we have this as a buffer – it'd really be awkward to drop straight back into the Emergency Department. For one thing, I'm going to have to get used to wearing pants!"

"At least you won't be tempted to drop a curtsey wearing pants," he pointed out with a chuckle.

"What are we doing for supper?" she asked, ignoring the comment.

"It should be similar to what we did for dinner last night. Remember that? About five months ago?" He tried to smile.

"That's not much of a smile. Maybe we can get Bart together with Gail. Normal conversation might help."

"Great idea! I'll work on it." He looked around. "Where's the phone?"

"Charging," she pointed to it. "I haven't had the nerve to look. Maybe tonight. Oh, do we have a tent?"

"Bart to the rescue. It's not white, but it is a tent. He went home to get it, and said he'll be back."

"I feel like we know him, he's so much like his great-grandfather," she said. "I'm glad we know our Bartholomew found someone. He really deserved the best."

"I know – none of it would have been possible without him."

***

John and Cathy made a point of sitting with Bart and Gail at dinner and as time progressed, they became more and more convinced that they were hearing a solid click of a relationship starting. Cathy decided their Bartholomew would be pleased, and didn't even feel silly with the thought.

"When are you two leaving?" Scovel questioned as the four of them strolled around the campsite.

"Tuesday or Wednesday. Cathy doesn't have to be back at work until Saturday, so we have a few days to play with. The drive is either two days or one really long day," John replied.

"Johnny, when does the re-enactment officially end?"

"Tomorrow is the last day of shooting and most of the camp will be gone by dusk, although some of the men left today," he answered. "By the way, Bart, thank you so much for the loan of the tent."

"Can we get a room somewhere? I want to visit the National Cemetery," Cathy stated. "We didn't have time before, and I think we should."

"I agree." He tucked her arm into his. "I'll see if I can find a place."

"My aunt runs a B&B in Gettysburg. Let me see what I can do – Monday night is usually her slow night, so there shouldn't be an issue," Gail offered.

"We'd be very grateful," John assured her. "I've found that after doing one of these weekends it helps to have a day or so of buffering before jumping back into your everyday life."

"Meaning?" Scovel asked.

"We spend at least four days in period costume, using the language of the period, and mimicking actions of over one hundred and fifty years ago. The camps have tents, no plumbing, and little electricity. To go from all this back to the high-powered world of university classes is benefitted by easing back in – I use the travel days to do it." John smiled at the other couple. "In Cathy's case, it would be almost impossible. To be here one day and in her Emergency Department the next would be too severe a contrast."

"That's another reason I'd like to see some of the sights in Gettysburg," Cathy commented. "I haven't worn jeans since we arrived here."

"I saw you wearing pants yesterday," Gail observed. "No, wait - they weren't jeans."

"No, they were period pants for a young boy," John said, chuckling. "I had fun picking them out."

"Here you are," called Randy Thomas, striding towards them. "I've been looking all over for you."

"Is there a problem?" John inquired.

"John, I'd like to borrow you for a few minutes since you seem to be up on what happened to Buford's men, you can all come – I don't want to break anything up."

The five walked across the campsite in the gathering dusk and approached what Cathy recognized as the setting for McPherson's Ridge. She tugged on John's sleeve. "Be careful, and take lots of deep breaths."

John walked the area with the others, listening to their conversation, but part of his mind was in the past. *This terrain is almost too accurate – it feels real somehow. Maybe too real.*

The re-enactment coordinator explained how they were going to line things up; Steiner was walking with the assistant director and assistant director of photography, discussing what units had been posted at the site. Cathy saw Thomas turn to John and start to speak.

Suddenly, John stopped with an odd look on his face.

"Uh-oh," Cathy murmured to herself as she moved closer to the men, "*now* he remembers."

"No, Randy." John's quiet voice cut through their conversation. "It was a push from the Mississippi men – their flag had a green tree on it. They bowed the line, right where the 9th New York was, not on the extreme flank opposite the 17th Pennsylvania." John's voice started to rise and his words came faster as memories flooded back. "Still no infantry in sight. I pulled every third man to reform the line at the buckle – we pushed back and held – Buford came up because he saw the line starting to break – I argued with him – told him he *had* to move back…. He did just as the Rebs' artillery fire swung our way – I was pulling my men back when a shell landed where he had been – I turned to check my men and…." He cried out, grabbed his right thigh, and crumpled.

Cathy ran forward in time to hear, "Take me to Catie," as she dropped to her knees.

"He passed out – probably the heat," she stated. "Does anyone have water? Please?"

Thomas handed her a bottle. "That sounded real, as if he had seen it," he commented, his voice shaky, as Cathy eased John to a position where he could sip water.

Steiner was looking at his notes. "I don't have Mississippi men being here."

"John's thorough. If he says they were Mississippi men, that was where they were from," Thomas stated firmly. "I didn't know that Buford made it this far up the line, but I'm probably wrong."

"Randy," John's voice was a bit groggy, "my apologies. I was getting into this, and let my imagination run away with me."

"Is he all right, Doctor?" Steiner questioned.

"Yes, he is." Cathy turned to push herself up and leaned too heavily on her left arm. "Damn it!" She stood, cradling it.

"Cripes, Catie, did I hurt you?" John rose slowly and dusted himself off.

"No, I managed all by myself," she replied crossly, "but the next time you fall down, I won't join you." She took a deep breath and let it out slowly. "Relax, Randy - we're both all right. I think he was just getting carried away. It's been a long, hot day." *Not like the cool November weather we were in yesterday.*

"Before you go, as long as you're okay, can you go over what you said before you passed out?" The assistant director was studying his notes.

John carefully and unemotionally explained what he had remembered. He repeated that the Mississippians had been in the attack and their artillery fire that had swung towards the 9th New York as Buford left the scene. The AD took notes and said he would pass them along to the director.

"Now, gentlemen, if you will excuse us," John said, taking Cathy's arm. "It finally became clear," he murmured to her as he moved away from the site. "How badly did I blunder?"

"You were okay until you started saying 'I' and 'we', but I think you bumped past it."

"Did your stitches open?"

"I don't think so – I think I just pulled on them."

"Ahem." The sound came from behind them. Two voices.

John and Cathy stopped and turned. Gail and Scovel, side by side, were staring at them.

"I know this is an 'I-Don't-Answer-Questions' Day, for you, Cathy, and I doubt John would either, but something very odd just happened." Gail made the statement firmly.

"We heard Cathy say, "uh-oh" right before you went into your dramatic recreation, and I'd be willing to bet that it *was* a recreation, although how you knew is beyond me," Scovel added. "I haven't even mentioned the reactions you two had when you first saw me, either."

John and Cathy exchanged glances.

"Let's return to our tent," John suggested, "where we shall regale you with the plotline of a book Cathy and I want to write. It's going to be a science-fiction time travel novel about two people who get drop-kicked back in time one hundred and fifty-two years, landing outside a town in Pennsylvania just in time to be involved in a major battle of the Civil War…"

EPILOGUE

Voice One: The teaming was balanced and their trust is perfect.
Voice Two: They garnered local support and maintained life.
Voice Three: They broke protocol but wisely.
Voice Two: Their judgment is sound.
Voice One: The teaming took the second task without hesitation.
Voice Three: Their solutions were well-reasoned.
Voice One: They stayed within the time field parameters.
Voice Two: They did well, much better than most on first assignments.
Voice Three: We should be able to use them again should the need arise.
Voice One: We have found a new team. Are we agreed?
Voices One, Two, and Three, in unison: Yes.

ABOUT THE AUTHORS

Aubrey Stephens is a retired teacher from Mississippi. He has Masters degrees in both theater and history, with certification in English, science, and special education. He is also a marine veteran and former military officer. The rumor that he has attempted to blow up the earth is just that a rumor, though he was on combat missile crew alert when the NORAD mistakes that caused a false report to believed that there were Soviet inbound missiles headed for the U.S. He is a trained martial artist with a second degree black belt in karate, brown belt in judo, and brown belt in Kendo. He also studied and taught European fencing for over 45 years. His hobbies include recreating the Middle Ages and the American Civil War. He is squired to one of the S.C.A.'s most well known knights and at this time holds the rank of Captain in Co. A – 2nd Mississippi Cavalry (Union and Confederate.) He has acted, written, directed, and done set design and construction for over 200 theatrical shows. He has written several articles on the history of the War Between the States for regional magazines. Since his retirement from teaching he has edited for Pro Se Productions and is now its Executive Editor. He has had published several stories and book. His anthology <u>Tales of the Interstellar Bartenders Guild</u> won the 2019 Pulp Factory Award for Best Anthology. He is currently working on two alternate history novels, one a different WWII ending and the other a terrifying day in the cold war of 1968.

A native of Manhattan, New York, **Dale Kesterson** is a writer, editor, actress, singer, and character voice artist who has been creating stories and putting them on paper since the age of seven; she wrote, produced, and acted in her first play at age twelve. Life, however, kept her busy majoring in science in college, teaching math and science, studying nursing, and managing a small home business with her husband. Her first s/f short story appeared in the award-winning anthology, *Tales of the Interstellar Bartenders Guild*, edited by her *Time Guards* co-author Aubrey Stephens. An avid Star Trek fan, she founded a Trek club and a convention, one highlight of which was performing onstage with the late Grace Lee Whitney (Janice Rand, ST:TOS). Besides writing and editing, Dale performs in community theater productions, everything from singing as Cinderella's Stepmother in *Into the Woods* to a variety of character roles most of which required accents. A seasoned traveler and professional photographer who has lived in six widely diverse locations, Dale settled down with her husband, their hairless cats and box turtle in the middle of nowhere in a town so small it doesn't even have a red-yellow-green traffic light. If she's not busy writing, editing, or performing, she does handcrafts — she hates being bored!